No Prisoners

A Leon Cazador Thriller

Nik Morton

ROUGH
EDGES
PRESS

Rough Edges Press
An Imprint of Wolfpack Publishing
5130 S. Fort Apache Rd. 215-380
Las Vegas, NV 89148

roughedgespress.com

Paperback ISBN 978-1-68549-138-3
eBook ISBN 978-1-68549-137-6
LCCN 2022941298

Dedicated to all the children abused and murdered by adults who should have known better and can never be forgiven.

With all my love to Jennifer, my spouse, mi amiga and first editor; and to our daughter Hannah and our grandchildren Darius and Suri; and to Harry, our son-in-law.

Thank you to James Reasoner, Mike Bray, and Jake Bray for believing in the character, Leon Cazador.

No Prisoners

Chapter 1

Golf Lynx

Southern Spain
September, 2019

Salty sea air wafted on the breeze and flapped at the flag on the green's pin, taunting. Leon Cazador's ball landed on the edge of the bunker of the twelfth hole—a bad lie. His blood ran cold but it had nothing to do with the way he'd just played.

Behind him, resplendent in bright yellow and red short-sleeved shirt and checkered chinos, Señor Javier Montoya was chuckling—until he saw what Leon was looking at. Then he went very quiet, thick fleshy lips zipped tight.

A tattooed forearm thick with fair hair and bloody right hand stuck out from the sand. Sun glistened on the bright red stumps of two fingers. The finger wearing an emerald signet ring had survived animal depredations. And all around were paw tracks.

"*Madre de Dios*, Señor Cazador, what did that?" Montoya croaked, his dark brown eyes watery, evasive. He wiped sweat from his brow with a linen handkerchief; the breeze did not diminish the heat of yet another hot day with a clear ultramarine blue sky.

"Wildcats of some sort took a bite or two," Leon said. "But I don't think they buried the body..."

"No, of course not. No..."

It was a reasonable assumption that the arm was attached to a body; otherwise the wildcats would have dragged it away and made a meal of it; then Leon might have been none the wiser.

Ignoring the specks of blood on the sand, Leon knelt at the edge by several paw indentations. The animals had entered the bunker from the right, their pads making an alternating pattern. The print size of the adult was similar to a mountain lion, he reckoned, and the footpads were obscured by dense hair and made up nearly half of the print. There were no claw marks. Their prints then clustered around the human arm. "Probably lynx, a female and two cubs."

"But—but what about the body? We should uncover it, no?"

"Definitely not! We can't touch it." Leon checked his Omega wristwatch—this would be the legal time of death, the moment of discovery; probably quite a few hours after the pathologist's estimated time of death. "I'll call the *Guardia Civil*." He pulled his cell-phone from his jeans back pocket.

"The *Guardia*?"

"Of course," Leon said. "Whoever the guy is, I don't think he died sunning himself on the sand."

"Yes, I see..." Montoya moved a hand over his heavy jowls and swore. "I will have to close Dimples while the cops investigate!" He owned this, the Dimples golf course plus two others, and yet he was still a poor player.

"Yes, I suppose you will," Leon conceded without sympathy. He turned his back on Señor Montoya and speed-dialed Juan, his brother, an officer in the *Guardia* . He told him what they'd found. Quite used to Leon's meddling in unsavory business, Juan didn't comment but ended by saying a unit would arrive in about twenty minutes. "And send Seprona, too," Leon added, "there's a lynx and her young out here somewhere. They disturbed the body."

"*Sí*, Leon, I understand." He closed the call. *Servicio de Protección de la Naturaleza* is the *Guardia Civil* group responsible for the environment, which included animal welfare.

Leon pocketed the phone.

Montoya scratched his thinning black hair. "What's so important about lynx?"

"They're an endangered species." Recently, he'd become quite conversant with endangered species of one kind or another. "There shouldn't be any lynx here on the coast. The last I heard, there are only nine isolated populations and they stay in the mountains, the Sierra Morena, or the Coto de Doñana, and Murcia. There should be none anywhere near us."

"Maybe they strayed."

"Maybe." Leon gestured at the bloody hand. "I think somebody else strayed, too." His tone was somber because he recognized that signet ring and the tattoo of a semi-naked female and beneath her feet, amidst the symbolic grass leaves, were the initials "RE-PG".

———

"Don't you worry that the tattoo will give you away?" Leon had asked a couple of weeks ago at the rustic El Meson restaurant in one of Torrevieja's back-streets.

Rod Wallace wore a checkered black and white short-sleeved shirt which revealed his muscular hairy arms. He brushed a hand over the tattoo on his right forearm. "It's a commonplace design. Actually helps me blend in."

He'd never liked his given name of Rodney, claiming he always got joshed over it. He blamed the popular British TV sitcom *Only Fools And Horses*. Maybe that was why he was comfortable to adopt any number of aliases in his work. Presently, he was going under the moniker of Roger Eastlake. He was about forty. Although they'd known each other since working on a case two years ago, they'd never been so close as to exchange birth-dates. Besides, in their line of work the sharing of too much personal information could prove fatal. Rod had been undercover for four years with the Metropolitan Police's SCO35 unit then he'd moved on: for the last three years he'd worked for the National Crime Agency. And it showed in his features. The eyes always wary, on the lookout for familiar faces from his past. Several UC officers begin by training together, establishing what is known as a 'universal standard'. There lies the hidden danger. Because sometimes one of those trainees might go rogue and if they encounter you on a case they could betray you.

Leon sympathized, having done plenty of undercover work himself. That and spying.

Normally, neither would divulge much about a case they were working on. Leon had been surprised when Rod contacted him and arranged this meeting over a dish of rabbit paella and a bottle of Rioja Gran Reserva.

"You seem troubled, Rod," Leon observed.

Rod looked rueful. "Have you ever investigated pedophile suspects?"

"No." Leon shrugged. He tended to steer clear of cases involving criminal youths. Despite being conversant in several languages, he couldn't keep up with their street lingo. "Whenever a case involves children or youths I refer them to Chico De la Fuente."

"He's the P.I. in Alicante, isn't he?"

"That's him. He's good with kids—maybe because he has six of his own!" Surprisingly, quite a few investigators were hired by Spanish families to keep an eye on their teenage sons and daughters. The rise in street crime and drug use was an ever-present worry for responsible parents. If the kids were sucked into crime, the shame could be devastating to the family; and the future for the kids was going to be bleak. At least these families wanted to know what their children were doing, unlike many parents from Leon's second home, broken Britain, who didn't seem to care.

"Well, you made the right decision, Leon."

"Oh?"

"Anti-pedophile work is debilitating. I didn't realize how bad it could get. It preys on your mind. Seeing those incriminating images all the time..."

"I can understand that. It takes special resilience and resolve, I imagine."

"I thought I had that. But this latest case, it's so sick I almost want to quit."

"But you can't tell me about it." A statement, not a question.

"I'd like to—you know, unburden myself. The luxury of catharsis. But no, I'll leave you out of it. Just breaking bread with you helps, even if I don't divulge any details. I tell you what, though—I'll never look at golf in the same way again!"

And with that cryptic remark he seemed to cheer up and they had finished the bottle of red.

If only he had quit the job, Leon reflected. Instead, the poor guy had quit this mortal coil.

———

BOTH LEON and Señor Montoya were interviewed in the Dimples club office and then told to wait in the bar area. Leon phoned his office and explained to Carlota Díaz, his bilingual secretary, PA and general assistant, and warned her he'd be late in. He didn't go into details. "I'll tell you all when I see you."

In the meantime the scene-of-crime people did their thing. A canvas screen was hastily erected round the bunker. Once the body was exhumed from the sandpit, more photos were taken.

Eventually, Leon was led into the club office where Inspector Teo Chávez sat behind Señor Montoya's desk. This golf course was in the Torrevieja bailiwick which fell under the jurisdiction of Chávez. "Come in, Señor Cazador," he said, his voice deep and authoritative. "Sorry to keep you waiting so long." His tone was formal, as was his address, though he knew Leon. His hat rested on the desk; he had close-cropped black hair, black bushy eyebrows and glinting dark gray eyes that missed very little. "Take a seat," he gestured; there was black hair on the backs of his hands. At first glance he might appear predatory with his hooked nose, black mustache, square chin, and a scar down the left side of his cheek, but Leon found him affable enough; they'd worked well together previously. Chávez was tall and handsome in a rugged sort of way.

As Leon sat in a straight-backed chair opposite, Chávez handed him a 10x4 color photo, a head shot of the victim. They'd cleaned off the sand, at least. Rod appeared quite peaceful. Sleeping. Never again to waken.

"Do you know him?" Chávez asked.

It was tempting to be negative; for Leon had considered embarking on his own crusade to find Rod's murderer and it would be easier if the police thought he had no connection with the victim. But he had too much respect for Chávez to be deceitful. "Yes."

"Really?" Chávez raised his right eyebrow. "That is a big coincidence, wouldn't you say?"

"Life's full of coincidences," Leon said. This one was chilling. "Rod Wallace. He works—worked—for the NCA. Used the alias Roger Eastlake."

"Yes, I know. He made his presence known to me when he first arrived, even though he would be working in the Guardamar area with Inspector De Vargas and had no reason to. A courtesy which I appreciated. Did you know him well?"

"Not really. We met occasionally over lunch or tapas."

Chávez stroked his mustache. "He did not confide in you regarding his work?"

Leon shook his head. "I'm a private investigator. He

works for a government agency. It would be dereliction of his duty if he confided in me."

"Of course." His facial expression suggested he knew Leon was talking bullshit.

"Can you tell me how he died?"

"It will be no secret." Chávez pressed a palm over his chest. "A single bullet in the heart."

"Sounds like a gangland killing? Which is worrying..."

The inspector shrugged; non-committal. "I don't know. Initial findings indicate that ante-mortem he'd been badly beaten. Impressions left on his flesh imply it was done with a golf club—a driver. A preliminary examination by the ME reveals several bones were broken in his arms and legs."

Anger swelled in Leon's chest, but he clamped down on it. He was used to concealing his emotions. "Poor Rod. Torture?"

"That is my guess. I do wonder what information they wanted to extract from him."

"He was undercover. They must have caught him out somehow." Leon knew only too well in undercover work you had to be a trained liar. And that entailed maybe remembering the same lies told to a target three or more years ago. The axiom was true enough: keep the invention to a minimum; too much detail becomes a slow-ticking time bomb. Because it's the little things that will always trip you up—ask Lieutenant Columbo. Treading a fine line, a tightrope act.

The job is to befriend the target, get the evidence, and then back out. "You need the ability to spin plates," Rod had said. "No matter how nervous you feel, you can't show it to the other guy."

Villains view undercover cops with extreme malice and drastic prejudice. Though not always while undercover using one of his aliases, Leon acknowledged he would be dealing with individuals who would kill. Those who had killed or were happy to order a murder. He remembered one of the last things Rod had said, after their lunch. "Not all of them are horrible people, despite the fact they arrange for horrible

things to be done in their name. People are many-faceted."
He'd snorted. "Though you'd have a hard time trying to tell
that to the 'cancel brigade' who believe everything is black-
and-white..."

Inspector Chávez pursed his thin lips then said, "We have
already tested all the golf clubs here and none have any trace
of blood on them."

No luminol fluorescence. "He might not have been beaten
and killed here."

"That too is a theory I am seriously considering; but we
have to be thorough." Chávez frowned. "I cannot fathom
what was to be gained by placing the corpse in the sand
bunker. It wasn't well concealed anyway."

"Maybe a player had a grudge against Señor Montoya?"

"Not according to him." Chávez didn't sound
convinced.

Montoya could be lying.

Chávez went on, "Only a few hours earlier we'd received
an anonymous tip-off that there was a body somewhere on
the course ... But the lynx found it before we could act on the
tip-off."

"Dumped to embarrass Señor Montoya."

Chávez nodded. "I think so, though Montoya insists he
doesn't know why anyone would do such a thing to him."

"Do you believe him?"

"I believe he is being economical with the truth, but if he
won't help me I can't help him."

"You've got quite a puzzle there, Inspector."

"Indeed. It is frustrating—Mr. Wallace was operating in
the Guardamar area, not mine."

"Yes, he'd told me that was the case. That's a mite
awkward for you, isn't it?"

"A little. We will work with Guardamar and overturn
many stones to find the slugs who did this. And disturb
many bottom-feeders in the cesspool in the process."

"Well, good luck with that." Leon handed the photo
over. "Can I go now?"

"Yes, Señor Cazador."

On his way out of the golf club office he spotted Montoya manning the reception desk; earlier, he'd dismissed all the staff after they'd given their statements.

Leon approached the desk. "What did you tell the police?" he asked.

Montoya's eyes were still watery and seemingly reluctant to look at him for any length of time. "Only that I have never seen the dead man before."

Was he lying? Why would he do that? "Any idea why he should be buried in a bunker on your golf course?"

Montoya hesitated for a fraction of a second and then replied, "No... The Inspector asked the same question. I suppose the culprits wanted to dispose of a body but did not bury it deep enough."

"That could be it. Mind you, there are less obvious places to get rid of a corpse."

"I wouldn't know, Señor Cazador."

———

LEON VEERED AWAY from the throng of lunchtime shoppers and made a beeline for a brownstone building and the marble steps with a large wood and glass door. On the wall in the entrance alcove a brass plaque stated:

Leon Cazador, Investigador Privado.
Horas: Lunes-Viernes. 10:00-14:00, 16:00-20:00

There were two more plaques for offices above his: one for a firm of accountants and the other for a psychologist. He'd seen the psychologist and he reckoned she did more than offer therapy of the mind.

He refrained from using the buzzer; Carlota was doubtless at lunch since it was the start of the siesta period. He slipped his key in the lock and opened the door into the shadowy lobby. He depressed the timed light switch and the door swung shut behind him with a loud clatter, echoing. His footsteps made no sound on the tiled floor as he crossed it to the stairs, eschewing the elevator. Stairs kept him fit, he reckoned. Good for the heart.

He climbed three flights, pressing the light-timers on the half-landings as he went, arriving at a landing with two doors. There were a further two flights of stairs to those other businesses. On a wall-notice between the doors was printed *Leon Cazador*: his suite of offices, which sounded grand, but there were only two rooms—one for him and an adjoining one for Carlota. Light showed through the frosted glass pane of the left-hand door, so she hadn't left yet.

He opened the door and stepped into Carlota's outer office.

Carlota Diaz had high cheekbones which flushed at sight of him. Her chestnut-coloured eyes shone as she rose from her reception desk. Tall and attractive, she was from northern Spain with the fair colouring from her Celtic ancestors. Her strawberry blonde hair was tied back in a chignon. She wore a fetching white poplin top and a lacy black bra was visible through the material. Her black skirt hugged a narrow waist and broad hips. He'd made a point of memorising her birthday from her CV; she was twenty-four yet had a mature head on relatively young shoulders, which had served her well in the police—until she was shot in the leg by an escaping felon. Afterwards she'd been offered a desk job but she decided to resign instead. Leon made her a better offer.

She sidled round the desk and limped up to him, her warm and smooth hands clasping his. "I waited in for you."

"Thank you. There was no need. You'll be famished." He gently released her hold and shut the door. He was pleased to see her. She was always full of life, a beacon of hope in the gray world he tended to inhabit.

They had a good relationship, despite the difference in their ages; God, it didn't bear thinking about: he was thirty-two years older! His heart held a special place for her, but they had not taken it further than the occasional kiss. That age difference inhibited him.

"There's plenty of time to grab a bite to eat," she said. "I'm surprised they kept you waiting all this time."

"It took them a while to dig out the poor guy and then take photos for identification purposes."

She shuddered expressively. "It must have been a shock finding a body there."

"Particularly since I knew the dead man."

She gasped. "You did? *Madre de Dios*! Who was it?"

He explained, briefly, ending, "From what Rod let slip, I think he was working undercover on a pedophile ring."

"That's—awful—that such things can happen here..."

Leon tended to agree. The Spanish were renowned for their love of children; it was in his half-blood too. "I didn't enlighten Inspector Chávez about that, however."

She sat on the corner of her desk and her skirt rode up to just above her knees. "Enlighten *me* then." She arched a dark eyebrow.

"A brandy first," he said and went through the connecting door into his office. He returned with two tumblers and a bottle of Chivas Regal. He gave her the glasses and poured.

While they sipped the blended Scotch whisky, he related the rest of the morning's events.

"Is it a coincidence?" She pressed the tumbler to her ample chest.

"I believe so. While it's possible somebody has seen me and Rod together, they wouldn't know I was going to play golf with Señor Montoya. And why would they leave the corpse as a warning? Warning about what, eh? The anonymous tip-off to the police implicates Montoya in something, that's for sure."

"So if the lynx hadn't unearthed the body, the police would have in a matter of time?"

"Yes, but as the tip-off was vague, it might have taken

longer—and caused more disruption for Montoya. He definitely seemed distressed."

"Well, that's not surprising," Carlota said. "His golf course was shut because of a murder. That's unsettling, isn't it?"

"Okay. He was evasive more than upset." His stomach rumbled. He checked his watch. "Time for tapas?"

"You're paying?"

He grinned. "Of course. Don't I always?"

"Considering the salary you pay me, you'll *always* owe me."

They found a table at the rear of their regular tapas bar; Leon had his back to the wall which gave him an unrestricted view of the clientele. Carlota sat on his left, running a finger down the condensation of her caña, a small glass of draft beer—La Caña Maestra, while Leon sipped at his usual Mahou doble—a tall glass, pleasantly cool.

An overhead television showed a quiz-game but the sound was muted and nobody paid it any attention.

The young waiter brought them assorted plates of pinchos: piquillo peppers stuffed with Basque shredded crab; small chorizo sausages in cider; curry chicken croquettes; salmon and Iberian ham skewered on bread; two portions of Spanish omelette; and a small dish of albóndigas—meatballs in sauce.

A nearby table was occupied by four tourists in shorts and garish T-shirts.

"I know that look," Carlota said. She nibbled on a croquette, brushed a crumb from her plump lower lip. "You're mulling over something."

"Rod's tattoo."

"What about it?"

"The naked lady was the same, complete with the tiny initials 'RE'. But he'd had a fresh addition made. Next to the 'RE' was a small dash followed by 'PG'."

"And they were definitely new?"

"They weren't there a couple of weeks ago when I last saw him."

"So 'PG' could be a new girlfriend?"

Leon shrugged.

"You could ask Jeroen," she said. "He might even have done it."

"I will."

———

Leon had first-hand knowledge of criminal tattoo styles. Hiroki, an ex-member of the Yakusa was someone he helped a while back; the man mountain was a prime example, with almost his entire body covered. Leon had also come across examples among criminals who indulged in the practice improvising with dubious equipment, even resorting to burning rubber to create ash which they then mixed with urine ostensibly to reduce the risk of infection. He was aware that some prisoners' tattoos conveyed details about their wearer, whether a drug addict, someone who could withstand extreme pain or perhaps the number of prison sentences served. Unfortunately, according to Jeroen, such amateur tattooing may be prone to the transmission of infection, mainly due to unsterilized makeshift equipment or poorly sourced inks; serious infections such as hepatitis, herpes, HIV, staph, and tetanus.

Jeroen was Dutch; tall, sinewy and of a lean build. He sported a chain-tattoo round his neck and round both wrists, "signifying I'm a captive of my skill," or so he said, anyway. He had a ginger goatee beard, eyebrows and hair, which was in a ponytail. His blue-eyed gaze was always intense, as if he was considering where to put in the needle next. He'd just finished with a client and shut the door, put up the 'closed' sign. As a reliable professional, he wore blue nitrile gloves and now peeled them off.

Leon described the tattoo on Wallace's forearm, giving the dead agent's alias.

"Roger Eastlake..." Jeroen nodded. "I know the name." He went over to his counter, pulled out a thick ledger and leafed through it. He tapped a finger on an open page. "Yes, I did his tattoo."

"What did the initials 'RE' signify?"

"That's my idea. I put the initials of my customer somewhere on the tattoo. In his case, it was amongst the grass leaves..."

"You do that for every customer?"

"Now I do, yes."

"But he was an undercover cop—the initials could have exposed his cover in a future case when he used a different alias..."

Jeroen shook his head. "Not really. Few people are observant enough to detect the initials. Anybody who does, the initials are meaningless, aren't they? Could be a lost love, a family member, anybody."

"Why do you do it?"

"Several years ago there was a sad case in Amsterdam, where I was working. The police showed me photographs of a corpse with tattoos but no face or hands. I was asked to identify the person by the tattoos. I couldn't. The artwork resembled mine, but I couldn't be sure—and, besides, some illustrations are very popular. The victim could be one of over a hundred customers. So I decided then that I'd always make a single alteration to each version of a specific tattoo and note it against the customer's entry in my ledger. And I'd also insert the customer's initials."

"Very public-spirited of you."

"I didn't do the dash and the 'PG', though."

"What do you make of that?"

"I would have to see a photo to make any judgment. Though I could guess..."

"Guess away."

"It might be a kind of initiation—or entry into a club."

"Like a nightclub stamp?"

"Maybe... It's a stretch. Most nightclubs use rubber stamps for a single visit only."

Leon exhaled. "Yes, but this looked like a permanent tattoo."

"Maybe he has to become a permanent club member?"

A glint of insight flashed. Leon said, "And the initials could signify the club's name..."

"And before you ask, Leon, I haven't seen any 'PG' tattoo on any recent customers."

A frustrating dead end for now, he thought.

———

CARLOTA LOCKED the office door and then descended the stairs. The landing light clicked off, thrusting upstairs into darkness as she crossed the atrium to the front door.

Stepping out, she closed the door after her.

Leon had related what the tattooist had said, and it worried her. Most cases that Leon took on didn't unduly concern her. But this did—for obvious reasons. Most of his cases didn't feature violent death.

She was hardened to the real world where criminals seemed to roam the streets with impunity. She'd joined the police to make a difference. And in her own small way she had put away a handful of miscreants over the years. But it never felt enough. Often, the criminals were out on the streets too soon. "Why let out murderers to kill again?" Leon had seethed when yet another murder was committed by an ex-prisoner parolled early.

"The keys should be thrown away for all child killers," she said with intense feeling in response.

"I can't fault you there, my dear."

Abruptly, as she was passing a shoe shop, she stopped walking and turned slowly.

A chill had run down her spine. It was a familiar sensation she'd experienced while policing. Being watched. Being followed—stalked.

But there was nobody suspicious anywhere in sight.

She returned her attention to the window, to look at the shoes on sale. The heels on so many were ridiculous. If the wearer had to flee an attacker, they'd have no chance! She was comfortable in her Mary Janes.

She scanned the reflections of passersby.

No, she chided herself, *there was nothing to worry about*.

Chapter 2

Gone Missing

MARTÍN DELGADO HAD CELEBRATED HIS FORTY-seventh birthday on the day of his release from Villena Penitentiary, Alicante Province. He didn't feel like celebrating, however, after five years behind bars in a place that housed some fourteen hundred inmates. He'd been banged up thanks to the efforts of Leon Cazador. He hadn't known him by that name at the time of his sentencing; the undercover guy had been using the alias Simon Caballero. His girlfriend Liliana revealed the truth of it only a month ago during one of her regular visits.

"A little bird told me that from time to time he works undercover to smash gangs like yours," Liliana had said.

"An undercover cop?" Delgado seethed.

"No, he's a private investigator. Works out of Torrevieja."

Wrinkles appeared across his prominent brow bridge. He swore.. "I lost five years of my life thanks to him!"

———

IF YOU'D GONE STRAIGHT, Liliana thought, *you wouldn't have been caught!* But it was in his nature, she supposed, he was weak-willed, wanted easy money that entailed minimal work. God knows she'd tried to wean herself off him, but they'd been together too long. In the last five years she'd bedded a couple of other men, one of them his best mate, Manolo, but none of them had excited her like Martín. That's why she still visited him. Her future life seemed bound to his. She bit her lip. All that must remain her little secret. He mustn't know she'd been unfaithful. "Cazador has been responsible for putting away others for longer, they reckon," she'd said in a mollifying tone.

His deep brown eyes turned hard on her. "Oh, so I should think myself lucky, eh?"

Yes! "No, of course not," she purred, pacifying. "Now don't go and do something stupid when you get out."

So help me, I'm not spending another five years visiting you in prison.

His complexion was sallow due to the years locked away, yet it was obvious that his thick-set body was strong with muscle tone thanks to the gym work he told her about. She longed to crush herself against his firm torso and feel those powerful arms hug her. "We can move away, start afresh," she promised earnestly.

He bit a fingernail, a bad habit she noticed he'd developed since he was sentenced. "Yeah, you're right. Can I stay with you in your apartment till we find someplace where we can be together for good?" He ran a hand through his short dark brown hair. "That's what I've wanted all these years. Thought of nothing else."

"Yes, of course you can. I'm looking forward to the day." That admission of his had pleased her immensely. He was worth waiting for, after all.

Now, she was waiting for him outside the prison gates.

For the occasion she'd put on a bright red dress, short enough to show off her legs from mid-thigh, and a frilly white blouse that drew the gaze to her substantial bosom.

She hurried into his arms, certain that her enticing perfume would invade his nostrils and excite his senses and put him in the mood.

Instinctively, he hugged her, and she knew he was pleased to feel her curvaceous shape pressed against him. She caught him glancing over his shoulder and grinning at the prison warders who watched. She flushed with pride as their faces reflected envy. She gave him a long lingering kiss, enjoying the taste of him, just to show them.

The gate slammed shut on his life there.

"I promised myself I wouldn't be going back, ever," he whispered in her ear.

"That is wonderful, dearest." She broke free of his embrace. "It's good to hold you!" she exclaimed, tugging at his hand, leading him to her waiting second-hand Seat Ibiza. "But come, we have lots of catching up to do!"

He went with her, his pitted cheeks flushed with anticipation.

As they reached the car, he said, "I have to make a stop at the bank in Guardamar. Stuff I need and money in the deposit box."

"No problem, lover," she replied.

They got in her car. Joy bubbled up in her as she started the engine.

The prison was situated on kilometer 66 on the N330. Within a few minutes she was headed south, on the Alicante road, then veer right towards Guardamar.

They were together again—for good.

Everything would work out alright, she told herself.

————

LEON'S OFFICE WAS UTILITARIAN, businesslike. His old mahogany desk held drawers on either side of the knee-well, a blotter pad to protect the polished surface, and a telephone with a connection to Carlota's. There was his swivel leather chair, two straight-backed guest chairs, a single window behind him with the Venetian blinds constantly lowered. On the wall on his right was an aging copy of a painting by Juan Romero de Torres: *Oranges and Lemons*. Behind the painting resided his wall-safe. There was a glass-paneled door in the wall on his left, connecting to Carlota's reception office. In the right-hand corner a four-drawer filing cabinet housed files from his previous cases, assiduously administered by Carlota; it also contained a bottle of Chivas Regal and four tumblers in the top drawer. Next to the cabinet was a small refrigerator standing on a little table, where he kept ice cubes and a couple of bottles of cava brut. He fancied a glass of cava now, but decided against it since it wasn't midday yet.

Standing in the interconnecting doorway, Carlota said, "There's a Beatriz Hernández on my line. Shall I put her call through?"

"What's her story?"

"Her husband Miguel García has been missing a week."

"And the police have no leads?"

"An elderly missing person? Give me a break, Leon."

"You're right, I guess. They either assume he's walked out on her or he's suffering from dementia. Inspector Chávez is always complaining they're expected to be social services as well as cops!"

"Señora Hernández tells me her husband hasn't got dementia."

"Unless she's forgotten?"

"Not even slightly funny, Leon."

"Okay... Though I assume you've told her the trail will be cold by now."

"I did. But I have every faith you'll crack it," she said and winked.

He picked up the phone and Beatriz began: Miguel had left their apartment in Edificio Donna Ximena, saying that, on his way to his latest job, he was going to drop into the *lotería* shop to claim his Euro *reintegro* from *La Primitiva*.

José on the lotto desk knew Miguel as a regular and was adamant that he had not come in that day. Miguel was supposed to go to the La Mata villa of the lawyer Señor

Rafael Morales, to fit a wooden carport in his drive. A three-day job, he'd estimated, but he never arrived.

Leon told her his daily rates and she agreed to employ him and then gave him her address. He promised to drop by.

Beatriz let him in. "I'm sorry to trouble you," she said, "but I fear something terrible has happened to my dear Miguel." It showed in her sleep-deprived, dark brown eyes and unkempt dyed-black hair. She was in her mid-forties, but seemed older since the clear complexion of her chubby cheeks was mottled after she had dried too many tears.

She'd been quite a catch. Her family had worked in the salt industry since the 1820s. Salt was another word for money in Torrevieja. Beatriz thought that Miguel was the salt of the earth, and she should know. In the middle of last century, Torrevieja was a small fishing village on the southeast coast of Spain that also thrived on "white gold", salt production. Today, Torrevieja exported a million tons annually. Twenty years ago, its population was about 20,000. Now it was a sizeable city with in excess of 100,000 residents, over half of them non-Spanish.

It was always delicate in these cases, but he had to ask. "Could he have left you for another woman?"

Stoically she shook her head. "We have always been close. Naturally, I thought it was a remote possibility and checked his closet. All his clothes and shoes are there. He has not taken a single thing—no mementos, nothing. He left for work and did not return."

"Do you know who his previous customer was?" Leon asked.

Beatriz shuffled papers in the sideboard drawer, its shining top filled with framed photographs of their son and daughter and grandchildren and nephews.

Family is important to the Spanish. But there was only one picture of Miguel, taken at least ten years ago. Next to this was a carved bull and matador, well executed. Leon picked it up.

"Whittling is Miguel's hobby, besides gambling," Beatriz

said, and continued to rifle the drawer. "Here we are!" She wafted a piece of paper. "Señora Astrid Hedstrom, a chalet," she said, giving Leon the paper with the address.

"Thanks." He pocketed it. "I'll try this later."

Beatriz leaned against the sideboard and looked up at him. "I informed the police, of course." She then shrugged.

That hunch of the shoulders expressed much. The police were stretched at any time of year and, besides, notices had been posted with the decade-old black-and-white photograph of Miguel. Some families never take photographs and this was the case here. Since their children left, their camera never came out, not even for anniversaries or birthdays.

There was little more the police could do. Naturally, the hospitals were contacted as a matter of routine. No accidents or deaths had been reported, suspicious or otherwise resembling Miguel's description.

In these types of cases, the trail soon goes cold, whether you're searching for a villain or a missing person. He should know, because in his time, he'd worked for several law enforcement agencies around the world. Now, as a private investigator, he was freelance, which he preferred and wondered why he hadn't opted for it much earlier. If he can bring justice to a few of the ungodly while he's doing his job, then he's happy.

Miguel had been an insurance salesman until he was thirty-five, when he'd decided he wanted to work with his hands, creating something. So he became a carpenter. He celebrated his fifty-second birthday a couple of weeks before he went missing.

Leon had to ask: "What mood was he in?" Sometimes bodies were washed up on the rocks further south—failed illegal immigrants, mostly, and, infrequently, the victims or even members of the Russian mafia.

Beatriz shook her head. "No," she said emphatically, "he would not contemplate suicide."

LEON TRIED THE NEIGHBORS FIRST. The police had already done door-to-door, so he didn't expect much.

No. 4, next door, was occupied by a German couple living together, which wasn't unusual in modern Spain—or anywhere else for that matter. Here, in this near-paradise called the Costa Blanca, you found couples starting out again. Everyone—with the exception of murderers, perhaps—should have a second chance.

With a ready smile and gray intelligent eyes, Emil Müller answered the door. He spoke only a little English and some Spanish— "though I go to classes to learn" —so in German Leon explained why he was there.

"My allegiance is split because I'm half-English and half-Spanish," he had explained more than once. "Mother had a whirlwind romance with a Spanish waiter but happily it didn't end when the holiday was over. The waiter pursued her to England and they were married." As a result he was one of those fortunate individuals capable of learning a foreign language with ease: he grew up bilingual, speaking English and Spanish, and soon learned Portuguese, French, Italian, German, Arabic, Chinese, and basic Japanese.

Emil asked him in. His partner, Greta Kauffmann, got up from the sofa and deftly muted the Eurosport television channel. On the coffee table was a chess game, halfway complete. White was being seriously threatened. "Who's white?" Leon asked.

"I am," Emil said ruefully. "Magnus, my old dentist, is my opponent here. Magnus Olsson. We visit each other's apartment alternate weeks."

"A long game, then."

"Sometimes, it is like extracting teeth, Magnus says. Sometimes, far too short! He may be twenty years older than me but his mind is sharp, quick."

Leon broached the subject of missing Miguel.

"Yes, I told the police," Greta said, "I saw him leave our

block at 9:30 prompt Thursday morning. I was just going to the *Centro de cultura Virgen del Carmen* to give a music class." She gestured towards her violin on its stand behind the sofa. "He said *hola* as usual and moaned about his meager lottery winnings. We laughed at that and parted at the street entrance."

Emil started speaking but suddenly it made no sense and his eyes rolled back. It was as if he were having a seizure. He was a big man but, between them, Greta and Leon managed to manhandle him to the floor and placed him into the recovery position.

"Keep talking to him, check his airway," Leon urged, grabbing his cell-phone.

Within three minutes the ambulance arrived and two paramedics hurried in. They were calm and competent and gave Emil blood pressure and ECG tests. As far as Greta knew, Emil merely suffered from tinnitus. He smoked like a chimney, though.

While the paramedics were taking Emil away, with Greta set to follow in her car, the neighbors at No. 5 had come out, showing concern. They were English, so Leon was more comfortable speaking to them.

Eric Jordan was weather-beaten and in his mid-sixties, the cliché image of an ex-merchant seaman, with balding ginger hair and a salt-and-pepper bushy beard. Beside him stood his wife, Gladys, her tinted glasses covering cool blue-gray eyes.

"I thought I saw him outside the swimming pool on Saturday," Eric said, shaking his head. *El palacio de la Infanta Doña Cristina*. "I sometimes walk off the pain—if I keep moving, it isn't too bad." Like many, he'd come here to benefit from the climate and ozone, anything to ease the joint pain and stiffness of osteoarthritis. "Better here than old Blighty, any day!"

Leon agreed, adding, "You spotted him almost three days after he went missing?"

"Well, I *thought* I did. I called out his name, *Señor*

Hernández, but he didn't answer." He shrugged. "Sorry, it must have been someone who looked like him."

As Leon was leaving the Jordans at their doorstep, he met Ludmilla Vasilev in the corridor; she lived alone at No. 6. She was a part-time waitress working in a pub-restaurant and had finished for the morning.

She was in a hurry, as she wanted to get changed and go to the swimming pool. A friend, Dolores García, was waiting below in her Seat Ibiza. Ludmilla hadn't seen Miguel, and suggested Leon try asking her boss, Patrick O'Keefe.

O'Doyle's Irish Pub was open and Leon grabbed a bite to eat. O'Keefe was sensible enough to provide Spanish tapas and food as well as fare for the British clientele. Halfway through his *albóndigas con salsa*, Leon recognised a wiry little man sitting at the bar: Ciro Jara. If he remembered correctly, Jara was wanted by the police on suspicion of car theft. He made a quick call on his phone and then eased up to the bar.

"Ciro, isn't it?" Leon asked.

"*Sí*, what of it?" His close-set dark eyes screwed up. "Do I know you?"

"You probably saw me in court. I got your brother, Diego, arrested a couple of years ago."

He made to move toward the door, but Leon restrained him, pressing his hand against his chest, pinning his back to the bar. Leon felt the man's heart pounding. "We're waiting for company, Ciro. Let's not disappoint them."

He spat two expletives but didn't move.

A few seconds later, the two cops arrived. Chico Gómez and Isabel Soledad. Isabel was a stunner with a black ponytail. Ciro was about to make a fuss but Leon suggested he go quietly, adding that Leon would go quietly with her too, especially as he'd fought her on the dojo "and she's good". Ciro went quietly, in handcuffs.

O'Keefe's live-in partner was a redhead, Bridget Brannigan, who'd taken over the shift from Ludmilla. Being an ex-teacher of French, she was proud of her French accent, which held no trace of Dublin in it, but Leon asked if they could speak in English. Adjusting her bifocals, she said that she knew Miguel. He came round Tuesday nights to play dominoes with two Spanish pals, Paco and Manuel, and a Dutchman, Johan Hoek. They had missed him this Tuesday, though.

Bridget was a survivor from breast cancer and knew Nurse Inma Escobar in Edificio Manumiso, where she lived with O'Keefe. "The police have tried the hospitals," Leon explained.

"Oh, of course," she said. O'Keefe was still at home in the apartment, sleeping in readiness for tonight. "Call on him at 5:30," Bridget advised, "not before. As for his domino partner, Johan Hoek, at this time of day you'll probably find him on his boat, the *Full House*, moored at the *Real Club Náutico*."

It was a pleasant stroll along the Paseo Juan Aparicio with the rocks and stone benches on his left. A tourist couple were having their photograph taken with the sculpture of Bella Lola, who perpetually stared out to sea for her loved one. The *ayuntamiento* had worked hard to eliminate the gratuitous splurges of graffiti, but they seemed to be fighting a losing battle. Ethnic and handicraft stalls were doing brisk business. It was still too early for the evening *paseo* of the townspeople. Torrevieja was well endowed with squares and monuments but it was nothing without its people, and this city had managed better than many to integrate an amazing international mix, with restaurants to match.

As Leon passed the port entrance, he waved to Pedro on Customs duty.

Now, the Paseo Vistalegre is attractive and modern, but it wasn't too long ago that it looked as though it had recently suffered its own little earthquake. Then a mindless vandal deprived the statue band of their trumpet: *I know where I'd like to stick the instrument if I ever found the culprit*, Leon thought. However, the band had now been re-sited and a new trumpet restored. Never let the senseless idiots win.

He turned left, and climbed the steps to the marina.

Halyards clanged against masts in the slight breeze. Johan Hoek was on his ketch, *Full House*, adjusting the after lower shroud. He was swarthy and overweight, with brown hair and a mousy mustache.

Leon mentioned Bridget and Johan welcomed him onboard and motioned for him to take a seat in a folding chair in the well deck and then he sat opposite.

While Leon explained the purpose of his visit he glimpsed the moored decommissioned submarine, S61 *Delfin*, a tourist attraction. It reminded him of the time he was clandestinely landed on a hostile shore a few years ago from a British conventional boat. But that was another story.

"Yes, Miguel is a gambler." Johan's teeth betrayed excessive smoking. "Just like me. Bet on anything."

"Does he have any money difficulties?"

"Don't think so. But we're all feeling the pinch these days, eh?"

Just then Leon spotted a sailing boat entering the harbor, the steering position was behind the mizzen, so it was a yawl. The water was almost reaching the gunwales. As he'd seen the same boat leave the harbor a few hours earlier during his mid-morning coffee and brandy, he wondered why it should be lying so low in the water now. Perhaps they'd landed a big shark.

"Excuse me, Johan, I must make a call." Walking to the stern, Leon phoned Pedro and he agreed to prepare a reception committee. It was not unknown for smugglers to leave their merchandise hidden on the nearby island of Tabarca for pick-up.

"Sorry about that. Is there anyone else I can talk to? Fellow gamblers?"

Johan said, "Yes, the *abogado*, Rafael Morales."

Leon knew Rafael. They trained together at the karate

dojo. He'd have to cancel a session tonight, since he was working on this case, but he could take ten minutes out to talk to him there. Apart from gambling, Rafael enjoyed playing billiards and watching bullfights. "Reminds me of the court-room," he said.

A bald man came up from below. He had leathery features and a Cadiz-style beard.

"This is Pavel Sokolov," Johan said. "He's staying on my boat while his house gets finished."

"If ever!" joked Pavel Sokolov.

Leon knew him. He was a rogue builder. Señora Mendez in Calle Ramon Gallud had issued a *denuncia* against him because she had paid for work he never even started. As he'd given a false contact address and phone number, the police hadn't been able to question him: he'd done a vanishing trick. The gall of the man, to live on the seafront virtually in plain view here.

"Unfinished work—that's something you know about, isn't it, Pavel?"

"Eh?"

"I'm sorry, Johan," Leon said, "but I'm going to have to make a citizen's arrest."

Pavel's best defense was extreme halitosis but he succumbed to a little jiu-jitsu manhandling. Leon persuaded him to accompany him to the police station, where he was charged with fraud and working without a licence.

So he had his martial arts workout, after all. He still went to the dojo.

Rafael had finished his session. He sat in the changing room, towelling down after a shower. He wasn't surprised when Leon mentioned Miguel's disappearance. "That would explain why he hasn't turned up." He brushed a hand through thick, tawny hair. "I telephoned, but his wife wasn't too helpful. In fact she seemed a little upset..."

"Yes, she would be."

"Of course, I can see that now." He adjusted his glasses with mirrored lenses, remembering. "No, it wasn't a three-day job—more like a day. The wood was delivered and his tools are still there."

"What about the gambling in O'Doyle's pub?"

"Harmless fun. Miguel is good, he gives nothing away. Keeps things close to his chest."

That's the problem, Leon thought. Nobody seems to know what he was thinking or planning to do. It happens all over the world, though. For no reason whatsoever, men and women just up and leave their home and family. The majority are found within days. Perhaps the most famous instance was the missing crime writer, Agatha Christie. She was gone for about ten days in 1926. Her reason was stress, the death of her mother coinciding with the discovery of her husband's infidelity.

But by all accounts Miguel wasn't stressed. He worked most days, but chose the hours that suited him. Starting about ten in the morning, he stopped for a light lunch at two and started again at four, and went on for a couple of hours and then returned home to Beatriz. Exceptions were when he worked further afield on big contracts, usually extensive fincas in the countryside or mountains. Sometimes he stayed at a small hotel to avoid excessive travel, as his VW van was rather ancient.

The van was found while Leon had been talking to Rafael. Beatriz phoned to tell him. She was very distressed. After Leon had calmed her, he got in touch with a contact, Concepción in *Agrupación de Tráfico* and learned that the van was discovered near Avenida Habaneras. Badly dented, hood crumpled, the offside headlight smashed, it was against a yellow curb, but there are so many illegal parking transgressors that it could have been a month before it was towed away. The cop on the beat had put a sticker on the windscreen. Concepción confirmed there was no blood and no sign of foul play.

Coincidentally, the van was found close to Edificio Encarnadino, where Roberto Ramos, the pathologist, lived. He and Leon were about the same age and, from time to time, he helped unofficially with investigations. Leon knew he was a keen chess player. He also whiled away the time knitting. It took his mind off the cadavers, apparently.

Like many streets in Torrevieja, there was a motley collection of apartment blocks, all of eye-catching design. It seemed as though no two were alike. The potential was there for it to appear an absolute mess, yet it didn't. Balcony rails were draped with washing, lines were strung between blocks; other high terraces were filled with bicycles while some were festooned with plants. Clearly, many balconies offered a retreat from the wear and cares of the day.

Roberto answered the door with a Marlboro hanging from his lips. He had a dark complexion and was prematurely gray.

"A little tame for you, this one, isn't it?" he said, pouring a coffee for Leon in the kitchen.

"From time to time I help friends." Leon shrugged. "It's what I do."

"You're a saint, Leon."

"No, not really. I just like to get to the bottom of puzzles and problems."

"Well, I can't tell you too much about Miguel. Yes, I knew him and we met occasionally in the bar."

Roberto also enjoyed dancing and his current dance partner—'purely platonic', he hastened to add—was Astrid Hedstrom, Miguel's previous customer.

Small world, Leon thought.

He went round to Astrid's chalet and asked about Miguel's work, which he had completed the day before his disappearance.

Astrid was a very attractive silver-blonde in her mid-sixties, with hardly any facial lines and a creamy white skin. He soon learned that she was an ex-beauty salon owner. "No, you are mistaken, Señor Cazador. He only spent two days on the work. He was fast but competent. I have no complaints."

There was a pattern here, he could sense it.

He arrived at the Edificio Manumiso and rang the Olsson's bell.

Magnus the dentist was quiet-spoken and his wife, Hilde, was a perfect advertisement, with faultless sparkling teeth. "I'm semi-retired now," she said, "but I still run a few sessions per week."

"What do you do?"

"Sex therapy."

Sex—frustration, obsession or whatever—could be a cause for leaving home. Sex and money are two strong motivators.

"And before you ask, no, I can't divulge who my clients are."

That told him straight.

Magnus, the chess-player, smiled. "Thanks for helping Greta with Emil earlier."

"Have you heard from her?"

"Yes, he had taken two contra-indicated medicines, which she didn't know about. He reacted badly, but he's going to be all right. They'll keep him in overnight for observation."

"Glad to hear it. Do you know anything about Miguel Hernández, anything at all?"

Magnus shook his head. "I've seen him about, from time to time. Never noticed him much, though. Sorry."

"Well, thanks," Leon said and shortly afterwards left.

Outside their door, he checked his watch. Five pm. Half an hour, then he'd call on Patrick O'Keefe. But first he'd try next door. The nurse, Inma Escobar, lived here. The door opened to his knock. Fortunately, she was in off her shift.

He showed his ID. "I'm looking for a missing person, Señora Escobar. Can I come in?"

"Yes, Señor Cazador, of course, though I doubt if I can help you." She ushered him into a neat little lounge and shut the door. "Most missing person enquiries are directed at the hospital."

"That's been covered already." He did a double take as he

noticed on her sideboard there was a familiar whittled bull and bullfighter. Plus some family photographs. He had to ask: "Who's the couple?"

"My cousin, Dolores, it shows her wedding."

"They look happy. What's her husband's name?"

"Carlos García."

Miguel's double.

Leon said, "You've been most helpful already, Señora Escobar, but I wonder if you could give me a little more information..."

———

ACCORDING TO INMA ESCOBAR, her cousin Dolores lived at the Edificio Encarnadino. He knocked on her door.

Miguel opened the door. He wore a faded green T-shirt, jeans and espadrilles. "Yes, can I help you?"

"*Hola*," Leon said, and introduced himself. "I'm working on behalf of Señora Beatriz Hernández and I'm looking for her husband, Miguel."

His brow wrinkled. "Those names, they sound familiar, but no, I don't know any missing person."

"Who is it, Carlos?" called his wife, Dolores.

He turned his head to answer. "A private investigator, he's looking for a missing man." On the back of his neck was a distinctive birthmark.

"Why's he come here?" she said, moving into view at the end of the hallway.

"Can I come in for a moment?" Leon asked.

"Very well," he said, "but don't take too long. We're going out."

Dolores walked up to Carlos and held his arm.

Leon introduced himself again.

"Why are you here?" she said, dark eyes wary.

"I'm looking for this man," he said, and showed them both the decade-old photograph.

The likeness was remarkable, even so. "But..." she stammered, "this could be you, Carlos..."

He wrinkled his brow again.

"I think we all need to sit down," Leon suggested, "and perhaps have a coffee."

———

IT TOOK a while and plenty of coffee to disinter buried memory and unravel the facts.

Miguel had met Dolores when he was an insurance salesman, and fell in love. Yet he still loved his wife, Beatriz. The relationship with Dolores became so intense that he changed career and married her. When with Dolores, he worked as a painter, often 'away on contracts'.

He always over-estimated the duration of his jobs so he could spend that spare time with one of his two wives.

That Thursday, his van had been involved in a minor collision. The other vehicle drove off, leaving Miguel disoriented. He'd knocked his head and all memory of Beatriz and his life with her was submerged. Guilt can do that. He'd obtained help from several passers-by to move his damaged van against the curb; then he went home—to Dolores.

He was surprised to learn that he was a bigamist, while his two wives were shocked and considerably annoyed when they learned the truth.

It had been a long day, but not that unusual: a day in the life of a private eye! Leon had been instrumental in getting a few ungodly to help the police with their enquires and he'd interviewed German, Spanish, English, Irish, Russian, Dutch and Scandinavian nationals, all of whom had tried to be helpful regarding Miguel's disappearance. It was interesting to see how they all seemed connected.

Elsewhere in the world there'd be ghettoes—Little Italy, and Chinatown, and countless other small 'nations', each maintaining their separateness within the greater metropolis.

But here, in Torrevieja, whether by accident or by design,

that hadn't happened. Here, he witnessed it daily, people from all nationalities rubbing along together and enjoying life under the Spanish sun.

———

THE TELEPHONE CALL from Inspector Chávez was brief: "Señor Cazador, I thought you'd like to know that I have been informed someone is being sent to replace the late Rodney Wallace."

Señor Cazador; this was formal, then. "What he was working on must be very important, Inspector. That's a fast response from the NCA, isn't it?"

"It is. I wonder why they haven't used the other NCA agent in place here in the Costa Blanca — Sebastian Okoro."

"I know him. Maybe his ethnicity would stand out?"

"That is possible."

"Do you know the new guy's name?"

"His cover name is Evan Tremayne, that is all I can say. You are not to approach him. He will be traveling with several potential suspects."

"Thanks for letting me know. But, Inspector, why are you telling me this?"

"In case your investigations should fall upon a certain Evan Tremayne."

"My investigations?"

"Unofficially I know that you are making enquiries about your late amigo Rodney."

Chávez was well-informed.

Leon said, "Just curious."

"Well, tread with care—we would not want you to, how you say, queer the pitch for Señor Tremayne, no?"

"Consider me suitably warned, Inspector."

Chapter 3

Blood Lust

Rome

Months earlier, American politician Harley Coleman was identified as a passenger on an Iberian flight to Rome. On the same flight was a certain Vanda Dinescu. But thereafter their trail had gone cold. Enquiries were made at Harley's home town, but he never came back and a new incumbent had to be voted in. His wife continued with her suit for divorce, changing the grounds to desertion; she was incensed to learn that Harley had siphoned off all his money, transferring the funds overseas. There should be a law against it!

Throughout their escape from the Hit-the-Target hacienda and Spain, Harley and Vanda had fumed over the disruption caused by that damned investigator Leon Cazador.

They disembarked at Fiumicini airport, purchased their tickets on the platform and validated them on the Leonardo da Vinci Express. The journey into the center of Rome took them thirty-five minutes.

Weeks ago, once they'd gotten clear of the hacienda, Harley had purchased a travel case each and a minimalist wardrobe so that they had clothing to change into while they traveled to their final destination, Italy.

Cosimo was waiting for them outside the train station. He was about thirty-five, with jet-black hair, an olive complexion, startling gray-green eyes and long lashes, and an easy smile. Vanda had enjoyed a one-night stand with him when she visited from Bucharest a while back and, though they enjoyed the experience, they mutually decided to be useful friends rather than lovers. "It's less complicated," he had admitted chivalrously but with some reluctance in his tone.

She spoke Italian with Cosimo as they walked to the taxi rank. "This is mine," he said, patting the hood of a parked white cab with its light on the roof. "I drive it when it suits." He loaded their small amount of luggage in the trunk and helped them into the rear. He got in, drove alarmingly fast, negotiating the traffic with skill. "I will drop you at a small apartment I have spare in my portfolio on Via Torino until you can arrange something else," he said over his shoulder. "Second floor, number 27."

As they traveled through the busy streets, Vanda explained to Harley that registering at a hotel was not a wise move. Their passports might be traced.

Harley said, "That makes sense, I guess, honey." His fluting voice was no longer so pronounced since they'd been together so long.Then he leaned closer and whispered, "How do you know this guy?"

She nibbled his ear. "If I didn't know better, I'd say you were jealous."

"Well, maybe I am. He's handsome. And Italian…"

"Cosimo and I are business associates. We do each other favors—in illegal business. He has a number of good contacts. I think he will help supply us with new papers."

"What, fake passports?"

"Yes. Does that worry you?"

"No, not really. I reckon it excites me, honey." He slid a hand over her thigh. "Everything about you excites me!"

At times like this she marveled at his naivety. He was eight years older than her yet behaved like a gauche guy in his early-twenties.

Cosimo drew up to a block of apartments. He got out, gave Vanda two keys on a ring and then helped them to the foot of the steps with their cases. "Give me a call when you need anything," he said. "*Ciao!*"

They climbed the steps to the front door and she inserted the key. They entered an echoing lobby with pigeon-holes for mail on the left. Number 27 had no mail, not even any circulars.

"I'll go and check the apartment," she told him. "Watch the cases." She climbed the stairs rather than risk what appeared to be a rickety old elevator with concertina doors.

The second key opened the door to 27. The place was basic, but clean: a bathroom with shower cubicle, a bidet and washbasin, a tiny kitchen, a lounge and a single bedroom. The color-scheme was bland, mainly cream and brown. She left the door open and skipped down the stairs, her footsteps reverberating off the walls.

Hugging him, she whispered, "It's basic, darling, but it's our very own love nest!"

He grinned and carried the two heavy cases, while she handled the smaller baggage.

Once inside, she suggested they dump their bags for now. "I'm famished. I fancy fast food, yes?"

"Makes no mind to me, honey. You lead, I follow!" They stepped into the street and he said, "I'll hail a cab, honey."

"No, you can't, it isn't allowed," she replied. "Over there," she cried, pointing, "there's a taxi stand in that piaz-za!" She asked the driver to take them to McDonalds, which happened not to be far on Via Barbieri, which she thought was just as well as the fare was exorbitant.

As Harley paid the fare, he said, "Hey, don't worry about it. I've got more than enough to treat you to dozens of taxi cab rides!"

She took his arm, pressed close against him. "I promise

you in due course lovely Italian meals in cosy restaurants, my dear," she said as they entered the world's most ubiquitous restaurant. "But for now, we need to eat quickly and settle into our apartment..." She clutched her shoulder bag to her; it contained her passports, snug in their ziplock polythene bags. "... at least until we can find somewhere else, ideally not far from the train station." *Always try to stay close to a means of escape.* That was her credo.

"I'm in your hands, honey. I don't speak the lingo."

The fact that she spoke Italian obviously proved useful. More importantly, it meant that Harley couldn't understand what she said to other people, which she had no doubt would also prove valuable from time to time. "I will be your travel guide, no?"

"Oh, yes!"

But their first night in Italy was almost their last as a couple. Harley woke in the early hours of the morning, his whole body shuddering. Disconcertingly, his owlish denim eyes showed abject fear.

"What is it, dearest?" she asked, fingers running through his auburn hair.

He wiped a hand down from his high forehead over his face; it came away damp with sweat. "A severed bloody hand was grasping at my throat, choking me!" he said, the fluting pitch of his voice increasing. He continued to shake and ooze sweat. "I couldn't stop it—and then I woke up! It was horrible!"

Though she found him distasteful to touch in this clammy sweat-soaked state, she forced herself to hug him and finally managed to soothe him. She marveled at herself; considering what she had done in life, and yet she slept soundly, and didn't even dream about snakes anymore. Though she still suffered a persistent itch over the scar where she'd cut the area of the snake bite.

Sadly, the wimp had the same nightmare most nights, which was quickly verging on being wearing.

Yet she wasn't ready to abandon him . He was attractive;

some might even say he was handsome. He had oodles of money, which he willingly spent on her.

No, in truth, he needed a distraction. Embrace *la dolce vita*.

"I've never been to Rome before!" Harley said, excitedly.

"Then let me show you the sights, my dear."

He was childishly trusting.

Their first morning, she took him to a typical café-bar and drank strong caffe macchiato and ate crumbly croissants. Then they strolled round the Colosseum; he was almost speechless at the size of the place. "Gee, seeing it on TV or in a movie doesn't do it justice, honey!" She agreed, licking her lips and reflecting how the sight of the place often awoke her dormant need for blood lust, which she frequently had to restrain.

They toured the ruins of the Roman Forum. Each time she trod this way, she experienced a frisson through her core, as if she could sense the thousands of ancient Romans who had walked and worked and bartered—and loved!—here so long ago. She would like to visit Pompeii again; since her last time there they had unearthed masses of erotic art that had been hidden from the public's gaze for years. But Harley wasn't keen on the journey.

One evening they had dinner at Il Falchetto on the Via dei Montecatini. She warned him, "The fish dish is a test for the squeamish."

He chuckled. "I can eat clams till the cows come home."

It transpired that the catch of the day was scorpion fish, a scarlet sea creature with nasty spines. "The fish's cheeks are thought to be lucky," the waiter explained, "and should always be served to a lady."

"I'll go for it," Vanda said boldly.

"Oh, I'll pass, I reckon," Harley said. Instead, he pointed on the menu to bucatini all'Amatriciana, a pasta dish of chili, tomatoes and crispy cured pork jowl.

She survived the scorpion fish.

In so many ways they behaved like tourists because they

were exactly that. They wined and dined, savoring the tastes and smells of the Eternal City.

Happily, the more they enjoyed the Italian lifestyle, the less frequent Harley's nightmares became.

She had to admit that even for her—to begin with—their sojourn in Rome had been an adventure.

Harley was infatuated with her, and she honestly revelled in his attention. And he was as good as his word when they had first escaped the ill-fated hacienda. He bought her clothes to replace those she'd left behind in their haste to get away, and also a Samsung smart phone. It seemed every Italian carried a cell-phone and was continually looking at it or sending messages or talking apparently into thin air.

After one gorgeous purchase of a diaphanous nightgown she said, "You keep spending money on me, dearest. I only hope you have plenty left." She kissed him on the cheek. "I wouldn't want to bankrupt you!"

"That's sweet of you, Vanda. Actually, the divorce was taking too long! So before I left the States, I opened another bank account so my grasping wife and her money-grubbing lawyers couldn't get their hands on my hard-earned dough." He sighed. "I have more than enough to tide us over, have no fear."

"That's alright, then." She pouted. "A pity we didn't go to the States," she said. "I could have put your wife's head on your trophy wall!"

His eyes almost popped. "Put the mother-in-law up there as well!" He chuckled. "Though it probably wouldn't endear me to my voters!"

They both laughed at that. He didn't seem upset to leave behind his political career. She had that effect on him, clearly.

"It's like a honeymoon!" Harley had said one day on the Spanish Steps. The tourists milling around paid him no mind. And he had eyes only for her.

"Why don't we make it official?" she suggested.

"What—marry?"

"Sure. Why not?"

"But—but I'm still married—the divorce hasn't gone through yet, remember?"

"Nobody needs to know, do they?"

"I suppose not. We're on different continents. It isn't as if she's on my passport! How do you go about it? What about the paperwork?"

"I can arrange that." Because she knew the right people. Using her smart phone she searched for old contacts. She'd visited Italy a number of times while living in Bucharest and established business links of the useful but dubious kind. Cosimo was one of those, and Enrico was another. It didn't take Enrico much effort to alter her name to Wanda Florescu on her current passport. She kept her other two passports spare, just in case. On the continent, often the "V" and "W" are interchangeable and sound the same, with a "V"; yet to the American and British, the "W" sounded as it should, in their eyes, "W for Wicked!" Harley joked.

When he learned about it, Harley went along with the name-change: "Hey, it's like having a new woman," he said.

That night she proved adept at behaving like a new woman just for him. He was besotted.

Fortunately, Harley had his original birth certificate as it had been required when he'd been recruited to the hacienda. Enrico produced a fresh passport for him in the name of Harley Doleman. "If you're not used to switching your name, it is easier to keep your first name—less risk of being caught out," the new Wanda explained to him. "You know it would have been easier simply to change my passport to my married name, Doleman," she'd said.

"No, no, that isn't proper—or romantic. I want the marriage to be real!" he argued.

"You bigamist, you!" she joked, and kissed him.

Her upcoming marriage would allow her to cover her tracks, in case she wanted to return to Spain, where her most lucrative deals had been made.

Any document could be forged for a price, and Harley

was obliging enough to pay Enrico what he asked. She arranged to obtain an affidavit or "Dichiarazione Giurata" sworn to before a U.S. consular officer accredited in Italy, stating that there was no legal impediment to Harley's marriage according to the laws of the United States.

"I'm impressed," Harley said. "I was going to ask how... but perhaps I shouldn't know, eh?"

"That might be best," she reassured him.

After that they visited the Legalization Office of the local Prefettura to legalize the affidavit. The marriage affidavit generally must be authenticated at a Prefettura within the same consular district where the affidavit was executed, which wasn't a problem where fakes were concerned. "They sure give you the runaround, don't they?" he said. They had to purchase a revenue stamp for a paltry sum of Euros from a tobacco shop and then present it to the clerk of the Legalization Office at the Prefettura for each document to be authenticated with more date-stamps.

"You cannot fight it, dearest. The Mediterranean is like this," she said. "The hoi polloi must jump through paper hoops. And they do so love their rubber stamps! And we're not finished yet!"

"Reno's a darned sight easier than this." He groaned. "It's almost as if they want to discourage matrimony!"

There were more hoops, as she had warned. The court official explained, "The Atto Notorio is a declaration stating that according to the laws to which you are subject in the United States, there is no obstacle to your marriage." It was sworn to by two witnesses, who happened to be associates of Enrico. Even though Wanda was fluent, they still needed the presence of an interpreter. "It keeps the interpreters employed," she whispered. They had to produce their plane ticket as proof of their legal presence in Italy. Finally, they presented all the documents to the Marriage Office of the town hall, and made a "Declaration of Intention to Marry" before a civil registrar. After that, they could finally set the date of the wedding! As neither of them was an Italian citizen or permanent resident, the public announcement which had to be posted at the town hall (normally for two consecutive weeks, including two Sundays) could be shorter. Finally, their civil ceremony was performed by the deputy mayor. Still more money was handed over, however: Harley also had to pay a rental fee for the marriage hall, no small amount.

"It was worth the effort and the cost, honey," he declared breathlessly afterwards. They lay on rumpled sheets, an empty champagne bottle in its iced bucket by the bedside.

She was pleased with herself. Before the wedding she'd made Harley happy. And now, after the event, he seemed like a changed person, even happier.

Although she concealed it, she wasn't so happy, though. His nightmares didn't stop completely, and whenever the night-shades disturbed their sleep, she found them exceedingly tiresome. *He* was becoming a nightmare. She yearned for a much stronger man.

Foolishly, immediately after their marriage, still swathed by conjugal euphoria, he gave her the PIN number access to his US bank account from which he regularly drew funds. She'd seen the balance on the ATM screen: even after everything he'd spent so far, the balance was a tidy sum.

Sadly, she had to admit that he was beginning to pall. Now, she wanted to be rid of him—and as a consequence withdraw all that money.

Before she made her final move, she spoke to Cosimo in Italian. They sat at the dining table while Harley watched a NFL game on the television.

"I feared you would tire of this romance business," Cosimo told her softly, nodding at Harley. "You need excitement and risk in your life. That is what drives you. I know this. And he does not provide it for you."

"What do you suggest?"

"I keep abreast of happenings on the Dark Web. There is a certain Spaniard who is seeking investors in a project. Iglesias could be an intriguing player."

"Intriguing, hmm? How?"

"It depends on your scruples..."

"Where business is concerned, Cosimo, I keep my scruples in a locked drawer."

"In which case it's probably going to suit you."

"Can't you be more specific?"

"He has certain safeguards on the Dark Web so he hasn't spelled it out. But it's dark. He knows law agencies trawl so he's careful. I'll give you his contact number. Tell him my name and he will talk to you." He gave her the number.

"Thank you, Cosimo. I appreciate it."

"That is what old friends and lovers are for, no?"

"You're a good *friend*."

His lips downturned, as if he'd hoped the mention of "lovers" might have relit an old spark; it hadn't. "Oh, well, I'll leave you both to your football match, eh? I'll see myself out. *Ciao*!"

After Cosimo had left, Harley muted the TV's sound. "What did he want? Not more money, I hope!"

She went into the kitchen and took a can of Coors from the refrigerator. She returned with it and poured into his empty glass mug, making sure she didn't create too much froth, which he abhorred. "He was telling me about a lucrative deal I could get involved in. I need to phone his contact."

He slurped the beer and reached out, squeezed her rump, half eyeing the silent game playing on the screen. "You'd better do it, then, honey."

"Don't let my business spoil your game. I'll phone him from the bedroom." She briefly kissed his wet lips. "Okay, husband?"

He grinned. "Okay!"

As predicted, she got through the ring fence by mentioning Cosimo's name.

Tomás Iglesias was in Alicante, on the Costa Blanca, Spain. "I'm interested in your project," she explained. "But I'd like to know more about it before I invest in it."

Iglesias sounded cagey. "Perhaps we should meet first,

before any decision is made, no?" His voice was deep, attractive.

"I can fly into Alicante," she offered.

"Rather could you make it Madrid tomorrow? I have business to take care of in Chinchón—do you know it?"

"Yes—it's not far outside the city."

"Meet me at the Aniseed Parlor at 5pm tomorrow."

Her pulse raced. "I'll be there," she promised.

In the very early hours of next morning, she and Harley strolled across the Ponte Fabricio footbridge that linked the Jewish Ghetto to Tiber Island. They'd spent a slightly inebriated time in a small yet cheerful bar-restaurant.

The ancient Tiber flowed beneath the arches.

As they'd left the bar, after he'd settled the check, she had picked his pocket and relieved him of his wallet and slipped it in her shoulder-bag. All other important documentation was in their apartment.

Adrenaline coursed through her in anticipation. It had to be tonight. She had to fly to Spain tomorrow if she was to meet with Iglesias. While Harley had showered before their planned night out, she'd booked her flight.

Throughout the evening she'd been keyed-up, wondering how she would do it. Probably push him in front of a car or autobus. But then fate and inspiration hit her. The bar-restaurant they visited provided a kebab speciality. The tasty lamb kebabs were served on metal skewers; one end of each skewer curved into a ring which fitted onto an upright carousel, and on their carousel they were served six skewers. After eating, she surreptitiously concealed one skewer in her napkin and shoved it in her bag.

"Look at the moon, dearest, glowing in the water," she now urged, and detected an uncharacteristic slight tremor of unease in her voice. She hadn't done anything like this for a while. She was getting soft!

Harley leaned forward against the parapet of the bridge and stared hazily at the dark running water. The silver trace of the moon reflected as streaks due to the onrushing river.

"Gorgeous," he slurred. "These weeks have been wonderful, darling. Makes me giddy to think about it."

More like a nightmare, dearest. She scanned left and right—all was clear—and then leaned close.

At this time of night, there was nobody else on the bridge. The street lights were not particularly bright here.

She leaned closer and quickly rammed the long skewer into his ear, forcefully.

He juddered where he stood, staring blankly. There was barely any blood.

Before he became a dead weight or fell back, she hooked her arms under his knees and hauled him up onto the parapet. He'd gained weight since they'd first met, she realized. She checked again—all clear. A hard push with both hands and he went over. She hadn't noticed when she did it, but she'd grazed her wrist on the stone parapet when she'd hefted him up. She ignored the pain, consumed with the euphoria of her action.

A faint splash sounded as her husband hit the water. Disposed of in the Tiber—the repository of countless corpses throughout history.

We had some good times, Harley. Adieu!

Another quick glance around revealed that nobody was in sight. She was in the clear.

Her heart pumped and adrenaline coursed through her. She was on a high.

Next morning, she went to a hair-dresser and had her hair cut short, a fashionable bob.

Then she flew to Madrid.

Chapter 4

Close Associates

Spain

Combining comfort and style, Wanda traveled in a black Balenciaga single-breasted blazer with matching pants and a light gold blouse. She retained her shoulder-bag, for it held all her important documents. Her two suitcases were swiftly processed. At Madrid airport she hired a car which had adequate space in the trunk for her cases, a yellow Seat Leon. When she'd signed for the car a shiver ran through her as it was the only vehicle style on offer at the time. Its name reminded her of her encounter with the damnable Leon Cazador. It briefly left a very bad taste in her mouth.

She was not in sight-seeing mode, but she could hardly avoid noticing the bronze statue of Don Quixote on Rosinante leading Sancho Panza on his donkey; both reflected in a pool in Madrid's Plaza de España. The stone sculpture of Cervantes loomed over his immortal creations. She drove past the Prado museum on the Paseo del Prado until she reached the great Arch of the Emperor Carlos. Wherever she looked Madrileños congregated, most of them stylishly dressed, few indeed in a hurry, chatting together or conversing on cell-phones.

Then she swung left to follow the Valencia sign, exiting the city on the A3. It was only fifty kilometers to Chinchón. But the multi-lane expressway soon narrowed to a two-lane highway.

The city disappeared behind as the sunburned hills of the Castilian plateau surrounded her.

About thirty minutes passed and then she came to the village of Villejo de Salvanes. She found a parking space and had a coffee and a tasty warm empanadilla.

After paying her check, she got in the car, found a turn-off, and drove on following the road clearly marked for Chinchón.

There were silver-green rows of olive trees, vineyards and grazing goats. The sky resembled those that Velázquez painted: pale, barely dense enough to support clouds. In contrast, the soil was a rich terracotta brown. It was good to be back in Spain, the real Spain—not the cities, not the beach resorts.

A half hour later after the turn-off she drove up a steep hill and then Chinchón suddenly loomed ahead. She slowed and motored down through narrow streets to the main square, the irregular vaguely oval plaza. It was a while since she'd been here. The place had not lost its charm, with its multi-tiered balconies, painted dark green, jutting out from whitewashed old buildings and wooden arcades which enclosed the cobblestoned plaza. In the shadows of the lower balconies were bars and shops and cafes. Even now she could see laundry still being washed in the town fountain. She wondered if bullfights continued to be held in the square; considering the controversy over the tradition, they might have been banned. The buildings were constructed with slim ochre-colored bricks, the kind seen all around the region.

Overlooking the town on a hill to the west was the ruined fifteenth century castle, the so-called Castle of the Counts.

She found a parking space with ease outside the Aniseed Parlor. The clock tower chimed the hour—5pm. The window was crammed with assorted bottles containing aniseed liqueurs and strings of local garlic. She grabbed her shoulder-bag and exited the Seat, locked it and entered the shop. A tinkling bell announced her arrival.

Two men stood behind a long wooden counter.

The elderly man was quite nondescript with a gray-streaked beard and wore wire glasses, while the younger one was quite attractive in her opinion. He had shining dark eyes, thick black eyebrows, a tanned complexion, a jutting chin with a dimple, a strong nose, and a fleshy mouth. His thick black hair partially covered his ears. He wore a bright blue floral shirt.

"Can I help you?" the elderly man said.

"I'm looking for Tomás Iglesias."

"Then you've found him," the younger one said. He lifted up a counter flap and walked through; he was wearing gray chinos, with matching gray stitched loafers. He offered his hand. "I am enchanted to meet you, Señora Doleman."

They shook; his grip was firm but not overbearing.

He turned to his companion. "I'll arrange for transport of the next consignment, Luc."

"Very good. Have a good day, Tomás. Miss."

"Thank you," she said.

Iglesias gently held her elbow and guided her to the door.

She couldn't place his after-shave or cologne but the scent excited her senses. "Where are you taking me?"

He grinned, an attractive non-threatening curve of the mouth. "For a business meal. We can then talk about your future investment, no?"

"Yes, I would like that."

He took her down a narrow cobbled street to a small restaurant. The building was ancient, its walls immensely thick, built around an airy green courtyard; glazed ceramic tiles, frescoes and antiques were scattered about, amidst three leafy green trees. It appeared to be a cool and shady retreat.

He led her to a round table in a corner. "Allow me to order," he said, holding her chair for her.

"Thank you."

"Can you stay overnight?" he asked.

"I haven't booked anywhere. But my suitcases are in my hire car."

"Good. The parador—it was the convent of San Agustín —it has rooms. Actually, I'm staying there. I only ask because you must try the wine—it's from the neighboring village of Colmenar. And it would be a shame to risk drink and driving, no?"

"I'd like to stay very much. Relaxation after the flight and the drive."

"My sentiments exactly." His heavy-lidded dark brown eyes glinted playfully. "I have a strong feeling we shall become close associates."

"I hope so." *Very close*.

The first course was brought promptly: *sopa de Almendros*. Light and creamy soup delicately flavored with almond, garlic and lemon, garnished with almonds.

"You are not averse to sea-food in all its guises?" he asked.

"No, I'm quite partial," She eyed him coquettishly. "Though I believe oysters are overrated."

He looked askance at her, smiled. "Then, for the main course I suggest *merluza a la Cazuelo con Almejas*." Casserole of hake with clams.

"Tell me a little about yourself, please," he urged.

She was comfortable talking about her past, suitably edited, naturally.

When she talked about Argentina—"I was there about eighteen months ago, lovely exotic country"—she noticed he could hardly keep his eyes off her. She knew only too well that she had that kind of attraction for men. And right now she realized that she desired this man, this Tomás. She shifted out-of-mind all thoughts of previous lovers, Nicholas Badescu, inadequate Lázaro Pérez, Francisco González Baeza and the hapless Harley.

Tomás took her hand in his and stroked it. "For dessert

you must try the speciality of the region: *yemas de Chinchón* —candied egg yolks."

It was delicious, she had to admit.

Finally, he began to talk of his latest venture.

"There's money in pornography," he began.

"Really?" She wasn't going to reveal anything about Baeza's organization and its blackmailing potential. "I'd have thought the Internet has more or less offered it all for free— even children have access!"

"Ah, children. They're the future, you know."

A mite trite, she thought. "Go on."

"Pedophiles are the new victims, I reckon. Greatly misunderstood."

She wasn't too sure about that, but she let him go on.

"They're hunted—more or less in the position that poor Oscar Wilde found himself in, you see."

"As far as I'm aware he didn't have sex with children."

"No, true, but he was hounded for certain frowned upon proclivities..."

"Homosexuality is no longer against the law. Pedophilia is, isn't it?" She didn't want to make it too easy for him.

"It is—for now. Laws change, eventually."

"What about the child's loss of innocence?" she asked.

He leaned forward, his gaze penetrating. "Why do you ask that?"

"Let's say I'm playing devil's advocate."

'You're a devilishly attractive advocate." He smiled. "My argument is that childhood innocence is a modern myth for most families."

"Oh?"

"Apart from the rich through the ages, of course. And even they had incest but it was never discussed... Poor children had little childhood to boast about. No formal education and early on in their short and grim lives they'd be helping in the fields, clambering up chimneys, and dodging dangerous machinery in noisy factories."

"But that's history."

"Modern times for thousands are no better. Look at the children working in the rare metal mines in the Congo, the sweat shops in the Far and Middle East. In truth, it's modern slavery. No innocent childhood for them—the West profits from their misery—and their loss of innocence. The real world denies them their childhood as we envisage it."

"But abusing them can't be better, surely?"

"I've heard some apologists argue that they're 'loving' relationships." He hunched his shoulders. "It depends how you define 'loving', I suppose."

"You condone it, regardless," she persisted, trying to get under his skin.

"I don't agree with it, but I can make a good profit by supplying what the market wants."

"The market's there so somebody must cater for it, is that it?"

"Precisely! That's commerce. It has always gone on. Before, it was small cliques, mainly underground; very secret. Now it's rather more accessible on Social Media and in particular on the Dark Web."

"That's how I located you, actually," she said.

"What were you looking for?"

"A new associate. My previous partner had financial problems."

"Do I know him—or her?"

"I doubt it." She'd risk it: "Francisco González Baeza."

He shook his head. "No, never heard of him."

Dismissed, as if he'd never existed. The thought of Baeza and all the rest was already a distant memory. "I'm not averse to what you propose," she said, resting her hand on his. The touch excited her. She hadn't felt like this for quite a while. Absently, she rubbed the graze on her wrist. *Sorry, Harley...*

"So you will consider going into business with me?"

"I find you intriguing, Tomás. I really do. If you believe in this venture, then I will too. I agree. This association might be mutually beneficial."

"Indeed. We can talk about terms tomorrow, perhaps?"

"Yes." She glanced at the restaurant clock. "Heavens, time is passing. I need to unpack. You'd better show me to the parador."

He insisted on paying the check. They returned to her car and he took her two cases and she carried her travel case and shoulder-bag across the square to the parador.

Though now a state parador, the seventeenth century Convent of San Agustín had retained much of its ancient character and charm, and she was more than pleased that Tomás had brought her here.

After she'd booked in and her cases had been taken up to her room, they strolled through the magnificent cloister and gardens, with cypress trees and rose-bushes in abundance. Although it looked picturesque with its shaded colonnades, she wasn't tempted to try the outdoor swimming pool.

The rooms were all tastefully furnished with antiques and decorated with paintings, tiles, and tapestries, with predominant earthy accents. Hers was very suitable. It had a modern oval bath-tub in the center of the spacious bathroom. The huge bedroom consisted of brown-tiled flooring, blue-and-fawn mats, and a generous double bed with a four-poster mosquito net. White ceilings were interspersed with modern wood beams.

That first evening they supped aperitifs of oak-aged Coloma Merlot on her own private walled-in balcony. She wore a multi-colored wrap-around jersey dress with a V-neck and tie-band at the waist. He'd changed into black and white striped Massimo Dutti shirt and pants.

When they kissed, she whispered, "I don't throw myself at just any man, you do realize?"

"I know. You are most discerning. And, of course, I am not 'just any man', am I?"

She broke their embrace and she led him to her bedside. "Let's form that association right now, hmm?" She pulled away the tie-band on her dress. She wasn't wearing anything else.

Rome

ON VIA DI San Vitale stood an impressive building with flags flying outside and a wall-plaque that announced: *Questura di Roma*.

Inside, in his office within the main police station, Superintendent Fabrizio Moretti of Italy's state police leaned back in his chair and raised his long legs, placing his feet on his desk. He trailed his hands over his vulpine features, an action that did not smooth away the lines around his eyes, nor was it meant to: he'd earned them. He leveled his gray-green eyes on his assistant, Riccardo. "So you've finally obtained a definitive ID for our cadaver?"

"We think so, sir. His dental work suggested he was American."

"Well, that narrows it down…"

Riccardo nodded. "We sent fingerprints to the embassy and they started the wheels turning. They resorted to their Automated Fingerprint Identification System and came up with a name. As a young man he'd been charged with a drink driving offense."

"And his name?"

"It's a Mr. Harley Coleman, a politician from the United States. There was an alert out for him some weeks ago from Spain, but at the time no trace could be found once he'd landed at the airport."

"What was the alert about?"

"Spanish authorities wanted to extradite him. It concerned that hacienda case, remember?"

"Ah, yes. Gruesome business."

"Fingerprints obtained from the hacienda confirm it, sir. It's the same man."

"Good. Next of kin?"

"His wife is flying here tomorrow, sir. They were in the middle of a divorce."

"Ah, the American disease." Moretti stroked his dark brown mustache.

Riccardo shifted from foot to foot.

"Something else?"

"I dug out the details we have about the hacienda case, sir. It's sketchy at best. Coleman absconded with a Romanian, Vanda Dinescu."

"So?"

"It may be coincidence, but using a Romanian passport a Wanda Doleman has just flown to Madrid."

"I admire your diligence, Riccardo. But I can't see us raising an Interpol file on this." He sighed. "Get the widow to formally identify her husband and ensure that the body is repatriated. As he was a politician we don't want any awkward publicity."

CHAPTER 5

CROCODILE TEARS

Southern Spain

LEON'S APPOINTMENTS BOOK TOLD HIM HE HAD A client in five minutes. Carlota stood at the interconnecting door, a pile of folders clutched to her chest.

"Do you know anything about this Señora Flores?" he asked.

"I know you don't take on missing children cases, but Adriana's my cousin. I thought maybe this one time you could make an exception and help her."

He chuckled. "After the last missing person case, which turned out to be a farce, I might welcome this. It's her child that's missing, is it?"

"*Sí.* Her daughter, Nadia." She added, but without the customary smile: "She's twelve going on eighteen..."

"That reminds me of my niece Jacinta at that age. Thankfully, she's twenty now! Has Señora Flores informed the police?"

Carlota bobbed her head. "Yes but—so far—they have *nada.*"

"Show her in, then."

Señora Flores moved hesitantly and sat on the edge of the upright chair, hands gripping a black leather purse on her lap. Her eyes glinted, a coffee brown. Pale, almost pallid skin. Long thin face with a narrow nose. Narrow lips. Raven-black hair swept back in a bun. She wore a flower-pattern short-sleeved dress, yellow Mary-Jane shoes. "It is good of you to see me, Señor Cazador. Oh, and Carlota has told me your daily rate." She fidgeted with the clasp on her purse. "The fees are high and it will be difficult, but I would pay anything to find my Nadia."

He ignored the veiled plea for a fee reduction; for now, anyway. It depended on how the case panned out. "When did Nadia go missing?"

"Two—two days ago I telephoned her friends, but she is not staying with any of them." Tears formed on the rims of her sleep-deprived red eyes. "This is the third day of her absence." Abduction—a mother's nightmare.

"And the police have no leads?"

"They are good, they telephone me each evening. They have even questioned my husband Matias—we are separated —and they confirm he does not know anything about her whereabouts... I have printed posters with her photo and my telephone number and put them in shops and on lamp-posts. I have only had two phone-calls as a result and they were from cranks." Her lips trembled. "I am at my wit's end!"

"Talk me through it, will you? Where was Nadia last seen?"

"There is not much to tell. She went to meet her friend María at the bookshop, *Librería Polgo*. It's only two blocks away."

"I know it. On Calle Apolo."

"*Sí.* I telephoned the shop owner, Señor Manrique, but he was no help. He confirmed the girls go to browse the books and read the comics on the racks but never buy any. I cannot afford to spend money on comic-books."

"Then what do they do?"

"Sometimes they go for a walk along the promenade, looking at the tourists—and cars in the lot by the amusements; Nadia's a bit of a car-buff. But that day María tells me she had a dance lesson so they parted at the bookshop."

"And that's all?"

Reluctantly, she nodded. "When Nadia didn't come home naturally I phoned María. She was upset to learn the news but of no help."

"Doesn't Nadia have a cell-phone?"

"No."

Which seemed most odd; he thought all kids carried them these days, almost an extension of their limbs. He paused for her to go on.

"My husband—he does not contribute any money... Once, when things were alright, she had a phone, but no more. It is in a drawer in her bedroom." She heaved a tremulous sigh. "I cannot afford—"

"Did you bring a photograph of Nadia?"

"*Sí*, Carlota asked me to." She unclasped her purse, handed him a color snapshot of Nadia dressed in her school uniform standing next to her mother in the entrance porch to their apartment.

Nadia was quite tall, slim, with a slight bosom pressing against the white shirt and tie. She had inherited her mother's long face and narrow nose. However, her lips were full. Her eyes were gray, her hair black and long, tied in pigtails, with two metal slides holding it away from her brow. She had brass studs in her earlobes.

A pretty girl, but he refrained from commenting. "Thank you. What was she wearing on that day?"

Agitatedly, she recited, "A yellow-and-blue tank-top, dark red jeans and sneakers."

"Does she have any boyfriends?"

She shook her head rigorously and lowered her gaze to her purse. "No, she is a good girl. She helps me around the house. She has no time for going out with boys."

Poor kid. But then again, she was only twelve. *Wait till she's a teenager*, he thought, reminded of Jacinta again.

He shoved his notepad and a pen across the desk. "Can you give me your husband's address, please?"

She nodded and scribbled it down. "His hours are erratic. He's a greens-man for the Green-Go golf course..." She added sourly, "When he's not gambling..."

"Thank you." He stood and she rose, too. He leaned across and shook her hand. "I'll be in touch."

After she had left Carlota came in. "Can you help her?"

"It's not going to be easy. I can try the bookshop— maybe the owner noticed something untoward."

"Untoward? I don't like the sound of that, Leon."

"If she has no boyfriend to abscond with, what other explanation is there?"

"Maybe she wanted a break from her chores at home?"

"But she has to stay somewhere, a place where she can sleep."

———

Outside the *Librería* *Polgo* stood several trestle tables with boxes of cut-price paperbacks, and beside them book-racks slightly blemished by a thin patina of dust from the passing traffic. There were also wire racks of that day's English, German, Spanish and French newspapers. A couple of browsers hovered.

Leon entered the bookshop and welcomed the contrasting coolness provided by the air-conditioning. He approached the counter on the right. A bespectacled man and a young woman stood in attendance, chatting.

"Excuse me, I'm looking for the owner."

"That would be me. Señor Manrique," the man said. He was about forty, balding and wore a creased white shirt and gray pants. His chin was double, almost triple, and his belly protruded over his leather belt. "How can I help?" He removed his glasses and blinked.

"Yes, of course. The police interviewed me and since then I

have heard nothing, " Manrique said after Leon had explained his reason for being there. "I know the two girls, Nadia and María, yes; they're regulars. They are not alone in browsing but never buying." He pursed his thin lips. "The worst are the youths who read the computer magazines and the girlie mags. I keep telling them to buy or leave. They just laugh. It is frustrating—sometimes they block access for genuine purchasers. Then I get annoyed and chase them off with a few choice words."

"Do you recall Nadia's last visit?"

"I do, for a very good reason." He shuffled excitedly. "Surprisingly, she bought a comic, which made a change—though it wouldn't make me rich, for sure. Wonder Woman."

"Did you see where the girls went?"

"I did. They chatted outside for a minute or two and then split up. Nadia went down the street to the left, in the direction of the harbor and her friend went up the street, to the right."

"Nothing else?"

"No. I was behind the counter. Another customer wanted serving. I thought nothing of it until Señora Flores telephoned me."

"Was there anybody lurking by the door?"

"No more than usual." He pointed to the outside tables. "As you can see, they attract browsers—our bargain selection. Alas, not so many buyers. I despair, the number of readers of books has diminished; all they read now is social media texts!"

———

AS HE STEPPED out Leon turned left and noticed further along the street was a jeweler's shop and above its barred and wire-mesh protected door was a CCTV camera. It was bound to be working; a firm requirement of the insurance company. He rang the bell and a matronly woman in black behind the counter waved at him. A buzzer sounded and the door was automatically unlocked. He swung it open and stepped in.

Approaching the counter, he brandished his card.

"How can I help, Señor Cazador?" she said, returning the card.

"I'm investigating the disappearance of a young girl." He thumbed at the shop door. "Is it possible to check your CCTV for the day in question?"

"When was it?"

"Two—three days ago."

She beamed. "Then it should be possible. The images are preserved for a week, so I'm sure it would be alright." She raised a hand, adding, "But you will need the owner's permission. Señor López is away until this afternoon. Can you call back then?"

"Certainly. What time?"

Compared to England, Spain was a long way behind in street surveillance. He marveled at the sheer volume of images disclosed during that Russian Novichok poisoning case in Salisbury.

"After siesta," she said. "Say, five o'clock?"

"Thanks. I'll return then."

———

MATIAS FLORES's apartment was on the ground floor; the door was in need of paint; it opened directly onto the side street. Leon pressed the buzzer and waited.

He waited almost five minutes until, finally, he heard locks being shot open and Matias cautiously opened the door. His body was short and stocky, his broad shoulders essentially blocking any thought of entering. He had black curly hair, a high forehead, deep-set gray eyes that boasted bulging bags under them, and a receding chin.

"What do you want?" His complexion appeared sallow, his lips downturned, as unwelcoming as his tone.

Leon held up his business card.

Matias squinted at the card. "A private investigator?"

"Your wife has hired me to find your daughter."

"Hired you?" He snorted. "She must be holding out on me, then. Last I knew, she said she had no money."

Against his own principles, Leon decided he didn't like Flores at all. "Can I come in for a few minutes?"

With a shrug, Flores stepped aside and waved a hand. "If you want, though it won't do you any good." He shut the door and led the way along an unlit somber passage and into a lounge. The furniture comprised a two-seater sofa, two straight-backed chairs, a television hanging on a wall bracket with wires dangling to the socket, and a coffee table. He was jittery. On most surfaces lay plates of partly-consumed food, most of it congealed or discolored; an open invitation to ants. Backs of chairs were adorned with various items of creased clothing.

Nicotine-stained fingers on his right hand signified he was a chain-smoker. A clutter of betting slips and the horse-racing pages of newspapers provided ample evidence that he was also a gambler. Judging by the squashed cigarette butts in an ashtray on the tiled floor by the sofa, he was gambling with his life, too.

Carlota had already warned Leon: "I can tell you one reason why they split up—his gambling."

"Any other reasons?" he'd probed.

Carlota had shrugged, hesitant, and then added reluctantly, "The usual—domestic abuse."

Leon wasn't surprised. Spain had an unfortunate reputation for domestic abuse; officials postulated that many men cannot handle women's new-found independence, which to Leon seemed odd since freedom for women began decades ago, when the old regime died with Franco in 1975. Yet *denuncias* for domestic violence in the Alicante province alone had tripled in the last ten years and roughly 56% of the cases attended to by the Offices for the Assistance of Victims of Offences were violence against women—some 8,500 on average. Leon tried to keep clear of those cases. Basic adultery

—by either party—was fair game and less dangerous than many of his other capers; it helped create the illusion that such work paid the bills. He was careful about where his considerable wealth actually stemmed from, since it had been illegal. In truth, he didn't trust himself where domestic violence was concerned. Usually the culprit was the man— and Leon knew he'd been tempted on those rare occasions when he'd been involved to teach the bully a severe lesson, which could have put him in court or even get his licence revoked. He detested bullies of all shades.

To look at him, you'd never think Flores was a wife-beater. It's not as if they have a tattoo on their forehead— more's the pity.

Flores slumped into a sofa but didn't offer Leon a place to sit.

Considering the unsavory state of the room, Leon preferred to stand anyway. "When did you last see your daughter?"

Flores played with a pack of Marlboros. "About a week ago, I think. You know, the police have already been around. Questioned me on that." He flung his big wife-beating hands in the air. "They even searched here!"

"Very thorough of them."

He snorted. "As if I would abduct my little girl!" Tears abruptly streamed down his cheeks. Crocodiles would have been proud of him.

———

Leon had worked with Seb Okoro a number of times, most recently the entrapment of Roland the Counterfeiter, who had been extradited back to the UK. Seb was in his early forties, with a dark ebony complexion. He had short-cropped black hair, flat nose—broken during an arrest, he explained; high cheekbones and a high forehead. He and Rod Wallace were the only two NCA agents on the Costa Blanca. Their main purpose was trying to track down British criminals in hiding. "Rod's body is being repatriated tomorrow," he said. "His mother will meet the plane."

Rod had no other family. He'd said often that he couldn't settle. "I'm not sure I'd want to be responsible for bringing a child into this dark forbidding world." He had moments like that, no doubt brought on by the nature of his work.

"Can you tell me what he was working on?" Leon asked Seb. "He let slip it was something to do with pedophiles...was it?"

Seb nodded. "He was in regular touch with CEOP."

"What's that?"

"Child Exploitation and Online Protection. The NCA took it over some years back—it's our specialist child protection arm."

"Ah. Online—the Dark Web, I guess."

"That's part of it. WhatsApp, Telegram and more secure conduits where they swap images... When images of abuse are intercepted, they actually have unique digital signatures that can be identified by search bots when found on servers or a pervert's computer. A Child Abuse Image Database is maintained—it can recognize if a seized image has been used before. Special bots spot trigger words by trawling through memory banks of giant server centers."

"This is going on all the time?"

"Yes. Crime never takes a rest, does it? Server firms are legally obliged to inform authorities if they find abusive images or suspicious communications. Although they do get stick about allowing too much filth to spread, they do act when they're able. So the server companies sweep messages and chat for keywords; they then notify NCMEC who hunts for the associated IP addresses and notifies CEOP."

"More acronyms... not that I can complain since most of my adult life has been involved with one sort or another!"

"NCMEC is the US National Center for Missing and Exploited Children. It's based in Alexandria, Virginia."

"Was Rod working with the local police here?"

"Yes. Only last week he'd been on a raid in Alicante. That swoop netted five pedophiles with hundreds of stored images." Seb shook his head. "But they're merely the tip of a very nasty iceberg."

———

THAT AFTERNOON, Leon returned to the jeweler's.

Señor López said to his assistant. "Hold the fort until I return."

"Yes, sir."

López removed his pince-nez and led Leon through the curtain behind the counter.

In his office, he tapped a few keys on his computer and said, "This is the day you told my assistant."

Standing behind López, Leon watched the passersby in the street. An electronic time-stamp appeared in the bottom right-hand corner.

"Can you move it forward to ten in the morning?"

"Certainly." López let the mouse glide over the mouse-mat and the curser moved along a thick line at the bottom of the screen. The images speeded up. Then he stopped as the line indicated the time: 10:00.

Thereafter he moved the image at a steady pace until about twenty minutes later on the recording. There she was: he saw Nadia pass the shop entrance and skipped towards the corner. About a half-minute after that she stopped at the curb as a black BMW limousine drew up. He couldn't see inside, the windows were dark, tinted.

The licence plate was clear to see, however. He'd get in touch with Concepción in *Agrupación de Tráfico* who regularly handled ALPR data.

———

SEÑOR MONTOYA WAS NOT PLEASED to see Leon at the golf course. Perhaps his presence was an unwelcome reminder of the gruesome find. "I'm just going out, actually." He was carrying a bulky briefcase.

"Have the police been back yet?" Leon asked.

"They phoned, said they had nothing to report." He appeared flustered. "Look, I've got a meeting. Sorry."

"No problem." Leon made his way to his F-Type Jaguar convertible and as he sat behind the steering wheel he watched Montoya drive off in a green VW Golf.

Leon decided to follow at a discreet distance; he wasn't driving the ideal vehicle for tailing somebody.

Into the countryside. There was the familiar sight of concrete water channels used for field irrigation, running alongside the road and criss-crossing the cultivated land, each with its own hand-operated sluice gate. The water usage of the farmers was decided by a combine, an irrigation association, and times were set; so there were the ludicrous instances when sluice gates were opened to flood fields while it was raining. He had heard that after Israel, Spain has the most land under modern irrigation; yet not enough rainfall was captured during severe wet periods. Go figure.

There was little traffic in either direction.

On the right there was an abandoned warehouse and a few other derelict out-buildings just off the main road. They sported several old metal-framed windows, most of them broken, saw-toothed. Montoya drove through an open gateway and parked.

Leon drove past slowly and swerved onto waste ground a couple of yards along on the left. He braked and switched off the engine.

He took his binoculars from the glove-compartment, adjusted the focus.

A man with a mustache exited a doorway in the warehouse. Leon didn't recognize him.

Montoya got out of his car and fidgeted with the briefcase.

The man made curt hand-gestures to usher him inside.

Montoya seemed reluctant to go in—but finally hesitantly went.

Leon slid from his car and crossed the road, dashed through the gateway, skirted round Montoya's car and rushed soundlessly to the side of the building they'd entered. He quickly located a window, low enough for him to peer through.

The light was reasonable: sunlight shone through a number of skylights.

There was no machinery or goods inside; only a little furniture: a fold-up table and a single folding chair. A man wearing wire-frame glasses, a gray pin-stripe suit and bow-tie stood by the table.

There were four other men standing in front of Montoya; one of them, the tallest with a stocky body, rested a hand on a golf club handle, tapping it idly against his ankle; its length signified it was a driver. From here he could see the man's features: heavy-lidded eyes, thick downy eyebrows, tanned complexion, a jutting chin with a dimple, a strong nose and a fleshy mouth. Thick black hair partially covered his ears.

Three of the men were probably in their twenties.

One was as ugly as a gourd, with a heavy jaw and a black cookie duster under his broad flat nose. He was the one who had welcomed Montoya. He wore a loose-fitting red-striped shirt and tight-fitting denim pants.

The other had a long face, lantern jaw, a dour mouth, bristles on his chin and black oiled hair. He wore fawn corduroy pants, a brown polo shirt and brown leather loafers.

The third man was dark complexioned with a shaved bullet head. He wore a white T-shirt and smart creased light green pants. He held a small off-white linen sack in one hand; at his belt was a knife in its sheath and a holster held a revolver.

On the floor at their feet knelt a naked bald-headed man,

cringing, his wrists tethered by electric cable. Leon couldn't determine his age—probably in his forties.

A golf bag cart was parked nearby, stuffed with clubs.

Leon was conversant with Inspector Chávez's rogues' gallery; he'd never seen any of these guys before.

Their voices carried in the cavernous place.

"I'm pleased you've seen sense at last, Señor Montoya."

Montoya nodded, seemed unable to speak, couldn't take his eyes off the kneeling man. Then, after a short hesitant pause he found his voice: "I've brought the deeds, Señor Fuentes." His shaky fingers unclasped the briefcase.

"Good. Give them to Raúl." Montoya flinched involuntarily as Fuentes lifted the driver golf club and pointed the big club head at the man in a suit. "He's the notary."

Montoya handed over the briefcase and stood swaying a little, as if his support had been kicked from under him.

"Andrés, take Señor Montoya's arm. He seems unsteady on his feet."

"*Sí*, of course," said the guy in the red-striped shirt. His voice was quite husky.

Andrés firmly grasped Montoya's arm and now sweat stood out on Montoya's forehead.

Raúl carried the briefcase to a fold-up table and a single chair. He emptied the contents of the briefcase on the table top, sat down, adjusted his spectacles and began to read the documents.

Montoya cleared his throat, dabbing a handkerchief against his temple. "It—it is all correct... Now, please, the—the money...?"

"When Raúl has checked the paperwork." Fuentes stepped a pace back and jiggled the golf club, made a couple of loose playful swings with it.

Montoya flinched again.

Abruptly, Fuentes jabbed the handle of the club forcefully at Montoya's chest. "You promise not to tell anybody about this arrangement, right?"

Montoya nodded again. Sweat glistened on his forehead.

"Good. I don't like snitches... Otherwise, *this* will happen to you..."

Deftly Fuentes swung the club and it slammed into the cringing man's head. Blood spattered. The victim whimpered and swayed with the blow but remained on his knees.

"I—I prom-promised..." Montoya stammered.

"Just remember." Fuentes turned, rested both palms on the club handle and gazed at the table. "Ah, Raúl nods. That is good, he is satisfied." He gestured at the dark-complexioned man in the white T-shirt. "Vicente—the money."

Vicente strolled over to Raúl and handed him the white linen bag. The notary untied the string of the bag and tipped its contents into the open briefcase. Then Raúl walked up to Montoya and handed him his briefcase. "The agreed amount is inside."

Fuentes said, "Don't insult me by counting it, will you?"

"No, no—I—trust you."

More fool you, Leon thought.

CHAPTER 6

LOCK PICK

LEON FOLLOWED MONTOYA, BUT THE MAN DIDN'T return to the golf course; instead he drove to his villa in a modern building complex with wide roads bordered by orange trees. He parked in his pink gravel drive, got out and went inside. The villa was set among similar buildings—an entire street of identical properties, each with a colored gravel drive and a garage set back at the end. The villa boasted a semi-circular balcony with stone balustrade, with Virginia Creeper climbing the white stucco stone walls. The roof had glazed blue tiles, which glinted in the sun.

Leon rang the doorbell.

Montoya answered the door. His face paled and he took a pace backwards. "What do you want?"

"How much were you paid?"

Montoya blanched. "How—how did you know?"

"I'm a private investigator, remember."

"Well, to answer your question, not nearly enough—but I am thankful for I still have my life—and my family is safe."

"You'll never be safe—nor will your family—while that scum calls the shots."

"I am not brave enough to fight him... If the law could only...oh, what is the use. There are too many villains these days, they have fingers in every business..."

"Why do they want your golf course?"

"They represent a syndicate, I was told."

"It's a cheap way to obtain a lucrative golf course, I suppose."

"At my expense," Montoya said in exasperation.

"Do you know the names of the men you dealt with?"

"Only two."

"The one with the bloody golf club?"

Gasped. "You saw?"

"I saw."

Montoya said, "He told me he was called Tomás Fuentes." He shrugged. "It might not be his real name. He has no reason to give me his real name, has he?"

"I agree, it's probably not his real name." Leon admitted. He didn't add, *That's why you're still alive...* He then said, "Do you know the notary Raúl's family name?"

"*Sí*, I have had dealings with him before." His mouth twisted unpleasantly. "Serrano. Like the ham." He spat. "The pig!"

———

FROM ACROSS THE street Leon cased the building that housed the office of Raúl Serrano. The brass plaque indicated that it was a partnership of three notaries. He wondered if all three were involved in crooked deals. It seemed possible.

Clandestine training often came in useful and this case was no exception.

He broke into the building at night, disabling the alarm system with consummate ease.

Sufficient ambient light percolated from high-placed windows, allowing him to see without using a torch.

Silently climbing the stairs, he came to the first landing where he found three adjoining but separate offices. He headed for Serrano's first.

The door succumbed to his lockpick, which he then pocketed.

He entered a small outer office: the secretary's domain; her name-plaque announced her as Lara Olonso. On her desk was a framed photo of an elderly couple—probably her parents. No other personal items were in evidence. Quite businesslike or soulless, depending on your point of view. A computer on her desk showed a red standby light. He hit the enter key and was surprised to find she hadn't password protected it. He did a search of the documents for golf courses and immediately found the files.

He checked for Dimples—and found it in a section labelled "golf course acquisitions". It gave the impression of being above board. Then he located Montoya's other two golf courses: Green-Go and Golf-Sur. Serrano had been a busy bee, acquiring fairway after fairway.

Notary offices would still rely on a paper trail, he reasoned; it was in their DNA. He went into Serrano's office and immediately noted the ink pad and several metal authorization stamps. Yes, bureaucracy was alive and well in twenty-first century Spain.

Behind the desk was a filing cabinet. He took out the lockpick set from his pocket and swiftly tampered with the filing lock: it was a basic system.

After a little rifling he found the three folders. Each one was quite thick.

According to the computer file they'd acquired four golf courses so far. Judging by the dates of the transfer documents Dimples was the newest in their portfolio. The fourth was Chip-away, owned by a Brit named Clifford Shaw. The course names probably appealed to British golfers.

Now he knew what to look for, he checked the filing cabinets in the other two offices. No golf course acquisitions. It didn't mean they were straight, honest notaries, of course. Each one might have different illegal goals, just as suspect.

He returned to Serrano's office and used the photocopier

on the four golf courses' paperwork—only the relevant documents revealing the purchaser was one Tomás Iglesias.

And then left the premises, leaving no trace he'd been there.

————

"THAT LICENCE PLATE number indicates the owner of the vehicle is Tomás Iglesias," Concepción said breathily over the phone. She gave him the vehicle owner's address.

So, not Fuentes. "Thanks for the feedback. Most useful."

"A pleasure, Leon," she said and hung up.

————

THE OLDEST ACQUISITION of Tomás Iglesias appeared to be the Chip-Away golf course. It didn't take Leon long to track down the previous owner Clifford Shaw, aged fifty-six. He was a rotund fellow with graying hair and a small mustache. His blue eyes were red-rimmed. Apparently, he was a widower. He lived in a semi-detached two-bedroom villa and had a black-and-white collie-cross dog. The sun was shining so Shaw had invited Leon to sit in his rose garden and have a cup of coffee—"percolated alright?"

"That would be fine, thanks."

When Shaw returned with a tray carrying two mugs and a small plate of assorted biscuits, Leon commented on two graves amid the rose-bushes: *Beloved Buster* and *Boisterous Belvedere*.

"My two dogs—poodles."

"As I explained on the phone, I wondered if you could tell me anything about the sale of your golf course."

"Don't mention that place to me!" Shaw spat.

"What happened?"

"I cannot say."

"Can't, won't or dare not?"

"The last of the above, if you must know."

"If you spoke about it, you'd end up like your two dogs, is that it?"

"You're very perceptive, Mr. Cazador." Shaw glanced around, taking an interest in the adjoining wooden fence of his neighbor.

Leon said, "If you feel uncomfortable about it, don't speak. Just nod."

Shaw nodded.

"Is the person who threatened you named Tomás Fuentes?"

A nod.

"That is not his real name, of course."

A shrug. *I don't care.*

"He acquired your golf course on the cheap?"

A nod.

"Under duress?"

A nod.

"What puzzles me is why he wants not only your golf course but at least three more..."

Shaw leaned forward. "*Three* more! By God!"

"It could be a land-grab," Leon suggested. "It's a popular criminal pastime—builders and town mayors indulge in it— even though the EU has weighed in with fines." He'd contended with chancers involved in such underhand dealings. "Land value always goes up..."

"True enough, but, no, it's still a golf course. I go there about once a month, just to look at it. I wouldn't play on the green, naturally. No way!"

Chapter 7

Hard Time

Two days earlier, on her way to meet María in the shop as planned, Nadia Flores had checked her *Frozen* wristwatch; she was on time. When she looked up and turned the corner of her street, she gave a small jump of surprise. "Papá?"

He sauntered to her side. For a change, he was smartly dressed in a tan jacket, trendy dark chino pants and boat shoes. His lips moved but it wasn't the usual smile he offered when they met. Those gray eyes didn't smile.

Instinctively, she thought something was wrong. "I'm not supposed to meet you until next Saturday."

"I know," he said, resting a hand on her shoulder. "I phoned your mother. She has agreed I could give you a special treat." He reached down to take her hand.

Abruptly, she pulled her hand away. "I'm too big to hold hands with you now, Papá," she chided.

"Oh, of course." He hesitated and then fished in his trouser pocket and gave her a couple of Euro coins. "Here, when you meet María you can buy a comic for a change."

She'd been excited. "Is that the treat?"

He shook his head. "No, sweetie. When you leave the shop, make your excuses and tell María you'll see her later. Then turn left and meet me at the corner of the street. The surprise will be waiting for you there." He'd leaned closer. "Don't tell María. It's our little secret."

"Alright."

When she approached María she was bursting to tell her friend that a surprise from her father was waiting for her. She found herself grinning stupidly. But she would keep the secret—at least until she saw María next time.

It was really good to hold the comic—her comic. The smell of its newness tantalized her nostrils. Wonder Woman was again in conflict with her arch-foe Cheetah!

As it happened she didn't have to make any excuse: María had a dance lesson and had to go in the other direction. So she waved goodbye to María and, brimming with anticipation, walked hurriedly to the corner.

A shining black BMW G11 limousine pulled up at the curb-side. It had tinted windows so she couldn't see anybody inside. But just then the rear window wound down electronically and she saw Papá sitting there. "Surprise!" he whispered.

He opened the door. "Come on, get in!" he urged.

She climbed in and he shut the door after her.

There was a woman on the rear seat on the far side. "Hi, Nadia," the woman said. "Pleased to meet you. Your father has told me so much about you." Her thin lips curved, toasted brown eyes lighting up. Her accented Spanish was good, but there was a hint of another country. She had high cheekbones and almond-shaped eyes. An oval face was framed by black hair that was cut short. Looped over her shoulder was the strap of her leather designer bag.

"Has he?" As she sensed the vehicle pull away, Nadia flushed and glanced at Papá and then at the woman. Was this his fancy woman? Mama had suggested he was living with another woman. The thought hurt her deeply. She smelled strong sweet scent. Cheap, she estimated. "Who are you?" she demanded.

"This is a friend," Papá said. "Señora Doleman."

"You can call me Wanda."

"H-hello, Wanda." Nadia eyed her father. "Is she your mistress?"

Wanda gasped and then chuckled.

He shook his head. "You shouldn't say things like that, sweetie. She's just a business friend, that's all."

The darkened windows prevented Nadia from seeing where they were going. Out of town, she guessed. But where? And why?

"Papá, where's my surprise? Where are you taking me?"

"Almost there," Wanda said.

Feeling uncomfortable sitting next to the Wanda woman, Nadia immersed herself in the comic and was soon lost in the graphic story.

Eventually, shortly after she turned the last page, the car braked.

The driver switched off the engine and got out, opened the rear door. "We're there, Señorita," he said.

Wanda stepped out and, one hand on her shoulder bag, offered the other to Nadia.

Reluctantly, she took it, and she was helped down. She hastily glanced around. They were in a parking lot. Signage indicated it was the *Green-Go Golf Club*.

The door shut with a heavy clunk sound; she noted that her father didn't get out of the car. He stayed on the rear seat, the window open.

Wanda delved in her shoulder bag and then handed him a thick brown envelope, which he shoved into his jacket's inside breast pocket.

"You stay with Wanda, sweetie," he said, his voice catching a little. "Until I get back, okay?"

"Will you be long, Papá?"

He looked briefly at Wanda and then at Nadia. "Not long at all..." Soundlessly, the window wound up and the car's engine growled and the limousine drove through the club's gateway.

"Come," said Wanda, clasping her arm, "I'll take you to a nice little room where you can read your comic."

"I read it in the car."

"Fancy that. What a bright girl! Sadly, I can't read in a vehicle, something about the movement makes me travel sick. You're so lucky! Come. You can read it again while you wait."

The main building appeared on the left, with entrance steps and a portico. She was led to a two-story building on the right.

They entered a small lobby with a reception desk manned by a woman; an oxymoron, her teacher might have observed. Wanda waved at the receptionist and strode with Nadia to the foot of a staircase. They climbed slowly.

Wanda escorted her along a carpeted passage until she stopped halfway at a door. Fishing out a key from her bag, Wanda unlocked the door and Nadia was led inside.

It was a small room and had little furniture—only a single bed with a mattress and sheets, a one-door closet and a bedside table holding a lamp and cluttered with two dishes holding scraps of food and a plastic knife and fork. Halfway up the wall there was one window, boarded with wood panels secured by screws that kept out the light and any view. An open door in the wall revealed a toilet, bidet and a walk-in shower cubicle.

"You wait there, honey," Wanda said. "Catalina will be glad of your company."

Wanda slid out, firmly shut the door and locked it.

Catalina? Then Nadia noticed a girl standing to one side of the closet, half-hiding, her wide brown eyes staring. She wore a flower-print dress, white socks and pumps.

"Catalina?" Nadia whispered, approaching warily.

The girl nodded her head of black hair. Tears had recently dried on her chubby cheeks. "Yes. But you can call me Cat." Her lower lip trembled. "What's your name?"

Nadia told her, adding, "How long have you been here?"

"A night and a day, I think." Cat's tone sounded so forlorn, without hope.

What was keeping Papá? He promised. Nadia wondered

about the food plates. Her stomach rumbled at the thought of food. All of a sudden, she feared that Papá was not going to return for her.

Gesturing vaguely, Cat said, "What's that you're holding?"

"A comic." Nadia held it out. "Do you want to read it?"

"Please."

Nadia sat on the bed and patted the mattress.

Tentatively, Cat sidled over and sat beside her. Nadia handed her the comic.

"Thanks, Nadia," Cat whispered.

While her new companion began reading, her eyes glistening slightly, Nadia absently fingered her hair, re-fastened her hair-clips, and studied her surroundings in more detail.

———

WANDA MUSED on those early days of their "association" as she lounged provocatively on a sofa in the downstairs office of Green-Go, watching Tomás pour Amaretto over ice in two glasses. Her cream Ralph Lauren georgette dress with a v-neck and matching tan leather belt was short, falling just above her knees. She liked to show him a leg to maintain his interest. "Not too much, dearest, I must drive to the airport. The next batch of clients for Golf-Sur is due in. I don't want to be over the limit."

"Get one of the boys to drive you." He stood in front of her and gave her the glass.

She gazed up at him and sipped the cool drink. "I like to drive myself."

"Fine, fine." He rested a hand briefly on her bare knee. "You know your own mind—a driven woman, indeed."

She blew him a kiss and downed the rest of the drink; it put fire in her belly. "Don't get distressed. I'll have a lot to do. I'll return tomorrow and we can enjoy the frivolities then."

Standing, she handed him the glass; the smooth cubes

clinked. On her way to the door she snatched her faux suede jacket and carried it in the crook of her arm. She slung her bag over her shoulder. "*Adiós*!"

————

AT THE ENTRANCE portico of the accommodation block Andrés and Bernardo stood ogling Wanda as she opened the door of her white Audi coupé. She turned to them, said, "Don't forget to feed the kids. Pizzas will do."

Andrés's features transformed into a scowl, displaying crooked teeth. "When do they get to see some action?" he demanded in his husky voice. "It might shut them up..."

"A few stroppy kids are upsetting you, Andrés? Shame on you. Be firm—but no spanking. In fact, no touching!"

"You promised we could get our share of the action..."

"When our next batch of golfers arrive and have broken them in. Not before."

His face went sour: he didn't like that.

She flung her suede jacket and shoulder-bag on the passenger seat, and ostentatiously flicked hair behind her left ear. The gold dangling earrings jangled.

Bernardo stepped forward, his dour mouth twisting. "Where are you going now?"

"It's none of your business, Bernardo. But it's no secret either. The airport. I'm meeting the next batch of clients for Golf-Sur. And a new batch of merchandise is expected."

She slid behind the wheel, showing plenty of thigh and slammed the door shut. In seconds, she'd started the engine and accelerated away.

Bernardo jumped a pace back as gravel shards landed close to his brown leather loafers. "We're fucking babysitters!"

"*Sí.*" Andrés passed a hand over his heavy jaw. "You know, this fresh young meat is wasted on the golfers."

Bernardo shrugged his narrow shoulders. "Yeah, but just remember what she said, they're off limits to the likes of us."

"For now..." Andrés hooked his thick thumbs in his knitted leather belt with its death's-head buckle. "To be honest, some of these golfing guys give me the creeps."

"Me as well. But, hey, they pay our wages."

———

Nadia sat on the single bed beside Cat. Her *Frozen* watch told her she'd been here almost an hour. Cat had read her comic three times already and now lay back on the bed with her hands clasped behind her head.

"How old are you?" Cat asked.

"Twelve," Nadia replied.

"I'm thirteen."

Nadia didn't see the relevance. She thought of Papá and that brown envelope the Wanda woman had given him. "How did you get here?"

"I was on my way to Mercadona for my mother. A woman came up to me and snatched me around the waist. Nobody saw. She bundled me into a car with a sliding door. Then she put a cloth over my mouth, it smelled awful and the next thing I remember is coming awake on this bed. The woman called herself Wanda. Didn't care that I knew her name. I decided to call her Wicked Wanda. She brought me my meals sometimes, at other times a man named Andrés did. But none of them would tell me anything else. What about you?"

"My father brought me..."

"Jesus, you poor kid! The bastard!"

"Why do you say that? Do you know why we are here?"

"Isn't it obvious?" Cat said.

"If Wicked Wanda thinks she's going to ransom me, she'll get a shock. My mother's got no money."

"Ransom?" Cat sniggered. "No, kid." She moved to a sitting position and swung her legs off the bed, walked over to the closet. She opened the door. Inside was a collection of colorful clothing. "We're being saved for the pleasure of *de mierda* perverts..." She rifled through the clothes—an assortment of children's princess dresses. "See?"

Nadia's stomach lurched and she feared she was going to be sick. A cold tremor ran through her frame.

"Are—are there other kids locked up here as well?"

Cat hunched her shoulders. "I figure there are. I've heard crying... And when the food comes, it's on a trolley stacked with quite a few plates..."

"Anything else I should know?"

"Usually once a day Tía Paloma comes in. Has a chat. Asks if I'm alright. She does seem to show genuine concern. When she leaves I've heard her open the room next door and dimly heard their voices. I assume she's there to look after us."

"That's really comforting, not!" Nadia snapped. "She's one of them!"

"Well, she's nice, anyway..."

"Well, I don't know about the others," Nadia croaked, "but we must escape."

"I considered that but we have no tools." Cat waved a hand at the plates. "The cutlery is plastic."

Nadia frowned, studying the boarded-up window. "Do you know what time they bring food?"

Cat shook her head. "I don't have a watch—I used my cell-phone to tell the time. But they took that off me."

"My cell's in my drawer at home. But my tummy tells me it's about time for lunch. I have an idea—but it'll have to wait until they bring the food." Horrible thought. "That is, if they bother to feed us."

"Oh, they'll keep us fed."

As if on cue, a moment later, the key turned in the lock and the door opened.

A man came in with a big tray holding two plates filled with pizza slices and two cans of Pepsi. He was quite ugly with a black cookie duster under his broad flat nose. His coarse brown hair covered his ears. Nadia didn't like the way his burnt almond eyes glared at her and Cat. He was powerfully built, with the thick short neck of a wrestler and a barrel-chest. To counteract his menace, she observed he was bow legged and walked with a lunging gait, at risk of spilling the tray's contents. He wore a loose-fitting red-striped linen shirt and tight-fitting denim pants.

"Hi, Andrés," Cat called and then peered at the second man who stood in the doorway, a wooden club in his hand. "Nice to see you too, Bernardo."

Bernardo had a downcast mouth and bristles on his chin. His black hair was oiled, slicked back. His almost black eyes glinted. He wore fawn corduroy pants and a brown polo shirt.

"Quit clowning around, kid," Andrés growled, his voice husky, angry. "We've brought food, not chat."

Standing in the passage was a food trolley, just like Cat had mentioned.

"Don't you have any Diet Coke?" Nadia asked.

"You get what we give you," Andrés snapped. "Take it or leave it, it's not my concern." He placed the tray on the bed

"Oh, finger-food from now on, eh?" purred Nadia. "Lovely!"

Bernardo slapped his wooden club in the palm of his hand. "If you don't show gratitude, you'll get nothing!"

"Nadia, stop antagonizing them!" Cat wailed, tears in her eyes.

Nadia shrugged and walked past Andrés over to the bed. "Chorizo and cheese—my favorite!"

Without warning, Andrés reached out and swung Nadia round to face him. He leered. "You won't be so funny afterwards!" Unexpectedly, both his hands pressed palms against her slightly budding chest.

Her cheeks flushed hot. She slapped at his hands but they didn't budge.

He squeezed and it hurt, made her gasp.

"I like 'em young as well!" he grated, his tone thickening.

Nadia trembled, fear rooting her to the spot where she stood.

"Please, don't!" Cat cried.

Bernardo rushed into the room and loudly banged his wooden club on the floorboards. "Hey, Andrés, that's enough inappropriate touching!" His voice was reedy yet forceful.

Grunting, Andrés let go and backed off.

The relief was instant. Nadia's cheeks burned; she massaged her chest.

Andrés laughed hoarsely and turned to face Bernardo. "Eh, where'd that come from? 'Inappropriate touching'? I'll do more than that! Who's to know, eh?"

"Tía Paloma will find out, be sure of it. And then you'll be chewing on your own pecker!"

"Tía, eh?" Andrés chewed on his lip, as if his mind was echoing Bernardo's dire warning. "Yeah, maybe you're right." He glared at Nadia and then at Cat. "But it sure is a waste." His shoulders slumped as he went over to the bedside and collected the old plates and cutlery from the cabinet.

The two men left and the door slammed shut. The key turned in the lock.

Cat let out a gasp. "That was too close. I should have known better. We're so powerless." With shaking fingers she opened a can with a hiss, guzzled a mouthful, "That wasn't clever, giving them a hard time."

"Giving *them* a hard time?" Nadia said. "You've gotta be kidding. It's us who're going to do hard time—unless we get out soon."

"Yeah. I wish."

Nadia bit into a slice of pizza. Chorizo, mozzarella, olives and tomatoes. "You know, this isn't that bad. Still warm as well."

"I don't know how you can be so cheerful," Cat moaned.

"I can because I have a plan," Nadia said, absently rubbing her chest.

"You have?"

Nadia nodded. "But first, eat up, then we'll talk about it and tomorrow we'll actually do it."

CHAPTER 8

RADICAL VENTURE

ALMOST AT THE LAST MINUTE, THE NCA AGENT
had been allocated to replace Rod Wallace. He'd been briefed
at headquarters and hastily registered on the Dark Web to
join a group of four men on a "golfing holiday" at the Green-
Go club. The very high fees were paid up-front with the
credit card in his alias, Evan Tremayne, aged thirty-five.
Tremayne's cover was simple—he worked in I.T. Hearing
that, most people changed the subject because it appeared as
boring as accountancy.

According to the web's instructions, he made himself
known at the check-in desk and, once they'd passed through
their luggage and golf bags and clubs, the five of them
repaired to the bar lounge "for a few bevvies".

The Heathrow to Alicante flight was called and travelers
were advised to go to the boarding gate.

He'd have thought the others would be reticent about
discussing their background, but not a bit of it. It had begun
in the airport lounge bar and went on from there after they
boarded the airplane.

Evan sat next to Danny Kneale who was in his mid-twen-
ties. He was the unknown quantity; he'd been entirely under
the radar. Of lean build, he had heavy-lidded tawny eyes,
spiky copper-coloured hair, an oval face, pointed nose and

thin lips. He confessed to being the novice in the group, and appeared a tad nervous.

"First time abroad?" Evan asked.

"Nah, I've been to Spain stacks of times with the family —Mum and Dad..." He hesitated, leaned closer. "It's my first time as a... a golfer, you know." His cheeks flushed.

"Well, there's a first time for everything," Evan replied.

As they chatted Evan soon learned that Danny was rich. "My old man owns a chain of supermarkets..."

In the airport lounge Evan had spoken briefly to Steve Weir, who was in his mid-thirties. Steve had protruding fog-gray eyes and neatly combed brown hair. He had a jutting chin, a button nose which he scratched constantly, and thin lips. His wiry physique was at odds with his professed job as a civil servant in Whitehall. "Hush-hush, you know, can't say more," Steve would whisper, tapping his hooked nose. Tremayne knew he was fantasizing—Steve Weir worked in human resources in the Treasury and was on a pedophile watch-list since no evidence had been procured for prosecution though suspicions had been aroused over several years. Perhaps this little jaunt would provide the necessary proof.

Curtis Falconer was on record, too. He was a heavyset fifty-eight-year-old with steely arctic blue eyes; crewcut ash-gray hair; a square face, and plump lips. At one time he'd been an American psychologist, but five years back he transplanted himself to escape the law in Charleston, South Carolina. He was an experienced con man, having started his career at an early age; by the time he was twenty-two he'd already been a director of twelve companies, of which five had been dissolved. He appealed to people's greed, getting involved in smuggling cartons of cigarettes, all of them prepaid for, only for them to be seized by Customs; he fled, leaving another shell company to collapse. He was known to associate with pedophiles but to date there was no credible evidence of him being involved. Breezily, he said, "Sexual relations between a child and an adult do not harm the child and may even be beneficial, if the adult partner is considerate." *Psychological claptrap*, Evan thought; self-justifying abominable behavior.

Nige Baxter was a successful interior designer who had recently celebrated his half-century. He had bedroom eyes of a hazel hue; short salt and pepper hair; angular cheekbones; an aquiline nose; thick lips; thick scraggly mustache; and five o'clock shadow. Despite his age, it was obvious he looked after himself and possessed a strapping build. He was a grandfather to two four-year-old twins, but so far there had been no concern about their welfare.

———

IN THE EARLY MORNING, between seven and eight, Paloma was permitted to take up to four children outside to the swimming pool. Each day it would be a different group. Here, they could let off steam in their swimming costumes, and play.

She was uncomfortably aware that the children could be observed from the dining room window by early-bird clients at breakfast. It had been Iglesias's brain-wave—entice the clients, looking at but not touching the merchandise.

Regular as clockwork, every day after the pool session, Tía Paloma conscientiously visited the upstairs rooms occupied by the children in Golf-Sur. And in the afternoons she would travel to Green-Go and perform the same visiting tasks. It was her job to ensure that none of her charges self-harmed and were suitably dressed in fantasy apparel and otherwise prepared in due time for the clients' attentions in the evening.

She hated that the children were referred to as "merchandise" but she could not openly object. She had her own cross to bear. Her ten-year-old daughter Gabriela was kept hostage by her ex-husband, a bitter man whose name would never again cross her lips. If she did not abide by the requirements of Señor Iglesias, she was assured that harm would come to Gaby. It was cruel of him. She was trapped.

In truth, she cherished the time spent with these captive children. She tried to ease their concerns and prepare them for the ordeal they would face. She virtually mothered them. If only Gaby had such attention! But she was alone, with that monster. Paloma knew where he lived, but he was too powerful, too strong for her to confront. Over the years she'd received any number of bruises from him. She only prayed he kept his fists off Gaby.

First today, in Golf-Sur she would call upon Carla and Juana in room 30—third floor, first room. She pulled the metal ring from her belt and located the key, unlocked the door and went inside. About to greet them, she stopped. The room was empty, the two single beds without sheets, the mattresses folded up. An emptiness engulfed her. The two girls had gone. Presumably sold on. She'd liked them so much. They'd been brave, despite what happened to them. Like most of the others, they divulged to her the details of their past and their abduction. Their stories wrenched at her heart, but there was nothing she dared do. They were not the first to vanish. Sometimes it was only one of a pair. The remaining child was often very upset and incapable of explaining or understanding the companion's absence.

She had been told to prepare for a fresh van load of children, which was due soon. So this room would again be occupied. And so it went on.

Downhearted, she left the room and locked it. Next she would see Michael and Lola in room 31. Brother and sister, they'd been orphaned a year ago, their parents killed in a traffic pile-up on the N332. Their elderly aunt had taken them in but found it difficult to cope. The aunt had mentioned her concerns to her hairdresser who in turn passed on the information to someone else. Before long, a charming lady called on the aunt and offered to look after the eight-year-old twins. They were brought here and groomed by Paloma's predecessor. Now, they were both traumatized.

The only way Paloma could convince the twins to carry

on was to encourage them to enter a fantasy world, where pain and hurt and loneliness did not exist. In their minds they were free.

She turned the appropriate key in the lock, opened the door, and stepped inside.

Though her heart ached for them she smiled broadly and said, "How is the weather where you are today?"

Michael returned her smile. "Sunny and warm, Tía Paloma. Sunny and warm."

"And the sound of the sea is so calming," said Lola.

———

EVAN TREMAYNE TENSED. Now it began in earnest. After clearing customs at Alicante-Elche airport, they collected their luggage and golf bags and wended their way through the concourse. They hadn't got far before Evan and the others were met by an attractive woman in a cream dress with a v-neck, a matching tan leather belt and leather shoulder-bag. She brandished the sign *Exclusive PG Golf-Sur Club*. *Innocent enough to bystanders, perhaps*, he thought. Until they realized that the "PG" stood for "Pedophile Golf". Not as blatant as the "PIE" of the 1980s—Pedophile Information Exchange which blatantly called for the legalization of child sex, with the age of consent lowered to well below ten.

"I'm Wanda Doleman," she told them. "I hope you enjoy your stay." They exchanged pleasantries just like any holiday group and then she led them out to a parked Hyundai midi-coach.

Even though it was September, it was hot. Evan had forgotten how hot and humid it could get.

The driver in peaked cap was introduced as Pedro. He relieved them of their luggage and golf bags, which he loaded on the back seats.

Curtis and Nige sat together.

Steve Weir sat alone and read a well-thumbed paperback, *Lolita*.

Evan took a window seat and Danny sat next to him.

When the coach started up and left, the air-conditioning kicked in. That made a huge difference; all of them cheered.

The coach joined the traffic, nipping in, overtaking.

"I've never done this before," Danny confided in a whisper. "I'm not sure I'm going to like it."

"Go with the flow," Evan advised.

"I know the golf terms but not how they mean them in the group, you know?"

Evan had heard Curtis and Nige chuckling, referring to the children they anticipated entertaining. Hole-in-one, par, bogey, cabbage-patch, lip out, shank, and bunker all related to various perverse combinations and positions they indulged in with "the merchandise". Oh, it was great sport! The thought turned his stomach.

Warping the language to suit clandestine or unsavory behavior was nothing new. Cockney rhyming slang and Polari were two such cases prevalent for decades, hiding in plain sight.

He had to tread a very thin line, showing enthusiasm for what they were going to do but not actually inciting it. The play-acting was difficult. Even in the age of Me-too, heterosexual men like looking at pretty women. But he had to remind himself that these people would not be looking at pretty women; they'll be looking at young boys or young girls in the same manner or even salaciously. So it stood to reason that they'd be watching him for his reaction to what he'd be looking at with them—in effect, "the merchandise".

Wanda strolled through the central aisle, trailing exotic scent behind her. "Make yourselves comfortable. It's a two-hour journey to the course." She handed them a sheet of paper and a pen embossed with *PG Enterprises*. "This is a questionnaire. Please tick the appropriate boxes to show your preferences on arrival." She smirked knowingly. "The usual—approximate age, gender, and so on..."

Accepting his questionnaire, Evan asked, "What's the itinerary?"

"First, I think you will want to wash and change. And then we shall indulge in a splendid typical Mediterranean meal and of course enjoy a few drinks together."

"When do we get to see the little darlings?" Curtis said.

She smiled indulgently. "All in good time, sir," she said, and then added brightly, "Tomorrow, actually. I would ask you to retire for the night and anticipate the next day, which will be all that was promised."

"I can hardly wait!" Nige enthused.

Eventually, the coach turned off the motorway and veered onto an unpaved road which sorely tested the suspension. The route led along a slightly raised track between expanses of fields of artichokes on one side and orange orchards on the other. Interspersed along the length were occasional cutouts to permit overtaking.

"Not long now, gents!" Wanda called from her seat at the front behind the driver.

At last the road surface improved, a wide area of blacktop, also providing space for a turning circle, because this was the end of this particular road. It only led here—to *PG Golf-Sur Exclusive Golf Course*.

The coach braked in front of high metal gates.

A man garbed in a green bush jacket and cargo pants stepped out of a small concrete hut with a flat roof; a gatehouse with a small window set in one wall.

Wanda pressed a button and the passenger door hissed open. She descended to the bottom step and waved at the sentry.

He waved back, gave her a jaunty salute and returned to the hut.

An instant later, the gates automatically opened.

As the coach drove through, Evan noticed a CCTV camera perched on a tall pole on the inside of the gates, aimed at the entrance.

The buzz of conversation heightened as the coach wound its way along a winding smooth drive bordered on each side by aloes and huge rhododendron bushes.

Ahead through the coach windshield Evan saw the buildings.

In the center were five wide curved stone steps that led to an entrance portico and an ornate dark wood door. On the right-hand side stretched a white two-story building with regularly interspersed windows, those on the lower level sporting curlicue bars. Four double garages were situated on the extreme left.

The coach pulled up and stopped and the engine cut out. The driver slid to the side and opened the door, stepped down and out.

Everyone stood at once, keen to get inside.

Evan was hit by the heat, in stark contrast to the air-conditioned interior.

They gathered round while Pedro handed them their luggage. "I will put the golf bags in the Fairway hut for use tomorrow," he explained.

"Sorry we don't have bell-hops," Wanda said, pointing at the personal baggage.

Carrying their own cases and bags, the five of them climbed the steps.

Behind a reception desk stood a young dark-haired woman in green and gold livery. Everyone signed the register and handed over their passports. She went through a door and returned shortly to return the passports, having photo-copied the relevant pages. She issued them with keys and a floor plan. Very efficient. Just like any modern hotel.

The client accommodation was on the next floor. There was an elevator, which made hauling their own luggage less onerous.

Once inside, Evan checked his room. There was a wall mirror—which might be two-way. He couldn't find any eavesdropping bugs or holes for a miniature camera lens, but he couldn't exclude the possibility that he and the others were being monitored.

The layout plan was comprehensive, which he found useful. This floor held twenty rooms allocated to clients.

Each the same dimensions and facilities. On the ground floor was the reception area, a gymnasium, a cinema, two bars, a lounge, a dining room, the laundry room, the kitchens, storerooms and a sauna. The basement was sectioned off into four large areas, all unspecified: perhaps they would warrant closer examination. Outside, at the rear, was a large swimming pool.

He undressed, showered and toweled himself dry. His stomach muscles tensed. He felt completely out of place, a fish out of water. If he was going to be convincing he must pose as a novice, he reckoned, like Danny. He put on a short-sleeved shirt, chinos, loafers. Dress casual, Wanda had said. Her voice and tone were sultry, commanding—even dominating, he thought.

The bedside phone rang. He lifted the receiver.

"This is reception. Dinner will be served in ten minutes, sir. Please follow the plan directions to the dining room."

He exited his room and headed for the top of the stairs. On the way he met Danny on the landing. "Going my way?" he said.

"Y-yes, if you don't mind my company?"

"Not at all. This is pretty new to me as well." Which was very true indeed.

When they got there, the others were already in the dining room.

Weir sat next to Wanda, Curtis opposite Nige. Danny and Evan sat opposite each other.

The first course was soup, hot or cold, followed by a choice of steak, pork or chicken, with various sauces and the ubiquitous French fries, plus ice cream, flan or cheese-cake for dessert. Plain food, but substantial.

Talk was strangely subdued until the after-dinner brandies were served. Cigars were permitted for those who indulged: only two bothered—Nige puffed on a cheroot and Curtis smoked a slim panatela.

Wanda stood up at the head of the table and explained: "You all may not appreciate that this is a fairly radical venture. For too long pedophiles have been shunned by society. You're probably aware that in the bad old days homosexuals were ostracized, hated and hounded, and yet, nowadays, they are widely regarded as ordinary, healthy people, no more 'ill' than people who are left-handed. It really is time that pedophilia should perhaps gain similar acceptance."

"I can't see that happening any time soon," moaned Curtis, blowing blue smoke. "I'm no youngster and I fear it won't happen in my lifetime."

"Oh, don't be so pessimistic," countered Nige, tapping the ash from his cigar. "What PG is doing is quite exciting! The fervent following of a popular sport—what could be more innocuous and acceptable, eh?" He sniggered and coughed on smoke.

"I confess I have difficulty with the meanings of the jargon you use," Danny admitted.

Wanda turned to him, eyes lighting up. "You know, I thought you were new, unsure."

"Just—just a bit." His cheeks flushed, as if a guilty secret had been exposed. Which wasn't far from the truth, Evan surmised.

Reaching out, she rested a hand on Danny's. "It will be alright. I will find a suitable candidate for you, to make it easy for a first timer. I might even help you, if you so desire."

"Er, n-no, I'm sure I will be alright when the time comes..."

"Alright on the night, eh?" Nige said, sniggering again.

Curtis cleared his throat noisily. "We all had to accept our true nature, son. Once you do that, there is no shame." He sucked on his cheroot and blew smoke out. "Believe me."

Evan slept surprisingly soundly that night, in spite of his concerns about being discovered.

———

THE NEXT MORNING, after Nadia and Cat had eaten the breakfast sullenly delivered by Andrés, they began their serious preparations. They cleared the table lamp and plates off the bedside cabinet and carried it across the room and placed it under the window. Nadia clambered on top of the cabinet with Cat's hands steadying her.

Nadia removed one of her metal hair-clips and fitted its end into the screw head. Slowly, she rotated the hair-clip. There was little resistance; she began to unscrew one, and then another.

Once the board was freed, Nadia handed it to Cat and she laid it on the floor.

By the time she'd unscrewed the last, Nadia's wrist ached. "Just as I hoped," she said. "The window doesn't have a lock."

Cat beamed at her. "We make a pretty good team, eh?"

Absently massaging her wrist, Nadia bobbed her head in agreement.

———

LEON DROVE his F-Type Jaguar convertible with its red soft top along a narrow country track generously endowed with pot-holes. After several yards, there was a passing point or cutoff. On either side were fields of corn though nowhere near as tall as an elephant's eye. He was glad of the vehicle's superior suspension; even so, he took it steadily. The map on his cell-phone was surprisingly accurate. He hadn't expected the GPS would recognize the address here in the country.

Then the surface improved, becoming a thin layer of blacktop and the track curved to the left. He slowed and, finally, up ahead he spotted the big metal double gates. The large brass plaque on the wall on the right showed *Green-Go Golf Course, Prop T. Iglesias*. The right place, then.

There was a small manned gate-house on the left. Leon lowered the window and leaned out as a man stepped through the gate-house doorway. He wore a peaked cap, green jacket and pants, and had a long lined face and humorless eyes.

"Your business, Señor?"

"My name is Knight. I have an appointment with Señor Iglesias."

"Ah, yes, he rang through earlier; you're a bit early."

"I'm keen."

The man smiled condescendingly. "One moment, please." He returned to the gate-house and abruptly both gates automatically swung open.

The gate-man came out again, leaned forward and lowered his head to the window. "Go straight for ten meters and take the left-hand fork which will bring you to the house. It overlooks the fairway."

"Thanks." Leon gunned the car in, drove to the fork in the road. A sign clearly indicated *La Casa* to the left and *El Hoyo Primero* to the right.

On the car's approach he took in the surroundings. Clusters of agave and red and pink rhododendron were planted amidst wood chippings, and behind them stood many conifer trees.

The house was grand, three stories. Only the downstairs windows were protected by ornate metal grilles. On the right another building was attached, comprising two stories. Attic windows were interspersed along the steeply sloping terracotta monk-and-nun tiled roof. The gravel drive swung round to that block which only had a single entrance portico and white door.

On the left side was an open garage wide enough for two vehicles; it presently housed one, a green Honda Odyssey MPV. A man was washing a black BMW limousine with a hose-pipe. The water-meter bill for this place must be huge; golf courses were notoriously thirsty.

Leon parked alongside the portico's three steps and killed the engine. He got out and climbed to the double doors. He was conscious of his lightweight Colt Officer's ACP LW automatic in its ankle holster. He didn't think he'd need it this visit, nor did he believe he'd be frisked. This was purely business. And as far as he was concerned, it was a fishing expedition. He needed to determine the layout of the place.

A burly man in smart tight-fitting green livery rushed to greet him. "Señor Knight?"

"That's me," Leon said.

"You are early." Sounded like an accusation.

"Punctuality is my middle name."

Unfazed, the flunky replied, "Is that so? This way, please. The boss is expecting you."

They crossed an echoing lobby flanked by marble statuary. A marble staircase swept up to a landing, where he glimpsed a couple of doors: apartments or bedrooms, perhaps.

He was led to a sturdy office door on the right.

The man rapped his knuckles just beneath the metal label stating *Gestión*. Management.

"Enter!"

The flunky opened the door and Leon was ushered inside. "Señor Punctuality Knight, sir," the comedian announced without benefit of a business card on a silver tray.

Tomás Iglesias had risen from a leather padded chair behind his large mahogany desk. "Very good, Paco, you may leave us."

"Sir," Paco said. The door closed behind him.

Iglesias had the rasping voice of a smoker. Cigar fumes lingered; a stub smouldered in an ashtray. This was definitely the man he'd seen wielding the driver to brutal effect. Leon's stomach roiled as he reminded himself that Rod had suffered massive blunt trauma at the hands of someone using a golf club as a weapon.

Outwardly unaffected, Leon strode forward, his arm extended. "Good of you to give me some of your valuable time."

"Happy to oblige." Iglesias walked round his desk and they shook hands. "Please, take a seat."

Leon sat on a straight-backed chair facing the desk. From his chair Leon had a view of the right-hand arm of the building he'd seen on his approach—presumably an accommodation block, with attic windows.

Iglesias didn't return to his previous position behind the desk. He set his rump on a corner of the desk. "Would you like a drink?" He indicated a trolley of assorted alcoholic beverages.

"Thanks, but no."

"To business, then. You said on the phone—by the way, your Spanish is fluent, Señor Knight –you had a business proposition for me..."

"I'm half-Spanish," he explained.

"I see. Mother's half, I imagine—hence your English surname."

"Indeed," Leon lied. Lying came easy to him and it always had. Useful in his chosen profession. "I'm part of a consortium. We're interested in buying this golf course. It's ideally placed for entertaining our foreign clients."

Iglesias pursed his lips and shook his head. "I wish you had told me the kind of deal you were proposing. I could have saved you the journey. Green-Go isn't for sale. My people have invested heavily in it. Now we are poised to reap generous rewards."

"That's a pity..." Leon glimpsed over Iglesias's shoulder movement outside, high up, contrasting colors. "We would pay top dollar, naturally."

"No, sorry." Iglesias stood and returned to his side of the desk and sat down.

At first Leon thought he was seeing things. But no, one of the attic windows was opening and a young girl appeared to be clambering through it, onto the roof. She was wearing dark red jeans and a yellow-and-blue tank top. He also glimpsed the head of another girl inside.

His mouth went dry.

Abruptly he stood up. He leaned across the desk and they shook hands. "Sorry to have bothered you."

He reached the door, levered the handle.

"One moment, Señor Knight!" Iglesias called.

Leon turned, arched an eyebrow. "Yes?"

"Do you want to stay for lunch? I offer it in compensation for a wasted journey."

Leon returned an apologetic smile. "That's kind of you, but no, thanks. Sorry, but as this deal is a non-starter, I must hasten to another appointment." He opened the door and stepped into the lobby.

He sensed his heart pounding.

CHAPTER 9

NO CHARGE

NADIA'S MOUTH WAS VERY DRY AS SHE CRAWLED over the window frame sill onto the roof tiles. The rough terracotta surface abraded the knees of her jeans. Mamá would be so annoyed with her.

"I'm coming out now," Cat whispered behind her.

"Alright." Carefully, one hand gripping the window frame, Nadia sidled to the left to make room for Cat.

The slope of the roof was more pronounced than she'd thought. She almost felt herself tipping forward and only stopped herself with an effort.

Her legs seemed wobbly. It was an awfully long way to fall.

How were they going to get down? There was no guttering, no drainpipe.

A hoopoe called, somewhere in the trees: repetitive, poo-poo-poo. She swallowed. Soon, she might be flying in the air —but without the aid of wings.

"It's so steep!" Cat wailed hoarsely.

It was tempting to climb up, on hands and knees, but that wouldn't help.

She glanced to her right and saw where the two buildings joined. If she could reach there, she could descend while hugging the wall of the main house.

"Follow me!" she whispered and began to edge across the sloping roof tiles. She was glad she wore sneakers.

"It's—my shoes—they're slipping!" Cat cried.

Nadia peered over her shoulders. "Take off your pumps —you'll get a better grip in your socks."

"Right. Good thinking. I'll try. But—wait, wait for me— don't go too far ahead."

———

Leon walked calmly but hurriedly across the lobby. Paco opened the front door for him and he said "*Adiós!*"

As the door shut, Leon raced down the steps and didn't bother with the car door but jumped in behind the wheel.

The engine purred and from a standing start he accelerated, the tires spewing stones behind.

Through the windshield he could now see two young girls traversing the roof.

Typical of so many Spanish buildings, there was no guttering or drainpipe. There was no way down for them.

Still on the move, he jabbed the switch, raised the convertible's roof.

Suddenly, a man appeared at the open window. Impossible to mistake him with that face resembling a bruised gourd and that black mustache. Iglesias had called him Andrés. Now Andrés hollered at the girls and slammed a wooden club loudly on the tiles.

The girl in the dress jerked round in alarm and lost her footing. Her hands scrabbled for support but found none. She screamed and tumbled forward, rolling down the sloping roof and, heart-stopping, into thin air. The other girl—he was sure it was the missing Nadia—shrieked.

The girl in the dress hit the gravel ground solidly and didn't move.

Leon braked beneath Nadia, changed the gear into neutral, and got out, the engine idling. "Nadia, jump onto the roof of my car!" He ran over to the motionless girl, checked the pulse in her neck. She was dead. A young life of promise snuffed out.

"Hey!" the man at the window shouted.

Nadia tentatively reached the edge of the roof. She'd run out of tiles. She hesitated and then pluckily jumped.

She squealed as she landed on the car's soft top roof; it ruptured and she fell through the material onto the passenger seat.

Leon sprinted to the car and opened the door. "Are you okay?" He gasped, slightly out of breath.

"Y-yes! But—Cat...!"

Two men he'd never seen before were running from the house entrance, heading towards the car. One of them was carrying a revolver.

This was not the place or time to engage in a firefight. The safety of Nadia was paramount. "Stay put," Leon told her and slid behind the wheel.

He revved the engine, put the car in gear and the Jaguar described a wide circle, gravel spitting everywhere.

Despite the shouts, the engine's throbbing, the wheels churning stones, he could detect Nadia's sobbing.

"I'm sorry about your friend," he said . "Now hold on tight!"

Leon knew the gates would present a problem. The man in the gate-house was on the other side of the fence. If he had no mind to open the gates, then they'd be stymied.

His luck held, however.

A white VW Caddy was entering the open gates as his Jaguar approached.

At this point there was room for two vehicles. He put his foot down, passed the van and raced through the open gateway before they could be automatically shut.

In his rear-view mirror he saw the gate-house man standing with a hand on hip, his other hand holding his cap and scratching his head, and then Leon had driven round the bend and the place was out of sight.

Clear. For now.

———

THE VW VAN driver swerved as a green Honda Odyssey MPV hastened past, heading for the gate. "Another one! Everybody's in a rush today," he mumbled.

Then he drew up in front of the entrance steps and braked. As he got out he noticed some men running around but paid them no mind since it was none of his business. He moved to the rear and unlocked and opened the back door.

Some children clambered to the ground, eyes blinking in the sunlight. Two boys and four girls.

"You can't bring them here now!" barked Iglesias from the top of the entrance steps.

"What?" The driver walked to the base of the steps. "I've got a consignment. It's been agreed. I need paying!"

"Didn't you see that Jaguar leave?"

"Yeah. So what?"

"He'll be sending the law on us, that's what!"

The driver snapped, "That isn't my problem. I've delivered. Now I need payment."

"You can't leave those kids here. We need to move all the others out now! Pile them in!"

"What about the MPV?"

"It's chasing after the Jaguar."

The driver spotted a man in a red-striped shirt carrying quite a large bundle wrapped in a blanket, heading for the gate. For an instant he thought he saw a hand flop down amidst the folds but then he was gone. "Was that a dead kid?"

"Don't be absurd, of course not."

"I draw the line at children dying."

"How noble of you!"

"Do you want my help or not?"

"I'll remember your attitude..."

It was pandemonium. Iglesias stood at the top of the

steps, barking orders. Men were rushing about like scalded cats.

————

LEON SPOTTED the MPV in his rear-view mirror. He cursed the pot-holes and slowed. Having the chassis ripped off wouldn't do Nadia or him any favors. He swerved to avoid one after another hole, the tire rims dangerously close to the edge of the track. He prayed there was nobody coming in the other direction.

Bouncing along, revving, slowing, slewing left and right, shoulder muscles aching, and Nadia's constant sobbing in his ears.

Finally, he reached the end of the track. The MPV hadn't gained on him.

As soon as the tires ran on firm blacktop, Leon slowed, yanked the handbrake and the Jaguar slewed to a stop effectively across the entrance to the track. He put the gears in neutral, lowered his window. The engine purred as he reached down and drew his Colt from the ankle holster.

"Stay low, Nadia!" he ordered.

Closer and closer the MPV came.

Leon rested both hands on the sill of his door. Two-handed grip. Steady.

He fired three times, two .45 bullets into the engine block and the third through the windshield.

The result was instantaneous.

The MPV abruptly veered to the right, left the track and ploughed full into a dense stand of corn.

Lowering his automatic to the floor well, Leon put the Jaguar in gear, swung the wheel round and drove on the refreshingly smooth road.

Sticking to the speed limit, Leon said, "Nadia, how do you feel?"

"Glad—glad to be free of that place... Sad—sad about poor Cat..."

"Cat—was that her name?"

Nadia moved closer to him. "Catalina. I don't know her other names."

"Were there other– ?"

"Kids?—Yes. I think so. They brought a food trolley, it had lots of pizzas on it..."

"That's all I needed to know. I'm taking you home."

"How do you know my name?"

"Your mother hired me to find you. Gave me a photo."

"That's fantastic. You are a detective?"

"Yes. Private. But it was mere chance I was there when you clambered... out..."

She sobbed, doubtless seeing again Cat falling to her death. She'd be traumatized for a while yet.

"You don't have to answer this, if you don't want to, but did– ?"

"No, they did not molest me. Cat said they intended to —there is make-believe clothing in the closet..."

He gritted his teeth, containing his anger. "Not long, and then you'll be with your mother—and father..."

"No—not him! Never him!"

Her sudden outburst almost made him lose control of the car for a fraction of a second. "What is it?"

"He—it was him who—who..."

He drove in to a pull-off and stopped the car. "Let's get out, stretch our legs, eh?"

He leaned against the hood of the car. "In your own time, tell me..."

She was trembling, clasping her hands together in front of her. "Papá—he took me there with his fancy woman..."

"Took you?"

"Yes. She gave him a brown envelope. I was naïve. I suppose it held money... Then he left me with her..."

He swore under his breath. "The bas— He sold you?"

She shrugged phlegmatically. "I guess so. That's what Cat thought, too." Her jaw clenched tight.

"It's up to you, of course," he said, "but I think you

shouldn't tell your mother what your father did. For her sake, not his."

She nodded, an old head on young shoulders. "I think you are right. It would be a terrible shock. There's no telling what she might do..."

"I take it you don't ever want to see your father again?"

She shook her head vigorously. "Never would be too soon!"

"Then I promise, he will not darken your life again."

"You can make such a promise?"

"I can be persuasive." He straightened up. "Shall we get on? It's not far to go now."

"Yes, please. But Señor—I do not know your name?"

"Cazador. Leon Cazador."

"Leon." Tentatively she reached out, her hand clasping his. "And thank you again."

And her eyes glistened with tears.

He wanted to console her, hug her, but thought better of it.

He tugged her hand instead. "Come on, let's go." He led her back to the car, opened the door for her.

She got in, belted up and her knuckles wiped away her tears.

———

AS HE DROVE, Leon pondered; he was in a quandary. His first priority was to return Nadia to her mother. Once that had been done, he had several options. Inform the police about the child Cat's fatal fall. Hope the police could trace Catalina's parents, and then break the awful news. Inevitably, Social Services would become involved in Nadia's welfare. Different branches of the law would be recruited and search warrants would be obtained after officialdom's tedious delays. In the meantime, he felt sure that Iglesias and his people would be busy removing any evidence. Alternatively, once Nadia was safe, he could return to Green-Go and disrupt their cover-up preparations. By the time he'd reached Nadia's street, he'd made his decision. Luckily there was a parking space near her apartment door.

Standing on the porch of the block, Leon champed at the bit. He wanted to get going. But first things first.

Nadia stood nervously beside him, anxiously waiting. She'd recovered well and on the final leg of their journey she had chatted about her mother's family and her school work.

The door opened and Señora Flores stood there, her puzzled frown immediately transformed into a joyous beam. There were tears and sobs and hugs and an unfamiliar warmth cascaded through his body.

"Oh, thank you, thank you, Señor Cazador!"

They went upstairs.

While Nadia went to her room and showered, Señora Flores wiped her eyes and took him into the kitchen. She opened a drawer and a shaky hand took out a black leather purse. "I have your payment here."

With trembling fingers she offered him the Euro bills.

He closed her fingers round them and said, "No charge, Señora Flores."

She gulped and sank onto a straight-backed chair, clutching the purse in her lap, staring at it as tears dropped onto her hands. "Oh, you are too kind."

"*De nada.*" It's nothing.

Then she lifted her chin and tentatively whispered, "Has she—has she come to any harm?"

"She says not, and I believe her."

"Oh, *Gracias a Dios*. And thank you."

"Nadia tells me you have a sister in Murcia."

"Yes?"

"Take her there—for a week or two. She has had a terrible ordeal. It would be good for her to get away. Until this business is settled."

———

WANDA DROVE her Audi coupé up to the entrance steps, cut the engine and got out. Slipping her bag on her shoulder, she mounted the steps and frowned. There was shouting coming from inside, and people running about. It didn't sound like they were preparing for tonight's frivolities.

Instinctively, she suspected that something was amiss.

Paco opened the door as she reached it.

"What's happened, Paco?"

"Lots, Señorita." As far as Tomás and his crew were concerned she wasn't married, and never had been. "And none of it is good, alas."

She strode into the lobby. "Where is he?"

"In the office, packing."

Packing? "I'll see him alone. I'm sure you have things to do."

"Very good, Señorita." He bowed slightly and moved to the opposite side of the lobby and disappeared through a doorway that led to the kitchen.

Wanda hadn't eaten and had been looking forward to a heaped plate of tapas and a couple of glasses of wine. All of a sudden she didn't feel hungry.

She opened the door and walked in.

Tomás was stuffing a wad of documents into a briefcase. On the desk were four piles of bank notes. The wall-safe door was open and the safe empty.

A log fire burned even though it was not cold. Assorted papers were burning. Burnt paper littered the hearth.

"What the hell's happened?" she demanded.

He told her.

"Who was this Knight character?"

"God knows. I think it was just chance he happened by when the two girls tried to escape."

"I'm not a great believer in so-called chance. It's a pity you didn't listen to me and install CCTV like I have at Golf-Sur. I'd have liked to see the troublesome Señor Knight."

"It's on my 'to-do' list."

"Couldn't you have phoned, told me, warned me?"

"I was busy getting Andrés to dispose of the girl's body. Then there was the MPV..."

"What about it?"

"It gave chase—but Knight shot it up and it crashed into the field. That took time to tow out. Fortunately, the driver —Diego—was only wounded."

"Chance? Again? Come on, Tomás... This Knight guy has a gun!" She snorted derisively. "Really!"

"Then I had to re-direct the five golfers that just arrived shortly after. They were not too pleased—we'd promised them your 'frivolities' tonight, remember?"

She ignored that comment as she paced left and right. "What about the kids?"

"I got Vicente to hire two coaches and loaded them all in. They also took the six new arrivals."

"That's something, I suppose. But this is a real mess. Where are you taking them to? Dimples won't be ready for ages."

"We're transferring our operations to Golf-Sur."

"But there aren't enough rooms for the kids and the clients!"

"Don't forget its big basement."

"Oh, I remember alright." She smirked and her high cheek-bones flushed.

"We can keep the kids down there," Tomás said. "That will free up enough rooms for the extra clients."

"That's a lot for Tía Paloma to cope with in one place, isn't it?"

"She does as we tell her. For good reason. You know that."

She sighed. "True, my dear. We'd be lost without her. I trust you've got her ex on a tight leash?"

"Yes. He gets paid enough."

She crossed the room and poured herself a generous measure of whisky and sank into a chair. She gulped the golden liquid and it burned all the way, leaving a warm glow. "All things considered, you've done well."

"Don't linger over that drink, dearest. I don't know how long it will take for the cops to get here."

She gulped it and stood up. Her empty stomach grumbled. "You're right. We need to leave very soon." *I need feeding!*

———

CARLOTA'S FACE lit up when Leon entered his office; as always, she was pleased to see him. "Did you learn anything from Señor Iglesias?"

He removed his jacket and put it on the back of his chair. "All that I needed to know, actually." He told her what had happened.

Impulsively, she embraced him. "Oh, that's wonderful! Adriana must be ecstatic!"

"I must confess it was sheer luck."

"You're too modest. What are you going to do about Iglesias and his people?" She'd dropped the *Señor*, he'd noticed. The man didn't deserve it.

"I intend paying him a return visit. Spoil his nasty operations."

"Is that wise? Couldn't you let the *Guardia* and the national police handle it?"

"I could. But... The delay officialdom imposes on search warrants and approvals and joint operations means they'll be too late and the bad guys will get away." He eased himself from her embrace and moved to the Juan Romero de Torres painting on the far wall. He swung it aside and quickly spun the combination and opened the safe.

He took out his Astra A-100 automatic snug in its black leather shoulder holster, and dumped it on his desk.

Then he strode over to the small closet in the corner of the office, opened it. He removed his shirt, bunched it in a roll and gave his underarms a swift wipe with it then dropped it in the wastebasket. From the closet he took a black silk long-sleeved shirt and put it on . He kicked off his shoes, unbelted his pants and replaced them with a black pair of cargo pants.

Carlota was unfazed. The first time he'd needed to change in a hurry, he'd asked her to go into her office. She'd complied but halfway through changing she'd entered with an urgent phone-call. "Don't worry," she'd said, "nudity is no big deal." So this wasn't the first time he'd undressed in front of her. Nor would it be the last, he suspected. He shrugged into his shoulder holster, checked the Astra and then the Colt in his ankle holster.

He selected a pair of black rock hopper neoprene shoes from a closet shelf and fastened them.

She delved into a filing cabinet and handed him two magazines for each gun.

He distributed them in the various pants pockets so they wouldn't make a noise knocking against each other. Finally, he pocketed two pairs of latex gloves and a set of wire-cutters.

"I guess you're ready to go?" she said, stroking his cheek.

"More or less." He kissed her lips. Moist, as inviting as ever. "Don't wait up."

She sniffed. "That's a laugh. You know I won't get any sleep."

———

LILIANA BLINKED, slowly emerged from sleep and stretched languorously. She felt warm, suffused with pleasure after their lovemaking. She brushed stray tendrils of black hair away from her face.

Her heart skittered as she saw Martín sitting on the stool at her dressing-table, still naked, his muscular back to her.

She wanted to call for him to return to her bed, for already renewed heat coursed through her veins.

But she was suddenly very curious. She sat up, let the sheet fall away. "What are you doing, lover?"

He swivelled round, surprise in his features. She could

see he was in the process of unwrapping a small bundle of khaki material. She remembered seeing it briefly when he exited the bank on their way here. He had that in one hand, and a thin bundle of Euros in the other. He'd looked left and right down the street, as if ensuring nobody had observed him, and then thrust them in his jacket pockets.

Now, as he watched her without any sign of passion, he peeled back the material to reveal the black metal of a handgun.

Her breath caught in her throat. "What are you doing with *that*?"

He held it up, smiling, and moved it from side to side, examining its contours.

She thought: *he used to look at me like that*.

"This, my dear, is a Tokarev automatic pistol. I'm told its 7.62mm slugs have sufficient stopping power for my purposes."

"Stopping power? You mean *killing*!"

He shrugged and released the magazine and then clipped it back into place. "If need be, yes."

"But you promised you'd go straight!"

"I will, when I've been paid what I'm owed. I reckon Cazador owes me at least ten thousand Euros!"

"But you lied to me!"

His lips pursed and he lowered the gun to the dressing-table. It seemed incongruous among her sprays, pots, powder and lotions. He stood, his deep brown eyes hard, his toned body rippling in the light. "*I* lied to you?"

"Yes. You promised..."

"Chica, you lied to me. While I was suffering in prison, you've been fucking my best pal, Manolo—and two others that I know about!"

She squirmed on the bed and absently tugged the sheet up to cover her breasts. Her mouth was dry. "How'd you find out?" she croaked.

Arms akimbo, he said, "A cell-mate got released. He'd promised to look you up. But when he saw you with

Manolo, he let me know. I paid him to keep an eye on you."

"You paid a crook to spy on me?"

"Yeah, that's right..." He walked to the bedside. "Now, if you know what's good for you, you'll do as I say."

She cringed, no longer desiring him. Her stomach roiled and she sensed a coldness skitter over her flesh. "This is madness!"

"Yes, I'm mad—mad as hell with you and your betrayal!" He slapped her.

Her cheek stung and her face burned. He'd never before hit her. Never. Tears began to form in her eyes and she blinked them away. She would not give him the satisfaction of seeing her cry. This was her place, and yet she felt trapped. He was powerful, stronger than ever as he'd worked out in the prison gym. And he had let his hatred fester. She rued the day she had told him about the private eye.

Martín turned back to the dressing-table and picked up the gun. "Get dressed. We have business to attend to!"

———

As usual, Carlota locked the offices and descended the stairs.

And stepped into the street.

As usual.

Annoyingly, she had that tingling feeling at the back of her neck again.

Recently, she'd found that was not usual. And it was the third or fourth time it had happened.

She checked the reflections of passersby in the shop window.

Nobody suspicious.

Her apartment was two blocks away. Convenient.

On an impulse she stopped by the mini-market. Entering, she hesitated and checked outside. Nobody seemed to be taking an interest in her or the shop.

She bought a pre-made tortilla, a carton of semi-skimmed milk, and a frozen Chicken Tikka Masala, which Leon had recommended to her; she used a fold up bag to put it all in, doing her bit to save the planet.

This evening she'd indulge herself with this and a bottle of Campo Viejo Reserva from her small wine rack.

And wait up for Leon.

It would be a long night, she reckoned.

Her shoulder blades still persisted in tingling all the way home.

CHAPTER 10

SIMPLY BUSINESS

IGLESIAS THOUGHT ABOUT THE KILLING OF Wallace. It wasn't the first, but it had been one of the most enjoyable. He had observed that Wanda had been strongly affected by it too. Her lips had glistened wetly and her chest heaved at each bone-breaking blow.

And it had happened all by chance. One of their clients, a Mr. Julius Peterson had approached him diffidently during post-prandial drinks at the Golf-Sur function room.

Peterson was short, wiry, with a bald head and sagging jowls. Probably in his forties. "I don't know how to say this, but I fear you have a cuckoo in your nest."

"Oh?" Iglesias had replied non-committally.

Peterson had nodded in the direction of Roger Eastlake. "He's not using his real name. I know him as Rodney Wallace. He was a member in the same gang as me in London. We were busted by SC035. I managed to get away during the cop raid. The others weren't so lucky. Before I scarpered out of the country and came here I heard Wallace had been working undercover for SC035..."

"Are you sure about him?"

Peterson nodded again, like one of those dogs on the back shelves of cars. "Yes. I got a shock, seeing him here..."

"Thank you for letting me know. You have done us a great service."

Yes, sheer chance had saved him and the organization.

Iglesias had sauntered up to Wallace and said, "You have been found out, Señor Eastlake. Or should I call you Wallace?"

Wallace's blue eyes glinted amusedly and he grinned good-humouredly. "Pardon? What do you mean, Señor Iglesias?"

Iglesias pointed to Peterson who hovered at the doorway, a stupid grin on his face. Peterson raised a thumb and then turned it down and shook his head.

Recognition lit Wallace's eyes. "Then there's nothing to say, is there?" Wallace didn't offer any resistance as Vicente and Andrés stepped to his sides and gripped him by the arms and frogmarched him out of the room. After a few moments, Iglesias had followed.

They took Wallace downstairs, to the basement.

The six rooms were all vacant at present.

Vicente opened the door with a key from the chain at his waist.

"Take him inside, strip him and put him in a chair," Iglesias ordered. "Don't hurt him. Wait for me to do that."

"*Sí, Jefe,*" they both echoed together and shoved Wallace inside.

Iglesias returned upstairs and went into his office. In the far corner behind his desk was his golf bag. He pulled out the driver and swung it experimentally. Yes, perfect.

Wanda came in. "Where are you going with that, dearest? It's a bit late for a game, isn't it?"

A frisson of pleasure shimmied through him. "Not for the game I'm contemplating. Would you like to come with me and watch what I'm going to do with this?"

She licked her lips and smiled broadly.

"Good," he said. "Come with me."

By the time he returned to the room with Wanda, Wallace had been stripped naked and was tied to the straight-backed chair, his arms fastened to the back, his ankles to the front legs. He was breathing heavily. Adrenaline was doubtless pumping away with nowhere to go. Sweat covered his face and soaked his hairy chest.

Wanda's breathing increased at sight of their captive.

Iglesias was impressed with her. She didn't raise any questions or express any concern. He gave her a glance. Her cheeks were flushed. She was going to enjoy this.

He took a step forward and stood in front of Wallace, resting his hands on the handle of the golf club. "You're going to tell me who you're working for and if there are any more of you lurking in the woodwork."

"I don't think so," Wallace replied.

"Well, I do." He pointed the club's head at the tattoo on Wallace's left forearm. "Pretty girl. Is she close to you?"

"No, it's just a tattoo."

Without giving any warning, Iglesias whacked the forearm viciously with the big head of the club.

Wallace made a seething sound between gritted teeth.

Behind him, Iglesias heard Wanda's breathing quicken.

"Brave. Very brave." Iglesias shook his head. "It will do you no good, however." He swung the driver around, pointing at the walls. "And this underbuild is sound-proofed."

Glaring defiantly at him, Wallace said, "You enjoy this aspect of your work, don't you?"

"Exceedingly." He gestured with the driver, pointing at Wallace's forearm; bruising already showed. "Now, what can you tell me?"

"I can tell you I work for NCA."

"That is good. You see, when you talk there is no more pain."

He detected a mew of disappointment from Wanda.

"What is this NCA?" Iglesias demanded. "Some kind of secret service organization?"

"British. National Crime Agency."

"But we are not in Great Britain. You should have no jurisdiction here."

"We are everywhere—fighting organized crime."

"I do the fighting," Iglesias said and hit Wallace's forearm again and there was a distinct crack of bone.

Wanda exhaled.

Wallace jerked in the chair and gritted his teeth, breathing heavily through his nose.

"You will do the dying, I think," Iglesias said. The head of the driver hit Wallace's left shin and bone splintered loudly.

Wallace wailed in agony, but nobody outside this place was going to hear.

Some time afterwards, Vicente stood in the lobby with Andrés alongside him. His dark complexion was ruddy. "I've just got back, Boss." He fingered the knife at his belt. "Montoya is playing up. Doesn't want to play ball."

"Then we shall present him with a gift, no?" Iglesias thumbed at the door leading to the basement. "Dump him and arrange for an anonymous call. When the cops spoil Montoya's day, that should scare him into compliance." Out of the corner of his eye he saw Peterson standing at the doorway into the lounge. His face appeared anxious. He turned to Andrés. "You stay with me."

Vicente opened the door, descended the steps to the basement.

Iglesias motioned with a hand for Peterson to join him.

"Did he tell you anything?" Peterson asked anxiously.

"Oh, Wallace said plenty." Iglesias nodded to Andrés who flanked Peterson. "He told me you changed allegiance, deserted your gang for another. The arrest of your original gang meant your new friends had a much bigger and wealthier patch to work on."

Peterson shrugged. "So? It's simply business."

Iglesias nodded again at Andrés.

Andrés clamped a hand on Peterson's arm.

"Hey, what's going on?" Peterson said.

"If you desert your friends so easily—for business—then I must protect myself from you, I think." He eyed Andrés. "Take him away and hold him. I may need him to use as an example to others later."

Sweat sprouted on Peterson's bald head as Andrés shoved him through the doorway to the basement.

———

Since his Jaguar was in the garage for repairs, Leon had hired a car—an inconspicuous white Toyota Yaris. He drove it close to the entrance of the track leading to Green-Go golf course and then halted and parked.

From here he would go on foot.

He noted that while the skid marks were there at the side of the track, the MPV wasn't.

They'd recovered it, moved it.

He jogged with care along the track, avoiding the potholes, most of which could rick his ankle if he didn't pay attention. The magazines and wire-cutters knocked against his thighs.

He made good time.

As he got near the bend he slowed his pace. He edged along and noted that the gate-house was unmanned at present and the entrance gates were shut. The sentry could be doing his rounds, perhaps. He would sneak through the trees on the left and, out of sight, tackle the wire fence while keeping an eye out for the sentry.

Underbrush and dead wood covered the ground. He walked slowly, lowering his heel first, then the flat of his foot, and finally his toe, attempting to avoid attracting attention.

He was no more than ten minutes into the stand of trees when he heard the rustling sound, not far ahead. He stopped and withdrew his automatic from its shoulder holster.

The sound continued unabated.

Slowly, he moved towards it.

He eased aside a bush.

The bastard. On the edge of a clearing was a man in a red-striped linen shirt, his back to Leon. It was that ugly bastard, Andrés, last seen in the attic window moments before the girl Cat had fallen. His denim pants were round his ankles and he was pulling up his boxer shorts. Laying in front of Andrés was a young girl's body, face down on a blanket, her back partly covered by leaves. The hairstyle and colour resembled Cat's; he'd been close enough to check her pulse, after all. The bastard.

Leon stepped out from concealment as Andrés was about to reach for his pants to pull them up.

"Don't move!" Leon snapped. "Stay very still!" He walked round to face Andrés.

Eyes widening in recognition, Andrés gasped. "Shit. You're that Knight guy..."

"Take off your shirt and cover her up."

Andrés hesitated.

"Now—or I'll put a bullet in your knee!"

Hurriedly, Andrés unbuttoned his shirt and took it off, flung it over Catalina. "I was just—just..."

"I know what you'd just done," Leon grated. He recalled a scandalous case in England a while back, when a hospital porter had indulged in sex with corpses of all ages in the morgue, even filming the act. It was no consolation that he would end his days in prison for his necrophiliac aberration. Considering the anguish he'd caused the many families of the deceased, it would be more fitting and just if he'd ended his days prematurely on a mortuary slab! Victims don't stop being victims once they're dead.

Leon controlled his rising anger with no effort at all, as he'd been trained by Hatsumi way back in Tokyo when he was attached to the Spanish embassy. He said with a level tone, "How many are in the house?"

"Two of us. Me and Bernardo."

"What about the guy at the gate-house?"

"He left with the others. We're the caretakers until they

return." He gestured vaguely at the pants round his ankles. "I have the keys."

"Where have the others gone?"

"Golf-Sur."

Leon nodded. Figures. He walked up to Andrés and could smell the despicable man's fear.

Glancing at the automatic, Andrés asked, "What are you going to do?"

"I'm not going to shoot you."

Andrés let out a sigh of relief and hastily crossed himself. Hypocrite.

Instead, Leon kicked Andrés between the legs, putting as much power and anger he could muster into the movement. The contact was immensely satisfying.

Andrés yelped and bent forward, wobbling with his pants round his ankles, trying to retain his balance while intent on clutching his damaged manhood. Next instant, Leon deployed the ninja Fudo-ken, the clenched fist slamming full into the bastard's nose, shattering the bone structure. While the bone and cartilage probably wouldn't penetrate this sick person's brain, the blow would undoubtedly cause subdural hematoma which was bound to deny the brain adequate blood flow. As a result, a biochemical cascade was in all likelihood happening right now as Leon dispassionately watched. Brain cell death was imminent. No great loss to humanity.

Andrés slumped forward onto the underbrush.

Crouching down, Leon replaced the Astra in its shoulder holster and then searched the man's pants' pockets and found the bunch of keys, a billfold and a cell-phone. No need of the wire-cutters, after all. He examined the wallet's contents: driving license, a hundred Euros in bills, which he pocketed, two credit cards in the name of Andrés Alonso; nothing else.

He ripped a pocket out of Andrés's pants and used the material to wipe the billfold clean of fingerprints.

Then, as he straightened up, unkinking his leg muscles,

he noticed an area of disturbed land about two yards away, among the boles of several trees. Animals had tampered with the earth, but for some reason hadn't dug too deep. Maybe they'd been interrupted. He walked over to the area and picked up a fallen branch. He used it to poke around and burrowed deeper. He didn't have to excavate far before he unearthed the intricate bone structure of a small hand with pieces of flesh still adhered to it—not an adult's. With a sinking feeling, he wondered how many were buried in this place.

Rage swept over him and his stomach roiled emptily and his chest ached.

Self-control. He calmed.

A reckoning was due.

He turned away. There was nothing he could do now.

Blindly he moved over the underbrush, that ache in his chest reluctant to depart. He'd rarely been so affected by death.

Finally he reached the road and shook the cold ire loose, if only temporarily.

He walked to the gate-house and unlocked the door and went inside.

The gate-switch was labeled; he operated it and left.

Eyes alert now, he walked through, leaving the gates open.

It was strange, returning to this place. Earlier, it had been bedlam. Now it was eerily still. He wondered where Bernardo had gotten to.

A Nissan truck was parked by the garage on the left. It hadn't been there last visit.

By the time he reached the entrance steps, night had fallen.

Before entering, he put on a pair of latex gloves.

The front door was ajar.

He went in and switched on the lights.

The lobby was quiet. His neoprene soles made no sound.

He found Iglesias's office door.

Inside, the place had changed since his visit. No longer tidy.

A whiff of burnt paper permeated the air rather than the aroma of cigar smoke. The fireplace was a mess with its gross carbon footprint.

Leon checked the desk drawers and the filing cabinets and found little of note.

Andrés had said "until they return" but judging from this evidence it was unlikely that Iglesias and his crew would ever return. They wouldn't write-off the buildings, they'd get their abogados to sell. In which case, they must be fools, to consider selling the place while those children's corpses were interred there. Unless they didn't know about them...

He switched on his own cell-phone and rang Carlota. She'd be anxious. She'd be pleased to know there was no confrontation with Iglesias and his men.

There was no answer.

Maybe she had gone home, after all, and had fallen asleep.

"Hey, what–?"

Leon looked up from his phone. "*Hola*, Bernardo."

Brnardo stood in the doorway. "You—you're the guy who—who—"

Leon withdrew his automatic. It felt slightly alien through the latex glove, almost as if he was disconnected from the weapon and any consequences of its percussive action.

Unconsciously, he had embarked on a crusade of revenge against Rod's killers—notably Iglesias. But he also wanted to wreak havoc on the lowest of lowlife who exploited children and left them in unmarked graves.

Leon pointed the Astra-A100.

Shoot Bernardo in cold blood?

He'd killed Andrés. That was cold-blooded. But *that* was in direct payment for the vile man's desecration of the poor girl's body.

Bernardo's reedy voice impinged on his thoughts: "Where's Andrés?"

"He's dead."

"Oh, Jesus..." He stared wide-eyed at the Astra.

Leon walked toward Bernardo, still undecided about the man's fate.

"Do you know about the children's bodies buried in the woods?" he asked.

The shock on Bernardo's face seemed genuine—or he was in the running for an Oscar. "*Qué*?"

"There are children's bodies buried among the trees..."

Bernardo's face paled and he shook his head repeatedly. "I—I know nothing about..." His eyes darted. "Tía... Tía Paloma, she's wondered about kids who have left without her being told... Oh, Jesus..."

Leon's cell-phone rang. It was Carlota's number. He opened the call. "Hi, Carlota," he said. "Everything's alright. I'll be on my way back soon."

"She'll be pleased to hear that," said a strange gruff voice.

Stomach-churning foreboding sent his pulse racing. "Who is this?" Leon demanded.

A throaty chuckle. Then: "Someone who owes you big time, Señor Cazador!"

He'd heard that gruff voice before, in his distant past, but he couldn't place it. "What have you done with Carlota?"

"Nothing—yet. It depends on what you do. If you do as I say, then no harm will come to her."

"Alright. What do you want?"

"Next time I phone, be prepared to pay me plenty of cash for her life. I owe you lots of pain, Cazador. Payment for five years in prison."

The man hung up.

Chapter 11

Shoestring Gumshoe

Leon got Bernardo to take him out to the garage at the side of the house.

"It's my Pa's," Bernardo said. "Borrowed it."

"Drive me to the end of the track where I've left my car."

Bernardo eyed him fearfully. "What are you going to do with me?"

"We'll see when I get there. Now let's go!"

Shakily, Bernardo clambered in. Leon got in the passenger seat, keeping the Astra leveled on him.

Bernardo switched on the engine and motored down the drive towards the gates, headlights glaring on the vegetation.

Once past the gates Bernardo braked. "The gates—I'd better lock them. It would not be sensible to leave the property open—"

Leon thrust the gun against Bernardo's ribs. "Not now. I need to get to my car pronto. You can come back and lock the gates when you've dropped me off!"

Bernardo seemed to physically relax then, absorbing the fact that he was going to be freed.

As Bernardo drove down the pot-holed track, Leon dug out Andrés's cell-phone and rang the local police. "I'm reporting a death—a young girl by the name of Catalina."

The woman on the other end tried to interrupt, ascertain his identity.

"Just listen! I don't know her family name. The man responsible is beside the dead girl in among the trees. Just outside the entrance to Green-Go golf course. Don't delay. There are other bodies buried there as well."

"But—but—"

He gave the address and hung up.

"I—I had nothing to do with her falling off the roof," Bernardo said nervously as he negotiated a large hole in the road. "She was a good kid—"

"Who you and your kind were going to exploit."

"My kind? No, no, it wasn't like that. I'm not like that. For me, it was merely a job. I would not touch underage girls. No way!"

"Obeying orders, eh?"

"We're there!" Bernardo exclaimed and pulled into one side next to the Yaris.

Leon put his automatic in its shoulder holster and got out. "Go back to lock the gates if you want," he told Bernardo. "Or get lost. But be quick about it. The police will be here soon—and I reckon you don't want to be around when they find all those corpses!" He slammed shut the door.

Leon ran to the hire car.

Evidently Bernardo no longer felt any responsibility for the Green-Go buildings. He drove off, exhaust fumes hanging in the vehicle's wake, the rear red lights diminishing.

Leon flung open the door and slid into his seat. He fitted his cell-phone to the hands-free bracket in case there was another incoming call from Gruff-Voice. He didn't want to be waylaid by any officious traffic cop. He switched on the engine and put his foot down.

Give you lots of pain. What did he mean by that?

His mouth went very dry. The knuckles of his hands were white as he grasped the steering wheel.

If he hurts Carlota, he thought, *he hurts me.*

———

BACK IN HIS OFFICE, Leon had changed into his gray suit and waited patiently for the call. He paced between his office and Carlota's, wondering what he could have done differently to safeguard her. Truth was, he couldn't. The godless were everywhere and had no moral compass. Anyone he cared about was a legitimate target in their eyes.

Leon phoned his brother and asked him to check on recently released prisoners who'd served five years. About an hour later, Juan came back with the information.

There were only two possibilities. Martín Delgado and Esteban Rubio.

The gruff voice he'd half-recognized belonged to Martín Delgado.

According to prison visiting records Delgado was visited by several individuals, but the most frequent and obvious was Liliana Cordero, his girlfriend, who resided in Guardamar.

"Oh, by the way," Juan added, "I got to the bottom of the mystery about the lynx being in the wrong area..."

"Tell me."

"A group of animal rights activists learned of a shipment of lynx being sold as exotic pets. They intercepted the vehicle and—foolishly—let the animals go free. Two of the cats were run over the next day, one was captured, but the rest roamed onto the golf course and a nearby housing estate. Seprona is tracking them now."

"And the smugglers?"

"Arrested—along with the activists."

"Let's hope Seprona finds the rest soon. This area isn't their natural habitat."

"I'll let you know. *Adiós*, brother!"

———

FINALLY, as daylight streaked across the skyline, Leon received the call from Delgado. Not that Leon saw the dawn. He'd actually managed to sleep in his chair and woke stiff-limbed.

Delgado was succinct: "Bring ten thousand Euros to me if you want to see your secretary alive. No police."

"I'm a private eye, not a millionaire," he retorted. In fact he had precisely that amount in his office safe, ready-to-use cash for unexpected outlay and the payment of informants. For a shameful second or two he wondered at the coincidence, Carlota being aware of the safe's contents and Delgado asking for that specific amount... And dismissed the suspicious thought immediately. Still, he needed to create tension and bargain. Tense lowlifes sometimes made mistakes. "Give me a break. I work on a shoestring here."

"Yeah, gumshoe on a shoestring," Delgado said unsympathetically. "You'll be playing a violin next."

"That's a lot of cash to get at short notice, and the banks aren't open yet. But I know I can get you five thousand cash *in an hour*." Emphasize it could be his soon.

Delgado paused at the other end; Leon could hear him breathing. He could almost see the man's mind turning, doubtless wondering about timing. The longer it took to obtain the money, the bigger the risk of being caught.

"A thousand for each year locked up," Delgado finally said. "Not a great deal... But I'll take it."

"Alright."

"You can bring it to my girlfriend's apartment. She lives at—"

"I know where Liliana lives. I was on my way to see her, as it happens."

"Aren't you the great detective, eh?"

"One tries..."

"Remember, your Girl Friday isn't here with me."

"OK. I'll bring the money in an hour. And no police."

"That's a good detective. And no weapons, either!"

"Agreed," Leon lied.

Chapter 12

Nineteenth Hole

Evan and the others in his group were all on the golf course immediately after breakfast, most of them dressed in bright colors, stripes, checks and special gaudy shoes. Evan dressed normally, mindful of Tiger Woods saying something along the lines that golf is a sport for "men dressed as pimps". They tossed coins to see who teed off first. The green always looked a long way off to him; Curtis called it "the carpet". Evan was asked his handicap, but he declared he didn't worry about such things; it all depended on the day. He just hit the ball.

"Why are you here, then?" Steve asked.

"Isn't it obvious!" Evan replied cryptically.

"So you're like Danny, eh?" said Curtis, the American. They christened him the Bogey-man since he proudly announced he was usually one above par per hole, which wasn't anything to write home about; "not exactly par golf, eh?"

"Thought so!" said Nige.

"Don't worry," Curtis said, "you'll ace it tonight. Hole-in-one!"

"Hey," Nige said, "did you see the kids in the swimming pool this morning?"

"When?" Evan asked.

"I saw them while I was having breakfast."

"I don't do breakfast," said Curtis. "I had coffee in my room."

"It was quite a sight," Nige went on. "Young bodies, all wet and slippery. I reckon they let them out like that to taunt us. It's positively cruel!"

Evan was by no means a scratch golfer; he didn't spend enough time on any green. But he found keeping abreast of the game worthwhile; he'd learned enough to get by; the pursuit was useful for keeping in touch with shady business-men, for example. He didn't have a distinctive waggle, unlike the elderly Curtis, who made a production of every attempt at a drive. Curtis professed to be two under par, but he wasn't having much luck today, it seemed. By the fourth hole, he'd been in the cabbage patch twice. Evan was a steady conscientious player and on the first three holes he managed an Eagle and two Birdies.

"A round of golf to put us in the mood, no?" Wanda had said. In the mood for what? He was in denial, but knew what she meant, and didn't see how he could avoid getting involved or found out.

By the time they got to the nineteenth hole, Evan was knackered. He recalled Mark Twain had said "Golf is a good walk spoiled", and he tended to agree. The clubhouse offered pre-lunch drinks. He settled for a San Miguel lager.

After the one drink, they repaired to the dining room, where a number of other clients were already seated at tables. The lunch food was laid out on several tables. Buffet choice, which was considerable. Among the dishes were mushroom and chicken croquettes and gazpacho; Evan found the cold soup most welcome and cooling after that round of golf. He wasn't keen on choosing grilled octopus, it looked too rubbery for his taste, so settled on albóndigas, which reminded him of the staple of IKEA cafeterias, pork meat-balls; he found them tender and very tasty, especially the sauce. Others selected paella—three varieties, one rabbit and chicken, one shell-fish, and one for vegetarians. Curtis went for a second helping.

Drinks on offer varied from still and sparkling water, which Evan stuck to as he needed to keep a clear head, and assorted Spanish wines: red, white and rosé, though Curtis insisted on calling the latter "blush".

As the dishes were being cleared away, Wanda stood up and said, "Now it is time for the film show!" She led the way. All she needed was a tour guide's umbrella or flag on a stick.

Suitably replete, they all wandered into the cinema room and spread out, sitting in plush seats. Not one sat next to another client; each seeming to treat this as an intimate private viewing.

Wanda stood arms akimbo in front of the large TV screen. "Gentlemen, I think you'll like the cinematic treat we've prepared for you all. It will get you in the mood, I'm sure." Here was that phrase again!

She raised a hand, a signal to the projectionist, who probably simply switched on the DVD player.

The lights dimmed, for which Evan was grateful. He felt uneasy in this company.

He'd seen pornographic films—both privately and as part of his policing work. They'd been made, presumably, with consenting adults, the performers actually getting paid. This show was nothing like that, however.

The films were amateurish affairs, beginning with shaky black titles on white card.

In color, but stark interior lighting, with unflattering shadows and unsteady camera-work.

Whoever had filmed the abuse had been careful not to reveal any of the faces of the abusers.

The same consideration was not given to the child victims, however. The distress, anguish and pain on the young faces were all clearly evident and shocking.

Over the years, Evan had become hardened to the inhumanity of criminals of all complexions with base appetites.

But this was in another league entirely. Depraved didn't cover it.

He was almost physically sick. A couple of the guys nearby shifted in their seats, as if uncomfortable. Or, were they overly excited?

There were six short films. It seemed an age, but it was probably only about twenty minutes in duration.

When the lights went up, nobody spoke. There was a subdued air about the place, a shared shame, maybe? Or was he kidding himself?

Wanda strode down the aisle to the front. "There will be a different film each day. You can purchase copies of the DVDs at the end of your stay." She rubbed her hands together and smiled. "Now, as promised, after dinner, you will see a parade of possible partners and, of course depending on demand, you may choose him or her for tonight and of course for the duration of your stay."

Dinner was scheduled for three hour's time; it was early by Mediterranean standards, but the itinerary required adequate time for the clients and merchandise to retire.

Almost everyone moved out of the cinema room and made for the stairs. There were no jovial comments, no jocularity as had been evident on the golf course. This was *the* serious stuff.

Evan noticed young Danny making a beeline for the gents. He didn't look too well.

Impulsively, he followed.

He swung open the door and saw that none of the urinals were being used. He heard someone vomiting in a cubicle. There were only three and the other two were open, unoccupied.

He waited.

Toilet-roll paper was torn and then there was a flushing sound.

The cubicle door opened and Danny emerged, his face quite pale.

"Are you alright, Danny?" Evan asked.

Danny mumbled incoherently and then he swayed and stumbled over to a washbasin, gripped it tight with both hands and heaved emptily. "Oh, God, I never thought it would be like that..."

"What? Like what?"

"I've got a huge collection of photos, but I've never seen... never seen..."

"Photos often lead on to acts, you know that."

"My dad told me to come here. Said it would make a man of me!" He laughed humorlessly. "A man?" He shook his head and stared bleary-eyed at his reflection. "A monster, more like."

"You should ask to be excused this evening," Evan suggested.

"What about my dad? He'll never let me forget the humiliation!"

"Nobody should dominate another person, especially where a father and son are concerned. Parents can guide, but should not compel."

"You tell him that, will you?"

"Ask to leave," Evan urged. "Delete or destroy all those images. Start afresh. A new life."

"That's alright for you to say. What about you? How do you manage to live with what is done to those kids?"

It was a risk. Foolhardy. "I don't. I'm undercover, investigating this organization."

Danny stepped back and gaped. "Shit!" He wiped a hand over his mouth. "Really?"

"Yes. Now, I've been honest with you. I'm asking you not to tell anyone."

Danny nodded vigorously. "You have my word, Evan."

"Fine. Now, rinse out your mouth, and then go and see Wanda. Tell her you want to leave."

"What will she say?"

I'm not clairvoyant! "They've got your money already. You should be free to go."

"Yeah, that's true... And I don't have to tell Dad I chickened out. As far as he need know, I did it..."

"I think you should seriously consider moving away from your father's influence."

Danny bobbed his head. "I'll think about it. Yeah."

Evan went to the door.

"Oh, Evan," Danny called softly.

Evan turned, his fingers wrapped around the handle.

"Thanks for being there for me."

"*De nada*," Evan said with a smile and left.

———

INSPECTOR TEO CHÁVEZ was driven to the site at the entrance to Green-Go golf course. Two ambulances and three Guardia Civil vehicles were parked at the roadside. He exited the Citroën C4 Picasso police car, put on his hat.

An area from the road into the wood had been cleared and yellow scene-of-crime tape draped along the route. Beyond, Chávez could see the green material tents concealing the crime scene itself.

Chávez strode up to the scene-of-crime officer, Lieutenant Sanchez. They exchanged cursory salutes. "What have we got?" he asked.

Sanchez had a pock-marked face and a bent nose. His countenance now reflected ill-concealed anger. "The anonymous tip-off was accurate, sir. Our sniffer dog found them almost at once. So far we've located seven bodies in a mass grave—children aged between five and nine, the M.O. estimates. We're presently scouring the area in case there are more..."

"And the man?"

"Driving licence and credit cards indicate he is Andrés Alonso. We sent a photo for checking and so far his picture and name are not known to us. The M.O. says superficial evidence suggests he performed a sex act on the dead child we found nearby; she was covered with his shirt, and his pants were still round his ankles..."

With an effort Chávez contained his anger and nodded. He didn't relish Sanchez's job. "This is grim, Lieutenant. Very grim. The press are not to be informed yet."

"Yes, sir. Understood."

"Keep me informed, however." Chávez glanced at the open gates of Green-Go golf course. He wondered what, if anything, the other investigating crew had found. He returned to his vehicle and told the driver to steer through the gateway.

CHAPTER 13

INTAKE TOWERS

LEON LEFT HIS SHOULDER-HOLSTER AND ITS ASTRA A-100 automatic in the office safe, in place of the five thousand Euros he took out. He put the money in his battered leather briefcase. He slid the lightweight Colt Officer's ACP automatic into the ankle holster.

Then he snatched his lightweight gray suit jacket from the back of his chair and put it on. He checked the inside pocket: his cell-phone was there and fully charged. He switched it off, then locked up and left the building.

His hired Toyota Yaris was parked at a meter and still had ten minutes credit. He got in and drove off.

It took him twenty minutes to get to Guardamar.

He arrived at the curb outside the apartment door. A number of cars were parked nearby. Shoppers sauntered along, all wrapped up in their thoughts, not paying him any attention.

He stepped out carrying the briefcase and rang the doorbell.

Seconds later, the girlfriend Liliana opened the door. She must have been waiting in the hall. Leon noticed the welt on Liliana's cheek. A bag was slung over her left shoulder. She didn't say anything. Behind her stood Delgado in a denim jacket. He carried a rucksack, its strap on one shoulder.

"You are prompt," Delgado said.

"Good business, Delgado, being prompt."

"You don't seem surprised to see me."

"I recognized your voice."

Delgado shrugged. "I've got a pistol in my pocket, so don't try anything."

"Why would I try anything? You're holding Carlota."

Leon held up the briefcase and Delgado took it with his free hand.

"Just don't forget that," Delgado snapped. "Liliana will drive."

Liliana opened the car door, sat behind the steering wheel.

Delgado told him to get in: "Sit next to her. I'll be covering you both from the back seat."

Both? So they'd had a falling out; the facial bruising suggested as much. He sat in the passenger seat and shut the door, fastened the seat-belt.

Leon glanced at the rear-view mirror and saw Delgado transferring the money from the briefcase to the rucksack.

"Okay, Liliana. Get a move on! You know where to go!"

Liliana started the engine and pulled away from the curb, quickly entering the flow of traffic. She drove the Yaris confidently; maybe she'd driven this type before so it wasn't unfamiliar. Her hands were clasped tightly on the steering wheel, her lips clamped shut, her high cheekbones flushed. Delgado sat on the back seat, an automatic pistol leveled on Leon.

This situation wasn't entirely new to Leon, though perhaps this was the most serious variant he'd experienced. Most undercover agents hit the same problem from time to time. When the targets realized they'd been betrayed, as they perceived it, and they'd been imprisoned for a number of years, they tended to harbor that grudge throughout their sentence. It was known that some passed on information to friends on the outside. Leon's evidence put them away, after all. They wanted payback. A small minority were psychologically damaged by the betrayal: the act had been so good they'd believed it hook, line and sinker.

Liliana entered the roundabout and drove onto the notorious N332, headed south, bypassing the turnoff to Torrevieja, and swung inland at the signpost for the CV95 in the direction of San Miguel de Salinas. Before reaching that town however, she took a sharp right-hand turn. Thanks to European Union funding, the roads were smooth.

The land continued to rise, with cultivated fields on both sides of the road, plus an equestrian center. Behind spread the conglomeration of scattered white buildings with rooftops of varied hues of red. The sun was high, the sky eggshell blue, the temperature in the eighties. Hard to believe rain was forecast.

She ignored the turnoff to Villamartín and Rebate and headed for the hamlet of Torremendo, which she skirted on the CV951, passing an old yet still functioning gas station and assorted builders' yards and whitewashed wayside hostelries.

And then they were on the approach, motoring on the CV950. No matter how many times he saw this panoramic view, it took his breath away.

Spread before them was a vast expanse of ultramarine water, in beautiful stark contrast to the tawny hillsides, several arms of the land pointing into the Pedrera reservoir.

In minutes she passed a sign on the right:

Embalse de la Pedrera—Presa
Confederación Hidrográfica del Segura

The reservoir's volume was about 247 cubic hectometers. The average rainfall was 275mm.

And then she drove across the gravity dam itself. Far over on their right could be seen two tubular intake towers poking out of the water.

On either side of the road the dam, comprising clay core, loams, rockfill berms, sloped away.

They passed a single dike and building, one of three used to close the storage area upstream, and then veered right.

"Pull in over there, in front of those two towers," Delgado ordered.

The two concrete tubular tower structures stood behind a high chain-link fence.

Throughout the journey Liliana hadn't spoken even once. She pulled up, braked and switched off the engine. She shoved the keys in her purse then, abruptly, she opened the door and stepped out. She left the door swinging open. She paced in high dudgeon to the fence and stood with her back to the car, arms folded across her chest.

"Sulky bitch," Delgado snarled.

There were no other vehicles parked here.

"Get out, Cazador. We've arrived." He got out the same side as Leon. He left the empty briefcase in the knee well but carried the rucksack over one shoulder. He waved the pistol; Leon identified it as a Tokarev which would hold eight rounds. "Move."

Leon didn't move. "First you tell me where Carlota is." He was on treacherous ground and he knew it. Delgado had the money. Carlota was nowhere to be seen. At present this place was deserted. A bullet in the back would be an easy option. But then Leon remembered Delgado's threat: *Give you lots of pain.* A bullet in the back would be over too quick. He turned to face Delgado. "Well?"

"In a minute. Walk ahead of me to that entrance gate." Then he shouted to Liliana. "Come on, woman, come with us now! We can talk about this later!"

Swivelling on rough stone, she stomped after them, striding with pent-up rage.

The chain on the gate had been cut. Beyond the gate were two concrete service bridges spanning the steep slope that led to the reservoir's water. Each bridge had a waist-high safety fence and led to a circular intake tower.

"Where the hell is she?" Leon demanded.

"You're in no position to demand anything, Cazador! Cross there!"

True enough. Did he mean she was across there? Or was he meant to cross the bridge?

A shove at the base of his spine gave him the answer.

"Alright, I'm going," he said.

They crossed the right-hand bridge. Leon first, then Liliana followed by Delgado.

"Carlota?" Leon hollered.

"D-d-down here!" Sounded like she was cold, not riddled with fear.

The concrete walkway and waist-high fence ran from the bridge and round the towers. A sturdy rope was tied to one of the fence uprights. Leon leaned over and saw Carlota below, up to her waist in water, her wrists tethered to the length of rope.

He swung round, faced Delgado. "I've paid your money —now let her go!"

Delgado shook his head. "No, that's not how it's going to work."

Give you lots of pain.

Delgado unslung the rucksack, put it on the floor and with a free hand unfastened it, pulled out a length of rope. He turned to Liliana. "Tie his wrists tight—and then he can join her down there."

"Martín, please don't do this," Liliana pleaded. "You've got the money. Walk away."

"No, I can't do that. I've been waiting for this chance for years!"

Leon said, "We'll die of thirst before the water level rises enough to drown us."

"Ironic, that," Delgado said, chuckling. "Dying of thirst with all that water so close!"

"At least let Carlota go!"

Delgado shook his head. "Sorry. I can't have her organizing a rescue for you." He laughed. "Oh, by the way you're likely to drown sooner than you think. I know their predictions are not always right, but the weather people reckon there's going to be an almighty *gota fria* due soon... The reservoir'll be topped up!" The *Gota fria*—the cold drop—often heralded torrential rain caused by a huge drop in atmospheric temperature that could result in devastating torrents and flash floods. Leon had been in a few over the years.

Delgado threw the bunch of rope at Liliana. "Now, do as I say!"

She caught the rope against her chest and immediately flung it back at his face. "No!"

Delgado flinched at the unexpected reaction and Leon leaped forward, his left forearm forcefully deflecting the gunhand while the heel of his right palm smashed into Delgado's nose, breaking bone and releasing a gush of blood.

The pistol fired wildly and deafeningly as Delgado fell against the concrete wall of the tower.

Liliana screamed.

Dazed and snorting blood, Delgado raised the gun, his eyes filled with tears, but Leon was too quick. He stepped forward a pace and jerked an elbow up into Delgado's throat.

With an alarming choking sound, Delgado staggered a couple of paces sideways like a drunk and then sank to his knees, coughing bright red blood.

Leon calmly put on a latex glove. Then he stood on Delgado's gun-hand and freed the pistol from the man's grip and dropped the weapon in his jacket pocket.

He looked over his shoulder.

Liliana sat with her back against the tower, nursing a bullet-wound in her side.

He'd been tempted to throw the pistol into the reservoir —doubtless to join countless other illicit weapons of murder; but it could be used as evidence against Delgado, should the man survive and not choke to death.

He crossed the space and knelt to check Liliana's wound.

Her eyes reflected fear. "Am—am I going to die?"

He shook his head and smiled. "It isn't fatal," he reassured her.

She nodded dumbly and then glared at the still form of her ex-boyfriend.

Leon stood and went over to Delgado, roughly removed his denim jacket. He came back to her side and jammed it against Liliana's wound. "Keep pressing there, it should stop the blood-flow."

She bowed her head and did as she was told.

Then he moved to the rail and leaned over it. He could see Carlota, up to her waist in the water, her arms outstretched above her head, wrists lashed together. The water was surprisingly clear; he could see her black skirt swirling underwater, but it obscured her feet. "Carlota," he shouted, "can you pull yourself up the rope?"

"No, he tied my ankles to a chunk of concrete. I guess he knew I'd try to climb up, even with my game leg."

"Alright, then, I'll come down!" He removed his jacket, dropped it on the concrete floor, then took the Colt out of the ankle holster and placed it on top of the jacket.

He stepped over the rail and his legs momentarily wobbled. It was a long way down. He could see Carlota gazing at him, fearful for his safety no doubt. He knelt on the lip of the concrete walkway and grabbed the rope and then gradually lowered himself over the edge. The actual concrete wall of the tower was too far away for him to abseil or use it for purchase for his feet. He found his leather shoes slipped on the rope, couldn't get a grip. He might have been better in bare feet. Too late now; he was committed. He'd have to take his weight on his arms alone.

Slowly, he lowered himself, hand-over-hand.

Finally, he was dangling directly above her. "Mind your head!" he warned as his shoes dangled close to her tethered wrists.

It was going to be damned awkward trying to clamber over her.

"I'm going to let go and drop. It's not far." No sooner had he said it than he let go.

His feet splashed into the water and he hissed in shock. It was uncompromisingly cold. He landed on what was a sloping solid conglomeration of stones cemented together. He slightly overbalanced, but windmilled his arms and straightened up. He stood thigh-high in the water.

His forearms and shoulders ached a little and he experienced a slight muscle tremor with the exertion and weight they'd supported.

Beside him, Carlota shivered. "N-nice—nice of you—to pop in..." she offered with a twisted smile through her upraised arms. He was aware that Carlota had been half-immersed in this cold water for several hours. Hypothermia shouldn't have set in yet, but she needed to get out.

No time to lose.

He grasped the rope that stretched taut from Carlota's ankles to the stone underwater. He took a deep breath and dove his head under. Through the clear water he saw the rope's knots around a slab of concrete. It would take too long to unfasten them, and cold fingers would fumble. He surfaced and gasped for fresh air. He withdrew the knife from its sheath on his left ankle and went under again. With one hand on the rope, he sawed through it slightly above the concrete slab.

Then he surfaced and caught his breath. "We'll have you loose soon," he promised and reached up, cutting through the rope binding her wrists.

The dangling length that was left was still within his grasp. He slid the knife into its sheath. "Do you want to go first?" he asked. "Or I go first and then I can haul you up?"

"I'll go first. But can you give me a lift up?"

"Sure." He wrapped his arms firmly round her thighs and lifted.

She reached up and grabbed the dangling rope with both hands. "Got it! Thanks!"

"I'm going to let go," he warned.

"That's alright, I've got my weight."

He let go and her sodden skirt clung to her legs and water sluiced off her, soaking him. He stepped back as she dangled. And then she began to climb the rope, hand-over-hand.

Finally, after what seemed an age, Carlota reached the lip of the walkway and heaved herself onto the firm concrete. "I'm there!"

He followed, and found it was harder going up than coming down. His arms protested at the strain, but he gritted his teeth and climbed. Climbed and climbed, swaying as he went up.

At last he reached the top and clambered over the rail.

He saw Carlota was kneeling beside Liliana, talking, while Liliana dipped her head a lot.

Catching his breath, feeling his age, Leon stood and shook his feet to get rid of surplus water. He replaced his gun and put on his jacket. Then he crossed over to Delgado. The man was unconscious, breathing shallowly through his nose; his mouth made odd bubbling noises as his windpipe was severely damaged. It was unlikely that he'd ever talk again. He'd be due another term in prison and when he was eventually released his days of being a velvet-voiced conman would be over. Leon intended leaving him there; he wasn't going anywhere.

With Carlota's help he raised Liliana to her feet. "I'll call an ambulance and then inform the police."

Liliana nodded.

He pulled out his cell-phone and contacted Teo Chávez. "Inspector, it's Leon Cazador here. Could you do me a favor, please?"

"What is it this time, Leon?"

Leon told him.

"I'll have a squad car there in fifteen minutes. The ambulance may take a little longer."

"Thanks, Teo."

He grinned at Liliana. "Give me the car keys." Fumbling a little, she hooked them out of her shoulder-bag.

He picked up Delgado's rucksack, crossed the bridge and took it over to the Yaris, put it in the trunk.

He went back and he and Carlota helped Liliana to the car, put her on the rear seat.

"Now we wait," he said, sitting behind the wheel.

As predicted by Chávez, the police arrived first. The two cops first greeted Carlota, her old buddies from when she had served.

On their way here the cops had been briefed.

Still wearing his glove, Leon handed over the pistol and explained, "Delgado's prints are on it. Liliana was forced to drive him here. Delgado was going to suspend both me and Carlota in the reservoir, ultimately to drown. Liliana's intervention saved us both."

Then the ambulance arrived.

The cops put the paramedics in the picture and then Delgado was lifted onto a gurney and wheeled to the ambulance. And then Liliana was helped inside too. One of the cops stayed with Liliana.

Leon and Carlota agreed to stop by at the station next day to give their statements. He told the remaining cop he was happy to drive the Yaris, though his forearms trembled with after-effects of the strain they'd been under.

Carlota sat in the passenger seat. Pools of water collected in the foot-well.

On their way to the office, Carlota said, "I'm impressed. You were going to pay five thousand for me?"

"I knocked him down from ten, actually."

She playfully slapped his upper arm and he winced. "You got me cut-price, is that it?"

"Not at all, my dear. You're priceless!"

It began to rain. Heavily.

"He wasn't wrong," Leon said.

"Who?"

"Delgado. Said we're in for a nasty gota fria."

She shuddered. The reservoir level would rise markedly if this continued.

Leaning forward to aid visibility through the windshield, he told her about the skeletal hand.

She shuddered. "That's gruesome, Leon. Those poor kids..."

"The police will find them, exhume them, I'm sure."

As they drove through the downpour, the windshield wipers had to be switched to rapid action, otherwise visibility was hopeless and they'd be forced to stop.

Rainwater splashed violently against the underside of the Yaris. He was glad the vehicle was slung higher than some vehicles. A flash sports car is not suitable for driving in flash floods.

Already muddy rivers of rainwater gushed down the gutters, almost reaching the tops of the curbs; many of the drains couldn't cope—either because they were clogged or the deluge was too heavy.

They'd both been in storms like this before. Fortunately they were not too frequent. But when they occurred the repercussions could be severe. Local flooding was evident now. A good number of underbuild garages would be flooded within an hour or so.

He parked outside the office.

The car rocked as the force of the water running along the gutter increased.

"Let's get inside."

By the time he'd retrieved the rucksack from the trunk, he was drenched.

Carlota kept fumbling with the key in the lock, but finally they burst in, dripping on the floor.

Chapter 14

Age Difference

Evan retired to his room. He didn't know how Rod had managed to cope for so many years in such an oppressive environment. Evan had been involved in investigations for a couple of years, but he'd never actually got close like now.

One of his most recent investigations had pertained to illicit transport of children for benefit fraud. A child was smuggled into the country and farmed out to individuals in the relevant community who claimed it as their own. Virtually the first thing they'd do then is register the child for school, since this would begin the paper-trail that sanctions the claiming of child benefit, which in turn triggers tax credits and other benefits, all courtesy of the downtrodden taxpayers. The school might never see the child because as soon as the confirmatory letters drop on the doormat, the child is moved to another family with a different name. On the odd chance of the school asking for a birth certificate, it is rarely adequately verified but taken at face value; besides, thousands of fake birth certificates are in circulation. Face-to-face interviews of the children are rare, and those that do occur will in all likelihood be with a hastily supplied substitute child, with the interviewer not being any wiser.

Last year he'd helped bust an Eastern European gang who had defrauded the British taxpayer of over £2 million.

Authorities reluctantly admit that it is unknown how many illegal immigrants go missing, being absorbed in the black economy. The gang had set up ninety-eight bank accounts to collect child and other benefits. Finally, someone noticed that an unusual number of claims emanated from only four addresses, and at last alarm bells began belatedly to ring.

A recent report stated that "it is possible to buy sex with a minor within a few hundred yards of anywhere in Britain, mainly thanks to Social Media." Life was made harder for the authorities by the increased use of the Dark Web until NCA cryptologists cracked certain access codes. Evan had been responsible for suborning one Dark Web user and taking his place using an alias.

Although thankfully it did not appear in his case-load, he was aware that some children, notably smuggled from African countries, were killed in rituals to instill fear in the superstitious beholders.

A disillusioned investigator had exclaimed, "I feel like Canute, helpless to stem this veritable tide of filth—sexploitation and murder for pecuniary gain."

What nagged at the back of Evan's mind was how had Rod been exposed, what mistake did he make that cost him his life? He dearly hoped it wasn't something simple, like revealing to a suspect that he'd been undercover! He didn't want Rod's fate.

———

ONCE IN THE OFFICE, Leon stripped off and toweled himself dry, while Carlota stood in her wet clothes shivering.

"I've told you time and again to leave a change of clothes here," he argued.

"Yes. Right. Like this happens all too often, does it?"

"No. True. But I need to get changed if I'm going to Golf-Sur."

She stamped her foot and water from her clothing splashed the tiled floor. "You can't be serious!"

He stepped into a dry pair of shorts. "I must go."

She gestured at the Venetian blinds, which thankfully were still closed. "In this!"

"Yes." He shrugged into a black pullover and donned his black cargo pants. "Those kids are stuck in there with a load of nasty monsters." He put on his neoprene shoes. "I can't wait until the rain stops." He picked up the rucksack, took out the money and went to the safe and opened it. He put the money inside and withdrew his shoulder holster and gun.

"I'll come with you!" she said.

"You'll catch your death in those wet clothes."

"Oh, you sound like my mother!"

He sighed, resigned, and pointed to the closet. "I've got a couple of spare shirts in there—and pants. They'll be too big for you, but at least you'll be dry and I won't have your pneumonia on my conscience."

She nodded. "Thanks."

Boldly, she removed her soaking clothing, which tended to cling.

She stood naked, unabashed, flesh glistening wetly under the light.

He got a dry towel from the closet shelf. "Here, let me." He vigorously rubbed her back and hair with the towel. In the middle of this process she turned to face him, which was slightly disconcerting with her being so close and without any clothes.

"Can't I be with you? I can handle a gun. You know that."

The age difference didn't seem to matter anymore.

But the children needed succour as soon as possible.

Selfishly, he realized he wanted to deal with Iglesias

himself. No arrests, no law courts. And that meant not calling Chávez and arranging a raid on Golf-Sur.

He gently moved from her and retrieved a black wind-breaker from the closet. He put it on and zipped up.

"Alright, you've got five minutes to get ready. There's a raincoat hanging in there as well."

He went over to the safe and took out a Llama Comanche revolver, put it on the desk. "You can use this. It only weighs about a thousand grams." He put a small box of .357 Magnum cartridges alongside it. He locked the safe.

She shoved her legs into a pair of his pants and rolled up the waist to shorten the legs. "I've used one before. Based on the Smith & Wesson design and none the worse for that, by all accounts."

"Ready?"

"Almost." She donned the raincoat and shoved the weapon and ammunition in its voluminous pockets. She had to wear her wet shoes; they'd be soaked all over again in this downpour in minutes anyway.

"Do you want to drive?" he asked.

"Yes. You can direct me."

"If the GPS is working in this deluge!"

———

Evan decided that he had to leave this place before dinner, before they paraded the children for selection that evening.

Was the knowledge that the pornographic films were on the premises sufficient evidence to justify an immediate raid? It should be. Inspectors Chávez and De Vargas had promised that they would act when he gave them the green light.

The basement was the clincher. From what he'd over-heard during his brief stay, the children were all now kept in the basement. If he could release one or more of them, they'd be living proof...

———

Iglesias beckoned Vicente.

"Yes, Boss?"

"Are you armed?"

"No, Boss. I must admit I feel naked without my knife... You said this wasn't one of those operations, remember?"

"Well, it's rare, I know, but I was wrong. I want you and a couple of your guys to carry from now on. Guns as well as knives. Alright?"

"You expecting trouble?"

"Possibly. You heard about the Knight guy?"

"Yes. He shot up Diego's MPV pretty bad."

"How is Diego?"

"He's okay. Happy to be back at work."

"Good. Tell him to be on the alert. He might get a crack at Knight."

"Yeah, he'd like that. Where do you want us?"

Iglesias glanced through the window. It was a howling gale outside, rain crashing against the glass panes. "That weather's not fit for a dog. Station a man in the hall, and one at the top of the stairs. Two should be enough."

———

"Miss?" Danny Kneale approached Wanda who was standing alone by the drinks table. The rest of the group were chatting at the far end of the room. "Can I have a word, please? If it's not too much trouble..."

"You don't seem happy, Danny," she purred, nursing a tumbler of ice and Campari. "You haven't got a drink, I see."

"I'm—I'm not thirsty," he managed.

She chuckled warmly. "We don't drink to quench our thirst."

"You were right," he blurted.

"Right? How?"

"I'm not happy."

She sipped her drink, her toasted brown eyes studying him over the rim of her glass. "How can I make you happy?"

Reticently, he took a step closer, caught a whiff of her perfume. His thin lips performed a smile, though he didn't feel like smiling. "I want to leave."

She placed a hand on his arm, brushed it gently. "Leave here—before the fun has started?"

He nervously ran a hand through his spiky copper-colored hair and gave her a nod.

She surveyed the room.

He could see that nobody was paying them any attention.

"Come." She put her glass down on the drinks table, gripped his arm, and tugged. "Follow me. We can talk about this in my room."

Obediently he went with her.

Her room was upstairs and its accents were brown and orange, not overly feminine. He observed that there was a well-stocked drinks trolley, a sofa draped with a faux leopard skin; well, he assumed it was false. The lounge opened into a bedroom with more animal motifs.

He was about five years younger than her, he reckoned. She was a mature woman. Alluring. If he went in for that sort of thing.

Once inside, she locked the door behind her. "Now, what is all this about?"

"I—I felt uncomfortable in the cinema."

"You've never seen anything like that before?"

"No. My picture collection is just that—pictures."

"Of what, exactly?"

"Young girls..."

"Not women?"

"No. Girls. Some are very young."

"Have you been with a ... female person before?"

"N-no..."

"Let me help." She began removing his jacket. He trembled at her touch. "Just be patient, dear boy." Slowly, tenderly, she undressed him.

Finally, she stripped. "I know I am not young enough for you, my boy. When you love me, think of your photos..."

Afterwards, as he lay exhausted beside her, she playfully stroked his pointed nose. "Did that help?"

He nodded, speechless.

"Now, do you want to do that to a young girl this evening?"

He gulped and croaked, "Oh, yes..."

"Then, that is good. There's no need for you to leave now, is there?"

He sat up abruptly and put his head in his hands. "But I promised him..." he mumbled.

"Promised who?" she queried.

CHAPTER 15

QUITE MASTERFUL

ALL THE WAY IT RAINED, AND HAD DONE SO MOST
of the day. They drove past the usual irrigation canals. Now,
though, they were edged by dozens of sandbags. "This is serious!" Carlota said.

Leon tended to agree. Already, the canals were overflowing in parts, the sandbags incapable of holding back the
water. Huge puddles were everywhere on the road.

Thankfully, there was respite as the rained stopped
minutes before they entered the approach track with a Golf-
Sur sign on the corner.

A short distance along, Leon directed Carlota to park the
Yaris in an overtaking space.

As before at Green-Go, he would make his way on foot.

Carlota followed, limping about a yard behind him.

The track's surface varied, old crumbling blacktop, clusters of gravel that had been inadequately deployed to infill
pot-holes, and clumps of mud and puddles of varied sizes
and depth. The sides of the road were inundated with water.
He was glad when he came to the smooth blacktop on the
final approach; it glistened with rainwater.

He walked towards the gates of Golf-Sur. It was a similar
layout, with a small gate-house for a sentry. Except that this
gate boasted a CCTV camera on a tall pole. He slunk to the

side of the track, and would go round the back of the gate-house, to surprise the sentry and keep out of sight of the camera.

Then he heard a vehicle approaching. Change of plan.

He turned to signal to Carlota but he needn't have worried; she was nowhere to be seen.

He darted into the undergrowth at the side of the track, close to the gate-house, his arms soaked from wet foliage.

It was a local police car in the town-hall colors and livery.

Were they going to investigate the place, even start a police raid?

If so, Leon was going to be disappointed. He would be denied his vengeance on Iglesias.

The two cops—a male and a female—got out and strode with care over to the gate-house, avoiding the puddles.

The green-garbed sentry stepped out, waved a greeting.

Leon was too far away to hear what was being said.

The female cop spoke to the sentry and motioned vaguely to the north-west.

The sentry gave them a desultory wave and went inside the gate-house.

The two cops climbed back into their car, started the engine and used the cleared circle at the gate to turn. Without a backward glance they headed along the track, their duty, whatever it was, done.

Leon broke cover, withdrew his Astra, steadied his aim, and shot the CCTV camera lens.

He then raced over to the gate-house and braced his back against the wall.

The sentry didn't seem to hear the shot. Was the camera hooked up to the gate-house or the house itself? Only one way to find out.

He heard Carlota close behind him as he opened the door.

The sentry had his back to the door and had just lifted the telephone handset. Hearing Leon enter, he said, "What do you want now?" and turned. Then he saw Leon and the automatic pistol. "Eh? Who are you?"

Leon said, "Put down the phone."

The sentry hesitated.

Leon gestured with the Astra. "Do as I tell you and you won't get hurt."

The sentry put the phone in its cradle.

"Good. That wasn't difficult, was it?"

No response. Eyes fearfully examined the gun.

Leon checked the interior. The CCTV monitor was on the sentry's desk, ignored. The guy probably rarely bothered to look at it. Perhaps it was used mainly for recording purposes.

"What did the police want?" Leon asked.

"Oh, some nonsense about the gota fria and a controlled release, whatever that is... Reckon we should all evacuate." He nodded at the phone. "I was going to call the house, tell them."

"Maybe later," Leon said. "Are you expecting any visitors in the next hour or so?"

"What?"

"Have you gone deaf all of a sudden?"

"No."

"I said, are there any visitors due?"

He shook his head. "Check the register if you don't believe me." He jutted his chin at a thick book open on a bench by the door. "All appointments have to be recorded. Them's the rules."

Keeping an eye on the sentry, Leon went over and checked it.

Nobody scheduled to visit. He noticed that the sentry had registered various arrivals—including "Boss Iglesias". That boded well, anyway.

"Sit on that chair."

"What?"

"I think you are deaf..."

"No I'm not... I don't know why I must sit."

"Because I say so. Now do as I say. Sit down!"

He sat.

Leon grabbed the cables linking the computer screen, uncoupled them and used them to tie the sentry's hands behind his back and then attached the cable to the chair back. Then he found more cables and tied the man's legs and looped more round his chest. "I'll let you go when I return."

The sentry nodded.

Leon found the bunch of keys. Much easier than using wire-cutters. He slipped out and used them on the gates.

Unheard, Carlota appeared by his side. "You were quite masterful in there," she said.

"Harrumph." He opened both gates wide and left them like that—in case a hasty retreat proved necessary.

Cautiously, he walked along the drive with Carlota limping by his side.

"Oh, great!" It began to rain again, quite heavily.

He should have come in a wetsuit.

"Alright?" he asked Carlota.

"I'll manage. I'm not here for my comfort, Leon."

All the way they clung to the shrubbery in case anyone happened to look out of the house windows.

He needed to find Iglesias. Make him pay. He was bound to be in the main house.

———

Evan left his room and moved soundlessly along the landing. His heart pounded as he almost bumped into Moreno who hovered at the top of the stairs and paced back and forth along the landing. Moreno was a big guy, his muscles rippling under his blue jersey T-shirt. He didn't conceal the revolver holstered on his belt.

Playing it nonchalantly, Evan descended the stairs, holding the floor plan in one hand.

He got to the bottom of the stairs and, not entirely unexpected, he encountered Domínguez ("just call me 'Dom', *mi amigo*" he'd said at their first meeting). He was broad-shouldered and had a lived-in-face and black curly hair. His side-arm was an automatic pistol, snugly tucked in a quick-draw holster. "Going for a stroll?" Dom enquired.

"Just stretching the legs, Dom. They feed you well here, don't they?"

"I wouldn't know, I'm hired help." Dom grinned, revealing that he'd lost two teeth.

The reception desk was unattended, which was not surprising. There was no reason for it to be manned if nobody was expected to arrive. Everyone was here, according to Wanda earlier. He had wondered about the frantic movement of people. It seemed that there'd been an unplanned influx of people.

He checked the floor plan. The door to the basement was at the back of the vestibule, under the staircase.

He waited until Dom paced across the tiled floor to the front door.

The basement door wasn't locked. Again, there was no pressing reason to lock it. As Wanda inferred, all the clients' needs would be catered for; they'd want for nothing. Checking that Dom wasn't looking his way, Evan opened the door and stepped onto a concrete landing with a rail. He hastily shut the door, as quietly as he could manage.

Ceiling lights were on and illuminated stone stairs that led deep under the house.

He put his ear to the door but heard no sound. Probably this basement was sound-proofed. He didn't want to dwell on the reasons for sound-proofing.

He descended.

At the bottom of the stairs he found himself in an enclosed square flagged area. There were four doors. He went over to one and tested the handle. It was locked. No surprises there, then. He couldn't hear anything beyond the door.

It was a standard door lock. He fished out his lock-pick kit which he'd bought on Amazon without informing his superiors. He'd tested it with a transparent lock, which came with the kit. After an hour's study, he felt quite adept. He inserted the two most suitable metal hook and picks. It took him two minutes, he reckoned, and was pleased with himself.

He pushed the door and it swung open.

There was a light on.

"Oh, my God," he breathed.

There were about twenty children, male and female, ranging from about eight to twelve, he guessed. Clothed in fairy-tale costume fancy dress. Wide-eyed, they stared at him. They sat on benches that ran along two walls of what amounted to a cell. A wooden table stood in the center and on it were four plastic jugs of water and a stack of plastic cups. In the left-hand corner was a cubicle; the rank smell informed him it was their lavatory.

No time to waste. Get them out, fast! He waved at them. "Come on, come with me," he urged. "We're getting out!"

"No, you most definitely are not!"

He pivoted round, recognizing the voice.

Wanda stood in the doorway, aiming an automatic pistol at him with one hand; her other clasped her seemingly precious shoulder-bag. "I suspected you almost at once. I studied you in the cinema. Your heart wasn't in it, was it?"

"No, it wasn't. Why did you wait until now?"

"Young Danny approached me, said he wanted to leave. I convinced him to stay. He told me all about you, Evan—or whatever your name is. I wanted to catch you in the act. Raise your hopes—and theirs. Now, sadly for them, dashed."

She waggled the gun. "Come along, you must have a talk with Tomás." She smirked at the children. "Sorry, kids, but we have to go for now. But be patient. Your new friends are very anxious to see you—after dinner."

Some of them who presumably knew what she meant moaned.

She pulled a mock-distressed face. "What, hasn't Tía Paloma arranged for you to be fed yet?"

Their response was a shake of heads.

"Don't worry," she told them. "If you behave later, you will get your reward."

None of them seemed overly pleased at that prospect and said nothing.

"Suit yourselves," she snapped. She shoved Evan ahead of her, out into the flagged square, and slammed the door shut on the children. The lock made an odd sound, which she ignored.

CLOUDS FORMED in the Atlantic Ocean. At this time of year there arose an extreme difference in temperature which caused more water to be stored in the clouds. And a great mass of cold air rotated and floated like a huge drop over a warm area, creating what amounted to an unprecedented situation. The Ministry for the Environment reported that record rainfall at this time was identified in six locations. The rain in Vega Baja del Segura was the worst in over one hundred years. Due to the severity, the authorities felt forced to act to preserve the dam's integrity: they ordered a controlled release for the dam.

It was said that the dictator Francisco Franco accomplished two good things for Spain: his regime was instrumental in building the Cenajo Dam and also enforced the requirement for all restaurants to offer an affordable *menu del día*.

The Cenajo dam's construction was in response to constant catastrophic floods of the Segura River. At the end of the Civil War the Patronage for the Redemption of Penalties for Work was created, which sought to rehabilitate the prisoners from the losing side. Between 1943 and 1952 the first works were carried out at Cenajo by about 350 workers, about a third of them being political prisoners and other inmates from nearby prisons. Rumor had it that the latter carried out the most risky tasks. Due to the terrible conditions in which they lived a working town was built, with a laundry, hermitage, barracks and shops. The construction group was also responsible for building the controversial Valley of the Fallen. Altogether, over seven thousand men worked on the project. It was completed in 1957 and opened by Franco on June 6, 1963.

Leon had visited the dam a few times. The reservoir's clear water and situation were photogenic and spectacular. Flocks of small birds flew around the immense construction, nesting in the adjacent cliffs, feasting on insects.

The force of the released water was formidable and devastating.

CHAPTER 16

NO PRISONERS

BY THE TIME LEON AND CARLOTA REACHED THE front of the house, the rain was torrential and whipped about by high winds. Worse, everywhere they trod the water reached their ankles. There was no shelter save in the house.

Carlota signed to him: *Go in the front door?*

He responded: *Why not?*

She shrugged and tried the handle.

It turned, and as she pushed her shoulder against it, fighting the wind, the door opened and was violently swung inwards, thrust by a strong gust of wind. She stumbled in with the door, spilling rainwater from her raincoat on the tiles.

Leon followed. He kept his right hand inside his windbreaker, covering his holstered Astra's grip.

A broad-shouldered man stood in the middle of the vestibule. He'd had his back to the door, walking away, when the door opened. Now he turned and snapped, "Who the hell are you?" He wore a quick-draw holster at his belt.

Leon closed his hand round the metal grip.

"Dom, that's Knight!" shouted Iglesias from the top of the stairs.

Dom reached for his holstered automatic.

Leon's Astra pistol was already out, and he aimed and

fired. Despite the howling wind and pounding rain through the open doorway, the blast reverberated in the vestibule.

As Dom tumbled backwards, arms splayed out as if he was playing at "snow angels", Leon spotted a woman who strongly resembled Vanda Dinescu emerging with a man from a doorway under the staircase. Her hair was shorter, but otherwise it was the same woman; he'd know her anywhere. She held a pistol to the head of a man he didn't recognize.

"Cazador!" the woman exclaimed, tightly clasping her shoulder-bag with her free hand.

So it was her!

Carlota's revolver exploded by Leon's right ear. Deafening. But he wasn't complaining because at that instant a man in a blue T-shirt staggered on the landing and then crashed through the balustrade and fell onto the tiles with a terrible thud. A revolver skittered across the floor.

"Nice shooting, Carlota. Let's beat a retreat!"

Warily, with their guns raised in readiness, they both backed towards the open doorway.

At present the only person with a weapon appeared to be the woman who resembled Vanda.

If it had been just her and no-one else, he'd have fought where they stood. But it seemed evident that the tall man with corn-colored hair was her hostage.

"Best to get the cavalry," he told Carlota.

"*Now* you see sense!" she exclaimed.

"I–" He never finished. Because everybody's world was transformed in an instant.

———

FLOOD-WATER BURST through the open door and almost swept Carlota and Leon off their feet. Instinctively, they grabbed at the door-jamb. The surge rushed over the vestibule floor, pushing the dead bodies of Dominguez and the other guy like so much flotsam.

The Vanda lookalike lost her footing and wrestled with the tall guy. She clubbed him with the pistol, unbalanced, dropped the weapon and fell into the water. She righted herself with difficulty and turned and trudged against the swirling eddies of water, making her way to the staircase.

"Wanda, come up, quickly!" Iglesias shouted. He descended halfway down the stairs, arm outstretched to her.

Wanda managed to get a purchase on the bottom stair and with the aid of a banister rail climbed, water falling off her onto the stairs.

At that moment Leon was distracted by a full-figured woman with a lavishly endowed chest. She emerged from a doorway in the vestibule wall, her colorful long-sleeved dress dragging in her wake like a distorted rainbow as she strode purposefully towards the foot of the stairs. She looked up, yelled to Wanda. "The children! My children!"

"They're not your children, Tía Paloma!" Iglesias snarled. "They're *mine*. My merchandise!"

Wanda glared at Paloma and turned her back and continued to climb the stairs to reach Iglesias.

The water was still gushing in.

Leon braced his legs against the thrust of incoming water. He raised his automatic and aimed at Iglesias, the killer of his friend Rod.

But the churning water pushed the corpse in the red-striped shirt against his thighs, buffeting him, at the instant that he fired. He missed by inches. The bullet ricocheted off the wall.

Steadily wading through the agitated water, Carlota called to the colorful woman, "Where are the children?"

The tall guy Wanda had clubbed spluttered to the surface, leaned against the wall and was heaving in air, attempting to catch his breath. Then he shouted, "The children—they're in the basement!" He pointed at the door under the stairs.

"I've got the keys!" Paloma cried.

Leon pushed the corpse away and took aim again. Iglesias and Wanda were higher now.

Carlota grabbed Leon's arm, said frantically, "*This* is what we came for—the children!"

The water was still gushing in. Elsewhere they could hear the shattering of glass, windows being forced in. The entire building was being inundated at an alarmingly rapid rate.

Leon shoved his gun in its holster and caught Carlota's hand. Together, slowly, laboriously they made their way across the flooded vestibule, wading waist-high in the churning water, until they finally reached the door beneath the staircase.

"Name's Evan Tremayne," said the tall man. His temple leaked blood, but he didn't seem concerned about it.

"Cazador—a friend of Rod's. This is Carlota." He grinned. "My Girl Friday."

Before Carlota could comment, Tía Paloma reached their side and held up the metal ring of keys. "The keys!" she said unnecessarily.

Carlota glared at her and then said forcefully, "Introductions over, let's get down there!"

Fortunately, the door was stuck wide open.

Water rushed through and cascaded over the stone steps.

There was no hand-rail so it was risky. Nobody said "Be careful" however; they were all grown-ups. Leon held Carlota's hand, Evan held Tía Paloma's.

By the time they reached the bottom of the steps, the square area they'd entered was almost half-filled with filthy stinking water and chunks of wood, bits of material, and several plastic bottles.

Tía Paloma led the way to the door on the left. "This one first!"

"Are you sure the children are here?" Carlota shouted above the roar of the mini-waterfalls tumbling down the steps. "I can't hear them!"

"It's sound-proofed," Evan said.

Paloma nodded absently and tried the appropriate key, but it didn't work. She tried again. No luck.

"Is it the right one?" Leon asked.

"Yes, of course it is!"

"Try another door," Leon suggested.

With the help of Leon and Evan, Paloma made her way against the stirring swirling water to the other wall and the door there. She tried the key and it worked and the door opened a slit.

It was difficult to force the door open any further; she was fighting against the weight of water.

Through the gap they heard cries of fear from children, which gave them added impetus.

Leon and Evan gripped the door and heaved, straining muscles.

Finally, they shifted the door sufficiently for the children to half-swim, half-wade through. The water level was getting higher by the minute. Fortunately, there were no little ones.

Paloma tried the third door, and again the key worked.

More straining and heaving, and then it was open sufficiently to let the children out.

As if from nowhere, someone came splashing down the steps, wading forcefully through the water. "Danny?" Evan exclaimed.

"I want to help!" Danny cried.

A key worked on the fourth door as well. By now they knew what was needed of them, and were familiar with their own strength and that of the onrushing water. They heaved the door open and children splashed out, gasping. Shockingly, a young girl floated past, head submerged.

Danny grabbed the floating girl, lifted her out, and turned her over. "Get the others, Evan!" he said. Then Danny left them and carried the girl toward the steps.

Carlota came out with a little boy piggyback, arms clasping her neck, his face crumpled as he sobbed. The rest managed to get out without any help.

The water was higher now, almost up to Leon's chest, and still swirling angrily.

Paloma returned to the first door they'd tried. She slotted the key in and it still didn't turn.

"I don't understand it," Evan said. "I picked the lock earlier—that's when Wanda caught me..."

———

THE FORCE of the water was tremendous. First, it had engulfed the guard-house, crashing through the door and window. Still tied to the chair, the sentry was buffeted against the desk with such violence that the structure of the chair shattered so that the restraints fell away with his agitated movements. Gasping for breath, he surfaced, waded out of the door and used the windowsill for purchase. He climbed onto the roof of the guard-house.

The barrage of water was not impeded by the fence; it continued on its way and burst through doors and windows of the lounge and kitchen of the main house.

While almost all of the clients were upstairs in their rooms when the surge hit, a couple of men had been reading magazines in the lounge and were caught completely unawares. Tables and chairs were upended, hitting against other furniture, some of it reduced to matchwood. The two clients tried swimming, but the frenetic chaos of the floating objects was too much, bashing against them, thwarting their attempts to keep their heads above water.

Kitchen staff had been in the throes of preparing the dinner when the water-surge gushed in, knocking them off their feet. One chef fell and hit his head on a marble central island and drowned, others scrabbled frantically, grasping the handles of drawers and cabinets.

A large American style refrigerator was pushed off the wall and toppled sideways. Pans of scalding sauces hissed and sank. Steam and smoke billowed. The electrics shorted.

An almost overpowering smell filled the place.

"TAMPERING WITH A LOCK can upset its mechanism," Leon said. "Stand back!" he barked. "There's no time to pick it now!" He pulled out the Astra automatic and fired twice at the lock. The sound was very loud, the bullets whined away.

"That was bloody dangerous!" Evan said.

"Yeah." Leon kicked at the door by the damaged lock and the frame crumpled and gave way. The two men grabbed the door and hauled, straining every sinew against the might of the water.

They shoved it open enough for Leon to slip through the gap. He dreaded what he would find.

"It's alright!" he called over his shoulder.

The children stood anxiously on the bench seats; a couple of them sat on the tabletop. Water lapped all around them, reaching their chests.

"Those who can swim, go for the door now!" Leon yelled in Spanish. He made breaststroke motions for those who didn't understand.

All but three of the children took the plunge.

Leon lifted one girl child on his shoulders and carried another, a boy, under his arm, keeping his head above water.

Evan waded in and carried the last child, a boy, in a fireman's lift.

Every one of them had to fight against the rush of water down the steps. The children who had gone ahead on their own had done very well, and helped each other up. Leon's thighs ached with the effort and the children's weight. He felt his age.

When they reached the top and staggered through the open door, Leon saw that the water wasn't rising any further here—it was about five feet high against the walls, but not rising, leaving a dirty tidemark. Of course a lot of the water was gushing over those steps and would fill that basement space. Once he'd moved away from the turmoil at the door to the basement, the water's agitation was minimal.

He carried his two charges to the stairs and climbed until he got above the water level.

On his way he'd noticed the guy named Danny on a stair tread giving the little girl CPR. Next to them stood Carlota and all the other children spread upon the stairs, all wet and bedraggled, and many of them shivering with cold or shock.

Leon lowered his two charges.

The girl lying on the stair coughed and spluttered and sat up with a jerking motion. "You're going to be alright!" Danny cried.

Evan came over with the child he carried and gently lowered the boy to the stair.

Leon looked at the wet and shaking children sitting on the stairs. He said, "Evan, go to the landing and try all the rooms. Grab any sheets or blankets you can find to wrap round the kids. Take a couple of the older ones to help you. And tell any clients you meet to stay in their rooms until they're told to leave."

"Good idea," Evan said. "Will do."

"And keep the children down here until I call for you." Leon began to make his way further up the stairs, working through the cluster of kids.

"Where are you going?" Evan asked.

"I have unfinished business!" he replied.

When he reached Carlota, he said, "Coming?"

She nodded. "Sure, I'll be glad to help in the arrests."

He shook his head. "No. There'll be no prisoners."

She looked askance at him, bit her lip.

"You don't have to. But I'll ask once more. Are you coming?"

Unhesitatingly, she said, "Yes. No prisoners."

———

WANDA AND IGLESIAS had burst through the doorway onto the roof. It was a tiled solarium, with a half-dozen sun loungers in one corner. A concrete bar area had been set up in a second corner. A brick chimney poked out from another corner. Puddles collected in the joins of some uneven tiles.

"What the hell happened?" Wanda demanded, catching her breath.

"A water surge—maybe from the Segura overflowing," Iglesias answered.

She hurried to the parapet and peered out. As far as she could see, there was water. It was as if they were in the middle of a lagoon. Tree tops poked out of the water in places, as did a few askew telegraph poles.

In the near distance she saw a couple of cars floating.

Rubbish clogged in many areas, forming artificial islands of plastic, material and fabric, while all sorts of other debris clustered against the walls of this building.

Her heart sank as she scanned the sky. Dark cumulus clouds gathered, promising more rain.

"We're stuck here!" she exclaimed. "We're trapped!"

"Don't worry, dearest, we'll be alright." He took her hand. "You'll see."

She pulled her hand free. "You don't understand, do you? That was Cazador down there! He'll be coming for me —and you!"

"Cazador?" He chuckled. "A hunter?"

"Yes, damn you, a hunter! That's who shot at you on the stairs. He's hunting for me and you now!"

Iglesias pulled a revolver from his coat. "Well, he missed me. Be assured, I won't miss him, you'll see!" He pointed the gun at the doorway in readiness.

———

LEON REACHED the top of the steps and hovered at the door's entrance to the solarium. Carlota was right behind him, her revolver drawn.

"The woman Wanda dropped her gun," Carlota said, "but Iglesias could be armed."

"Agreed. You crouch low and cover me as soon as I dash through the doorway. I'll dive to the left."

"Got it."

"Ready?"

"Yes," she said.

He braced himself for the leap and felt his heart-rate increase, his breathing intensify. He darted through the doorway, diving sideways to the left as two shots were fired, whanging off stone somewhere, following by two shots behind from Carlota's revolver.

Leon had spotted Iglesias by the parapet on the far side of the rooftop as he landed jarringly on his left side. He steadied his arm and fired twice. The first shot hit Iglesias in the right leg, the second in his torso as he fell. The shock must have been severe, for he dropped his weapon and sank to his good side, face twisted in pain, his back propped against the parapet.

"I've got him covered," Carlota said.

Slowly, Leon stood, his left hip protesting at the mistreatment. His Astra leveled on Iglesias, he walked toward him.

A couple of yards to the right stood Wanda on top of the parapet. She was clutching a shoulder-bag. This close, there was no mistaking her. Her chest heaved and her eyes lanced hatred at him.

"How many children are buried in the wood outside Green-Go?" he demanded.

Wanda's face paled; she put her head to one side. "Children buried?"

"How should I know?" Iglesias said, hissing air between his teeth.

"Weren't you missing any?" Leon persisted. "Children who'd gone missing?"

"No." Iglesias's eyes subtly altered shade, appeared shifty. "Maybe Tía Paloma can tell you more."

"You're lying!"

"Tomás!" Wanda snapped.

He peered up at her.

"You knew, didn't you?" Wanda said.

Iglesias shrugged, which made him wince. "Accidents happen. A few clients got over-zealous, they got carried away. Unfortunate incidents, that's all..."

"Name the clients responsible!" Leon demanded.

"I've already said too much. But it won't be allowed in court. It was forced under coercion." He grimaced. "I'm still bleeding, for pity's sake!"

"So?" Carlota snapped.

"I'm not saying any more till I speak to my lawyer."

Wanda's face clouded. "I didn't know about any kids dying—except that one I heard about who fell off the roof..."

Leon tended to believe her. He waved his gun at her. "Now, step down. You're wanted for—"

Abruptly she half-turned on the parapet and flapped her arms to maintain balance, her bag slapping against her hip.

"I wouldn't jump if I were you, Wanda," Leon said. "The water's only about five feet deep. You'd be lucky if you only broke your legs."

"I'll take my chances!" She pivoted round.

"Stop!" Carlota screamed. "Or I shoot!"

Wanda jumped feet first and Carlota fired.

Leon rushed to the parapet and stared in disbelief.

Wanda plunged feet-first into the filthy water, displacing floating garbage, and sank from sight. Seconds later, she emerged and swam with a measured breaststroke away from the building, the shoulder bag dragging behind her.

Carlota fired twice but the bullets missed, zipping soundlessly in the water behind Wanda.

"So much for 'no prisoners'!" Carlota seethed.

Iglesias laughed aloud.

Leon swung round. "What's so funny?"

"She got away, didn't she?"

"For now..."

"Where she jumped is the deep end of the swimming pool!" He winced.

"She may have escaped but we have you. You're going to pay for your crimes."

"You think so? Wait till you see my lawyer."

"You killed Rod Wallace." Leon said.

"Prove it."

"You're so arrogant you don't clean your sticks. The driver will still have some of his blood on it..."

"Maybe. But anyone could use that club."

"I bet we'll only find your fingerprints on it."

"Fat chance finding that after this flood." Iglesias shook his head. "He was a stubborn brave fool. Of course he talked in the end." He gestured at the recently vacated parapet. "Wanda enjoyed the session." He peered at Leon. "Was he a friend of yours?"

Leon gritted his teeth. "I'll ask the questions!"

"I have nothing more to say. Get me a lawyer—when the water level permits, of course."

Leon took a menacing pace forward and placed his foot on Iglesias's wounded leg and pressed hard.

Iglesias hissed in pain. "You won't get away with this! I'll make a complaint of brutality!"

"I'll continue to press until you tell me who supplies you with the children!" He stamped hard with his foot and Iglesias screamed.

"Alright, alright!" Iglesias hissed air between clenched teeth. "You'll pay for this later—police brutality!"

"I'm not police," Leon said. "Now, talk!"

"I have... two main suppliers... Basil Doukas in Tangier and... Roman Kurilo in... in Malta..."

"That will do, I suppose. It wasn't too hard, was it?" Leon said. He kicked the sole of his right foot and Iglesias moaned and swore.

"Now, tell me more about Doukas and Kurilo."

"I know little about Doukas, except he's Greek—he's a ghost, but he delivers what he promises."

"What about Kurilo?"

Iglesias shook his head. "You don't want to go anywhere near him. He's sick..."

"Well, you'd know, I suppose." He kicked the foot again.

"Alright, alright! He's ex Russian army, served in Chechnya. Word is he started torturing little boys there and got a taste for it... As I said, he isn't nice to know... He takes his pick of a couple from each shipment of merchandise to keep his hand in..."

"Sick bastard!" Carlota said.

Leon glanced at her and mouthed *enough?*

She nodded, her glare steely.

"Very good, Iglesias," Leon said. "Let's get you up." He and Carlota helped Iglesias to his feet.

"Have a care, that... that *hurt*!" Iglesias said between clenched teeth as they stood him up between them, his back to the parapet.

"Not as much as this," Leon said and pushed hard with both hands against Iglesias's chest.

The man's face instantly drained of blood and his arms were outstretched, fingers frantically grasping, but both Leon and Carlota had taken a step backwards. The backs of his legs hit the parapet and his body tumbled backwards.

He screamed as he fell and then the screams stopped, replaced by a dull splashing sound.

Leon moved to the edge and looked down.

Iglesias wasn't as fortunate as Wanda. His head was buried in mud, which created a dirty brown bloom round his legs that stuck out of the water. "That's for Rod, you bastard!"

Then he noticed Carlota at his side. "You alright?" he asked.

"Yes." She shook her head dramatically. "A pity, the fool attempted to escape like his confederate but miscalculated..."

"Quite so."

Tears glinted in her eyes.

"Are you sure you'll be alright?"

"Yes. I just keep thinking about the children. It's not

only the physical trauma, which we know is usually considerable, but it's the very loss of irreplaceable innocence, their childhood stolen..."

He hugged her briefly, and whispered in her ear, "You helped make a difference, Carlota."

She gulped and gently broke the embrace, wiped her cheeks with the back of a hand.

Leon said, "Pop down and get Evan to bring up the children and Tía Paloma so we can arrange to fly them off here by helo. Anybody else is to stay on the landing for now." He pulled out his cell-phone and prayed it would still work. "I'll arrange for the air-transport."

As Carlota left, he dialed Chávez and they exchanged cursory greetings.

"I know your men are pressed at present doing rescue work, Teo, but I have about twenty abducted and abused children on the roof of the Golf-Sur golf course main house. They need airlifting to safety and given priority care. Oh, and Agent Tremayne is here as well."

"Is he... alright?"

Evan came onto the roof with some of the children. They exchanged thumbs up.

"Worse for wear but he'll live," Leon said.

"Good. Can you put Tremayne on, please?"

"Certainly." Leon beckoned to Evan.

Evan took the phone, listened, and then said, "Can you tell Inspector De Vargas that the ground floor is flooded, but it's likely the cinema's pornographic DVDs will still be intact and prove suitable material for incriminating the individuals here. There are a good number of clients who can be prosecuted. They're trapped below." He nodded. "Yes, I'm sure he will be pleased." He noticed Leon gesturing in pantomime. "Oh, Leon would like to speak to you again." He handed over the phone.

"You've thought of something else?" Chávez queried.

"Yes. I'd like two seats booked for the next flight to Malta —Carlota and me."

"Now you want me to be your holiday arranger?"

"It's strictly business, sir. We're following a lead which might result in closing down a child-trafficking ring."

"But neither of you has any jurisdiction in Malta."

"We're only going to pay a social call…"

Chávez sighed. "I'll see what I can do."

CHAPTER 17

MARSASKALA BAY

WANDA DRAGGED HERSELF OUT OF THE MUD AND onto a bank that sloped up to a raised road. The bank would normally have been grassy but now it was clogged with detritus, mainly plastic and splinters of wood. Clutching her shoulder-bag, she stood shakily, swaying with the effort she'd expended to swim through the gateway, and keep going, until she got here.

She looked at her watch, but it had stopped. Yet she couldn't have been standing on the roadside more than ten minutes before a truck rumbled along and stopped.

"You want a lift?" the old gent behind the wheel asked in English. He was alone.

Dumbly, she nodded.

"Hop in. You're the fifth survivor I've picked up so far."

"Thank you," she said, clutching her bag. And she meant it.

He took her to the nearby town's school hall where dozens of survivors mingled.

Already, people were getting organized. Clothing was being contributed and distributed to destitute families, toys being provided for the children who'd lost everything. Pizza parlors and other eateries were donating their food.

Unexpected tears trickled down her cheeks; she was overcome by the kindness of strangers.

She had survived.

When the waters receded, as they must, she'd get away. She still had plenty of contacts. She could start over. She had access to Harley's money.

INSPECTOR CHÁVEZ HAD BOOKED them on a Vueling flight from Barcelona-El Prat airport because Alicante-Elche was closed due to the floods. They left their weapons with the helicopter crew.

Fortunately they didn't need passports since they were traveling within the European Union. They both carried Spanish ID cards, which would suffice at a pinch. And Leon had his credit cards, which took a little hammering at the airport since they hadn't been able to return to their apartments for fresh clothing and what they'd been rescued in was filthy and stank.

"Just a change of clothes for now," Carlota insisted. "Airport prices are far too high for my liking. I hope we can buy more in Malta without bankrupting you."

"Don't worry about the expense," he said. "You're worth it."

Her cheeks flushed. "I hope this detour is going to be worth it."

"We'll see."

Eventually, she exited the airport outlet wearing fresh underwear, a pair of stone-washed jeans, a white T-shirt, a denim jacket, and Reebok trainers. Leon settled for chinos, a polo shirt and boat-shoes. Their ruined clothing was binned and then their flight was called.

On arrival at Malta International Airport, they were treated as VIPs and passed through customs with haste. At the gate they were met by Detective Inspector Francis Attard. He was in his mid-forties, Leon knew. He was still slightly portly, and still wore the usual crumpled tan suit with open-necked white shirt which showed a chest of curling black hair.

"Good to see you again, friend," Francis greeted him in English with a light bear-hug.

Then disengaging, Attard bowed to Carlota and shook her hand. "Welcome to Malta, Miss." His gray eyes shone. "I'm only sorry my Spanish isn't too good…"

"That's alright. Leon told me most Maltese speak English and I'm comfortable with it, too."

"Good! Is it your first time?"

"It is," she said. "It's a working visit, Inspector, which is a shame. Leon tells me there is much to see and enjoy here."

"That is true. A mixture of beautiful scenery and eventful colorful history. Many of our visitors keep returning, the place captures their hearts. Oh, and call me Francis," he ended with a smile.

She nodded. "Carlota."

"Carlota. A fine name, ta?"

"I believe so. I'm content with Carla or Carlota."

"Well, as Leon favors your full name, so shall I. Come, I will take you both to my home for a meal. My wife Monica is looking forward to meeting you, Carlota. And of course seeing you again, Leon."

Attard married Monica four years ago; Leon had been invited to the wedding and had managed to attend despite his commitments. He'd only been to see them a couple of times since though they'd kept in touch by phone.

"There I can give you the details you asked for, ta?"

"That would be helpful, Francis," Leon said.

About to climb into the car, Attard pulled his coat tail over his belt holster to conceal his 9mm Beretta pistol. His brow wrinkled. "What, no luggage?"

"I'll explain on the way," Leon said.

"Intriguing. Let's go."

Francis lived in an apartment on Triq San David close to

the Mtarfa clock tower. It was an estate built on what had been the grounds of the Royal Naval Hospital Mtarfa.

Outside Attard's front door was parked a Land Rover. Attard said, "I took the liberty of assigning one of our pool vehicles to you. Less conspicuous than a hire car, no?"

"Appreciated, old friend," Leon said.

"Monica will have the keys indoors."

Leon turned to Carlota. "You'll like her."

Attard chuckled and unlocked the front door. "Monica keeps me young but not slim—she's too good a cook!"

They climbed the stairs, their steps echoing up the well. They reached the top landing where Monica stood outside the open wooden door. Her generous mouth smiled and her green eyes twinkled. She greeted Leon effusively. "Come in, come in!"

They all trooped into a spacious lounge and she shut the door.

She'd been twenty-eight when she wed Francis, quite late for most Mediterranean women. She'd been a nurse but left the profession after the marriage. Even now she had not lost her generous curves, so clearly she did not have as great an appetite as her husband. Her dark brown hair was swept into a bun. She had tanned features, a hooked nose, and a high forehead. "It is too long between times for you to come and see us, Leon!"

"My work, alas..." He turned to Carlota. "Let me introduce–"

"His Girl Friday," Carlota supplied, grinning.

"Ah, Carlota. Francis told me about you. Is that all you are, though?" Monica teased and winked. "You perhaps could convince him there is more to life than work, work, work!"

"He brings the ungodly to justice," Francis Attard said in his friend's defense.

"Oh, we could do with many more like Leon, I know!" She patted his hand. "But now is not the time to talk about beastly work. Let us eat!"

Monica said, "This is my signature dish, *Fenek tal Cazador*."

Leon whispered to Carlota, "It's 'Hunter's Rabbit'—her little joke, a variation on the Spanish *conejo a la cazadora*. And rabbit is the national dish of Malta!"

They talked about their mad rush to the airport, the chaos caused by the floods and their need to purchase fresh clothes tomorrow morning.

"Your best bet is Valletta—best for choice," Monica advised Carlota. It was evident that both of them were getting on well. They chatted throughout most of the evening meal.

After the meal, Attard took them upstairs to their private solarium, while Monica washed the dishes. "You talk crime business, while I clear up," she had insisted. They brought their wine glasses and a bottle.

There was a small table and four chairs. Before sitting down, they took in the view.

The vista was splendid. In one direction Mtarfa valley stretched for what seemed miles. And in the other direction there was the sweep of cultivated land and towns leading to the distinctive Mosta dome. Beyond that was lost in a heat-haze.

Carlota and Leon moved to the table and chairs and sat while Attard poured from a bottle of Delicata Cabernet Sauvignon.

Taking a seat, Attard pulled out a color photograph from the breast pocket of his shirt. "This is Roman Kurilo."

According to records, Kurilo was fifty-five. Ex-Russian army, ex butcher of Chechnya. Of stocky build, he had a puffy face, small gimlet eyes, a shaved head, and an old scar on his brow.

"He is known to us," Attard went on, "but only as a rich benefactor."

"That's not promising," Carlota said and sipped her wine.

"How does he do good?" Leon asked warily.

"He runs a charity for orphan immigrant children. They find homes and adoptive parents for them."

Leon exchanged a knowing look with Carlota. "Fancy that..."

"I've been to his villa a couple of times. It is well appointed. He lives well. He holds two or three cocktail parties a year. Many of the wealthy Maltese attend—as well as a number of ex-pat Russians. Apparently, they give generously."

"How altruistic of them," Leon observed.

Attard chuckled.

"What's amusing."

"I just remembered. Their butler, Alexei, he's also Kurilo's accountant!"

"The man who knows where the bodies are buried, hmm?"

"Possibly... Well, thanks to his charity, Kurilo is quite popular in influential circles."

"I bet he is," murmured Carlota under her breath.

"Where is his villa?" Leon asked.

"Triq Is-Salini overlooking Marsaskala Bay. A nice spot. His big yacht's moored there, too."

"Really? Thank you, Francis," Leon said and finished his glass of wine. "We must do this again some time."

Monica brought up a tray of cups and a coffee percolator. "Finished your crime talks?"

"We have," her husband said.

"I'm clearly in time, then," she said. "Now we can share other gossip!"

———

THEIR FIRST MORNING had been spent in Valletta. Carlota was enchanted by the ancient city, the sun reflecting on the ancient stone. The view across Grand Harbor to Fort St. Angelo was breathtaking, the contrast with the golden sandstone and the azure of sea and sky.

The narrow streets were crammed with shoppers and tourists.

"We can visit here as tourists one day," he suggested, "if you'd like to?"

"Yes, I would like that very much..."

Leon insisted on purchasing everything: two small carry-on cases and fresh clothing. He enjoyed shopping with Carlota, and she seemed to derive great pleasure choosing clothes and seeking his opinion and approval.

Then it was time for work to intrude.

On Triq Zondadari, Rabat was a row of old buildings, each with a door opening direct onto the narrow street. Leon had parked the Land Rover at the end of the street as he didn't want to block the access. He stood in front of a green-painted wooden door and announced his presence by slamming the brass dolphin knocker three times.

The door opened almost immediately and a short wispy thin man in his forties stood in the dark passage. "You don't have to knock so loud, Leon," he said in a mellow voice and indicated a small camera on a bracket across the street. "I saw you." He had a pointed nose, high cheekbones, dark hair to his shoulders, and eyebrows that met. He looked Carlota up and down, stroking his cleft chin. "And who's this lovely lady you've brought with you?"

"Carlota, meet Mr. Fixit, otherwise known as Mirko."

"Charmed." He had glinting brown eyes, kindly, even while appraising.

She nodded acknowledgement.

"You'd both better come in," he said.

The hallway passage was dark, the walls tiled dull grays and blues and greens. The floor was made from terracotta flagstones; cool in summer, warm in winter. After shutting the door he walked ahead of them in a loping gait in khaki shorts that did no favors for his spindly hairy legs.

At the end of the passage was a tub containing a large cheese plant, with doors to left and right. He turned right into a large high-ceilinged room crammed with metal shelving and a vast array of equipment: scuba gear, buoyancy compensators, mouth-pieces and regulators, spear-guns, rifles, pistols, knives, wetsuits, face-masks, weight belts, torches, and electronic items whose purpose eluded most observers.

"You're well equipped!" Carlota said.

"Thank you," Mirko said. "Not many women tell me that..." He smirked. "Seriously, this is truly my Aladdin's cave!"

Leon was beyond being impressed. He'd seen it all before. "Have you got what I asked for?" he said. After leaving Attard's house, he'd made a list and phoned Mirko.

Mirko waved at a pile of items in the far corner. "All of it is ready."

"Well done. Payment has been wired to your account, as usual."

"Thanks. Appreciated."

———

MYRIAD STARS and a full moon shone in the deep blue night sky and reflected in the waters of Marsaskala Bay. Other reflections, from the odd occupied moored boat and buildings, bars and restaurants, diminished the magical effect. Their Land Rover was discreetly parked out of the way in a side-street. Dressed in their gray-and-black wetsuits and wearing their buoyancy compensators, an air tank each, and neoprene gloves and footwear, Leon and Carlota carried the rest of their scuba gear down to the rocky shore. Here, in the light of the moon they did their pre-dive checks on each other—air switched on, all quick-releases and straps secure, visible and within reach, and contents gauges showed "full". Then they put on their fins and face-masks and swam a short distance into the wide bay and then submerged.

Leon used an illuminated wrist compass to orient himself and trailed a line behind him which Carlota held. She was an accomplished diver but had never swum at night.

After twenty minutes, he stopped swimming and waited for her. Then he signaled to go up.

They broke surface together.

His bearings had been accurate.

They had emerged abaft of the luxury yacht; its name written across the stern was in Cyrillic, meaning *Free*, which was ironic considering what the owner practiced.

There was a short metal ladder attached to the stern.

Leon disengaged his mouthpiece and raised the face-mask. He signed to Carlota, and she gave him the thumbs up sign.

Normally, the ladders of diving boats are angled so that divers can board wearing their fins; the ladder here was close to the hull, only suitable for divers with bare feet. Holding onto the ladder, he removed his fins and then climbed the ladder and clambered soundlessly over the side. With the utmost care, he removed his buoyancy compensator and air-tank, lowering them to the deck on one side with his fins. Then he took off his weight belt and left it on the deck as well.

Carlota climbed over and divested herself of her equipment too. Both had leather shoulder-holsters strapped on, though they were empty at present.

The saltwater dropped from their suits and created puddles, but they would not be out of place here.

They both unfastened the waterproof bags that dangled from their belts, opened them and removed their automatic pistols fitted with silencers. The guns were slim lightweight Russian-made PSM blowback pistols, carrying eight rounds; the unusual bottle-necked cartridges had unremarkable velocity yet good penetration power.

Earlier today Leon had scoped the yacht and reckoned there were only two crew members presently on board.

On a scale of size, this boat probably was medium for a Russian oligarch. The ultra-rich, living off the bent backs of the majority of poor Russians, would boast a boat twice this size. But this one could comfortably accommodate twenty people. Not too ostentatious, but not quite modest.

On shore, there was a small wooden jetty and then steps that led up through an exotic garden to the villa, a white stucco three-story building where lights blazed in four windows.

Silently, he moved across the deck and reached the open hatch that led below. Light spilled out from there.

Carlota would stay here, on watch.

With no sound at all, Leon descended the steps into the wide cabin, with accents of orange and gold, and brass fittings everywhere.

A thick-set crew-cut man was sitting at a table playing patience. He wore a black T-shirt that bulged smoothly where his muscles touched, and a tan leather shoulder holster. The gun was a revolver. He must have detected movement out of the corner of his eye for in the next instant he reached for the weapon.

Chapter 18

Mute Testament

Leon shot him. The silencer was not entirely effective in this closed space. He slumped, the playing cards scattering everywhere.

A door opened further along the cabin and another man stepped out. He swore on seeing Leon. He reached for the pistol in his shoulder-holster.

Leon shot him in the heart.

Were there more to spring out of the woodwork?

He waited five minutes.

Nobody.

Carlota probably heard the bodies fall, but she didn't duck her head in to learn what was happening. She trusted in his ability. She was proving to be a formidable companion.

He made his way along the companionway, past the second corpse. At the end there was another door. He opened it and came upon a hatch with a ladder leading down. Lights were on below, too.

He descended.

And opened the first door.

It wasn't locked because the six children here were chained to the bulkhead. What hit him was the smell, rank and overpowering.

Their eyes blinked against the light that entered from the

passageway, and one or two raised hands or arms to shield them.

A couple nearest showed alarm in their faces on seeing the silenced automatic in his hand. He hastily holstered the gun.

"Anyone speak English?" One hand was raised, a boy's. "Anyone speak Spanish?" Two young girls raised their hands.

He said in English and Spanish: "If you can, tell the others what I'm telling you."

The three of them nodded.

"I'm making arrangements to free you from here. For now, sit tight. Help will come!" He found the light switch and flicked it on.

He checked the three kids and they sheepishly grinned. Then they turned to the others and started gabbling and gesturing in the air and at Leon.

He ducked out and tried the second door. This was a cabin but it was empty.

A third door opened onto a further six chained children; the smell of the confined place was just as bad. He repeated what he'd told the others and then left.

Retracing his steps, he stopped off at a cabin and grabbed a couple of bath-sheets, then climbed up to the deck.

"Anything to report?" Carlota asked.

"Yes. Twelve children, all chained to the bulkheads."

"Oh, the poor things!"

"We'll come back for them when we're done here."

"Yes. Of course."

He tossed her a big towel. "Here, dry yourself as much as possible so we don't leave big puddles indoors."

"Very considerate," she said.

"We don't want scene-of-crime to get confused," he explained.

She nodded and dabbed the towel over her wetsuit; they dried each other's backs.

Then, still soundless, they walked down the gangway; he

felt the non-slip ridges through the soles of the neoprene shoes. They jumped onto the jetty. Together, like shadows, they swiftly rushed to the stone steps that led up to the villa.

"What's the plan now?" Carlota asked.

"Play it by ear. From what Francis told me, there are usually two heavies who patrol the property. I imagine when Kurilo holds his parties there are a lot more armed sentries about."

They passed evergreen honeysuckle, horn-of-plenty, black nightshade with its distinctive small poisonous berries, assorted geranium, and a number of castor oil bushes.

They slunk up to the rear patio which held several large planters filled with shrubs and a table and four chairs; the front door and portico was on the other side of the building, facing onto the street, with its entrance gate, sweeping drive and garage; he'd Googled it.

Here, which was obviously not on Google, there was a French window; the drapes inside were drawn.

From his waterproof pouch Leon fished out the lock-pick set and got to work. Within thirty seconds he had unlocked the door. He opened it a crack and paused and listened.

Nobody seemed to be in this room.

He tweaked the drape aside a little and peered through the small gap.

Not a soul.

The lights were on. So somebody might be returning any time soon.

They gently brushed aside the drapes and moved into a dining room. On a highly polished long mahogany table was a silver tray containing two glass tumblers and an empty vodka bottle. Sustenance for the troops?

The far door opened and a man walked in carrying a full bottle of vodka.

Replenishment time.

He saw them immediately. He was right-handed and the bottle was in his right hand. He fumbled. Instead of dropping the bottle—which would have smashed on the tile floor—he grabbed it with his left hand, clutching it to his chest, then reached for the revolver in his shoulder-holster.

Leon fired once. His bullet went through the vodka bottle, shattering it, soaking the man, and penetrated his chest, the vodka doubtless anesthetizing the wound in the process. Not that it would do any good. He collapsed noisily to the floor amidst the shards of glass and liquor, dead.

"No prisoners," Carlota whispered behind him.

"Where's the other guy?" he wondered.

"Might be doing the rounds like a good security man."

"Stay alert." He crossed the dining room, reached the door, stepped over the body. Through the open doorway he could see the circular atrium. Doors opened onto the large space; over on the right was the sweeping marble staircase. A brass life-size statue of Donatello's David stood on a plinth at the foot of the stairs, next to another door. On the other side of the door was a statue of Michelangelo's David. Clearly, Kurilo had a thing about the Biblical giant-killer.

He pointed across the atrium. "Let's try that door—it seems important with those two statues acting as sentry."

She followed.

Tentatively, he turned the handle and pushed the door inwards a smidgen.

There was no sound at all inside the room. He opened it wide.

On the far side of the room was another door. This one appeared to be solid metal, and it didn't blend in with the rest of the décor. On the right-hand wall by the door-jamb was a keypad. On the right of the door was a chaise-longue. All around the room was ornate antique furniture.

They reached the door. Carlota covered his back as he studied the keypad. He was tempted to blast it with a few bullets.

"Don't stop!" Carlota shouted in English. "Keep on walking in!"

Curious, Leon spun round.

A man had come in the same doorway from the atrium. He was carrying a laptop and a couple of big ledgers. He was cadaverous, with a toothbrush mustache, long thin nose and face, a jutting chin, narrow shoulders that tended to stoop. He obviously understood English as he started walking forward. In a calm unflustered voice, he said, "What are you doing?"

If he had registered the weapons, they did not disconcert him. A cool customer.

"We're here to see Roman Kurilo," Leon said. "Is he in?"

"Have you an appointment?"

Leon waved the gun. "Does it look like it?"

"No, I thought not. Your request would have to come through me anyway."

"I suppose you're Alexei."

"Most astute of you, sir. Who might you be?"

"If you don't mind, we'll leave the introductions for another time." Leon pointed to the laptop. "Is it connected to Wi-Fi?"

"Yes. Do you want to do a Google search or something?"

"Something. But later."

"Anything else, sir?"

"The combination for this keypad would be a big help."

"I wouldn't go in there if I were you, sir..."

"I insist."

Alexei's narrow shoulders hunched. "Very well. It's your funeral, as they say." He put the laptop and ledgers on the chaise-longue. Then he went to the keypad and fingered three numbers—666.

"You must be joking!" Leon exclaimed.

"No, it's Roman Kurilo's little joke."

The devil it is! It's no joking matter!

The door clicked and swung open slightly; ajar. It was thick, definitely metal; sound-proofed.

"Will that be all?" Alexei queried.

"For now. Thanks."

As Alexei turned to pick up the laptop and ledgers, Leon

hit him on the back of the neck with the ridge of his hand, stunning the man. Then he applied a choke-hold, counting off the seconds. Sufficient to render him unconscious but not dead.

When Alexei went limp, Leon lifted him in his arms with ease and dumped him on the chaise-longue. "Sleep tight."

Carlota stood by, watching, amused, but with one eye on the other doors.

He went through the doorway and stepped onto a concrete landing. Another keypad was on the wall, presumably in case anyone was accidentally locked in. Stone steps descended into a well-lit tiled basement. The tiles were predominantly different shades of blue; it conveyed the impression the place was under water. He caught the stomach-churning stench of the charnel house, an abattoir.

Why do the bad guys always hanker after a basement? Is it to get them closer to the fire and brimstone at the center of the earth, nearer to Hell and the devil? Perhaps they could take up residence in St. Paul's catacombs instead, among all those bones? Maybe that could be arranged.

A man in a bath-robe began climbing the stairs. Even from this angle Leon recognized him. It was Roman Kurilo. He walked with a bow-legged gait. Black hair bristled on his chest in the "v" of the robe. Behind his bulk was a huge underbuild wet-room. Somewhere on the left was the sound of a shower running. Probably his wife, Belka. Washing away the latest crime.

"Go back down again," Leon ordered, holding the silenced automatic.

Kurilo paused mid-step and looked up. There was a mixture of consternation and puzzlement on his face.

"Go back down!" Leon ordered again.

Slowly, Kurilo negotiated the steps backwards.

I didn't mean it literally! With any luck he'll tumble and break his neck!

"Who are you?" Kurilo said when he reached the bottom of the steps.

He speaks English. Well, he understood the order, and, it figures, he supposed, since the majority of Maltese do also and he'd need the language to get by.

Leon descended after him, and as he did so he took in the rest of the basement.

On the right was a locked glass cubicle with two young boys tethered by rope in a sitting position on the floor. They only wore boxer shorts.

There was a white vanity unit nearby and a matching stool. Next to that was a large oak table which in its former life might have graced the kitchen of a country cottage but clearly now served as a butcher's block. It had been recently washed, but many stubborn stains remained.

A series of long mirrors adorned three walls.

Between two mirrors on the left were two swords, a carpenter's saw and a bone saw, all held by metal brackets; a fifth bracket was empty. Here too was a door, presumably leading to the shower room.

In pride of place, directly in front of the steps in between two long mirrors, hung an enlarged photograph of Russia's president. As a result of his dirty wars in Georgia, Chechnya and Syria, he had lost the "Mr." and was referred to only with his surname, much like Hitler. Bare-chested and disdainful, Putin was riding a horse. A horseman of the Apocalypse?

Now Leon could see traces of red—blood, most probably—swilling away on the floor, into the central drain. Near the drain was a large green plastic bin with a few dark red splashes on its sides. Leon suspected that was the source of the abattoir stink.

"You're not a vampire by any chance?" he ventured.

Kurilo looked completely blank, bemused.

"No, you can't be, you'd suck the blood, not drain it away. And on reflection they don't like mirrors." Levity here seemed misplaced, but in a minor way it shunted the horror aside just a little.

Leon was convinced he'd entered the lair of a pair of

sadistic sociopaths. In 2000 he'd been attached to the United Nations and on a couple of occasions worked with the FBI. At the time he'd gained personal experience of investigations of multiple sadistic murders committed by two men shortly after they'd been paroled from prison. What they did to their victims, and what they forced their victims to do, turned the stomach. Similar inhuman atrocities had occurred in the Bosnian war zone when he'd been on special operations.

"Eh, what are you gabbling about?" Kurilo growled. "And who the hell are you?"

Leon sighed. "Hell is right here, I suspect. Nice touch, the combination code for the door."

Clenching and unclenching his fists, Kurilo seemed very exasperated. "How did you get in?"

"Your manservant obliged."

"Alexei wouldn't dare..." Then he gave a start as Carlota descended the steps behind Leon. "You haven't explained... yourselves..."

"We don't have to explain anything to you. As it happens we're here to put a stop to your business."

Kurilo let out a forced laugh. "What business? I'm a private citizen enjoying my well-earned retirement. I'm a feted philanthropist!"

"Fated, maybe. Ill-fated."

Confusion on his face.

Leon pointed to the two boys who stared wide-eyed, curious, fearful. "That kind of business."

"Oh, they're merely guests..."

"A blatant lie. You Russians are good at that..." Leon moved forward swiftly, adopting the ninja fist, boshi-ken, with his left hand. The fist is formed with the thumb protruding, and the hand in a position resembling that used to grip a golf club. A driving jab, reinforced by the curled index finger, deep into Kurilo's solar plexus, below the "v" opening of his bath-robe. Kurilo stood groaning for breath, as if paralyzed.

Leon noticed that the shower had stopped running.

Kurilo's wife Belka came charging out of the shower room, still dripping wet, pendulous breasts wobbling obscenely. She carried a shiny meat cleaver. "Leave him alone!" she wailed in Russian.

Out of the corner of his eye Leon saw Carlota raise her gun, about to aim.

"No, Carlota, let me!" Leon shouted. He swiftly unscrewed the silencer and lifted the automatic.

Behind him, Kurilo continued to rasp hoarsely, frozen to the spot.

She was about a yard away, the cleaver raised, and her visage twisted and ugly. The slap of her feet on wet tiles sounded louder and louder, nearer and nearer.

Calmly, he fired.

The bullet hit her between the eyes and exited in a mess of brain, bone and blood.

She stopped mid-stride, her head jerked and she fell backwards, dropping the cleaver. It made a metallic clatter on the tiled floor while her body made an unpleasant splat sound.

Still gasping for breath, Kurilo stood helpless, distress in his eyes at seeing his wife's sudden death.

Without any further thought Leon grabbed Kurilo's right hand and raised it unresisting to head-height; then he put his pistol in Kurilo's hand, making sure he had a good grip, and pressed its muzzle against Kurilo's right temple. Kurilo stood gasping and wheezing, in shock. Leon pulled the trigger. Surprisingly, the blood splatter missed Leon's wetsuit but covered two fingers of his gloved hand.

Vaguely he heard Carlota gasp behind him. He paid her no mind.

Kurilo crumpled to the tiled floor and lay still, blood trickling from his skull, dribbling towards the drain.

Staged: he killed his wife and then himself. The powder burns on Kurilo's hand would be conclusive.

And the bin filled with limbs would be mute testament to what had transpired here.

He stood and turned to Carlota. "Are you alright?"

She nodded but seemed unable to speak. Her usually attractive face was a mask, almost as if it was carved in stone.

The Kurilos were aware of right and wrong but didn't care. They lacked the internal prohibitions or conscience that keep most people from giving full expression to the most primitive violent impulses. They lacked even a veneer of civilization. Doubtless they had graduated from minor torments to full-blown sadistic torture and death with sexual gratification merely a bonus but not the primary aim.

A massive bolus of extreme distaste swelled in his chest as he scanned the wet-room.

The two boys cowered, peeking behind forearms resting on their knees. It stood to reason if the Kurilos wanted access to the two boys at some point, the key to their glass cage would be close at hand. Leon strode over to the vanity unit and checked the drawers. The top drawer held a pair of pliers, a whip and electric cables and a continental two-pin plug. He found a bunch of keys in the bottom drawer; evidently keys for more locks than these glass doors.

He unlocked and opened the glass door and clipped the bunch of keys to his belt. Quickly he knelt by the boys and used the knife from the sheath at his calf to free them.

With difficulty they managed to stand. They shuddered and shook against his side as he led them out.

Standing at the foot of the steps, Carlota gestured for him to hurry. As he reached her, she said, "We've still got at least one security man unaccounted for."

"Agreed." He gently shoved the two boys to her side. "Look after them."

Hands on their shoulders, she said, "Of course."

"Now," he said, "give me your gun and then follow me at a safe distance."

He took the automatic, checked the magazine: eight, more than enough. He peered up the steps. The door was still open.

He began to climb, soundless.

When he was near the top he slowed. His head was level

with the concrete floor of the landing and as he peeked over the lip he could catch a glimpse through the door.

Alexei sat on the chaise-longue, massaging his throat. Sitting beside him was a hulking giant, a shotgun resting across his knees. The missing security guard. He wasn't looking in the direction of the door. Perhaps he hoped to hear anybody coming up.

Soundlessly, keeping his eye on the security man, Leon climbed the last few steps, Carlota's automatic ready.

At last the security guard discerned movement in the doorway. Too late. Leon held his gun-hand steady with his left hand and fired. The bullet smashed into the security man's left eye and made a terrible mess of the chaise-longue. Splashes of blood and brain spattered Alexei.

Exclaiming in disgust, Alexei jumped from his seat, hesitant about what he should do next.

"Stay there, Alexei," Leon advised. He stepped through the doorway and called over his shoulder, "You can come up now!"

Alexei was visibly trembling. There was a large wet patch in his crotch area. Not so cool now.

"I have one last task before I let you go," Leon told him.

"Let me go...? Yes... Any—anything at all—I'm hap— happy to oblige..."

Leon pointed at the laptop. "Log on to the bank Kurilo uses—used."

"Wh—why?"

"I know you deal with his finances. So do it."

He hesitated, perhaps wondering if he could deny it. "There's no—no need to look like that at me... Y—yes, of course, I'll do it... Right away..." He grabbed the laptop and sat on the far edge of the chaise-longue, as far as possible from the dead security guard. He opened the laptop and tapped with two fingers on the keyboard.

"Are you in yet?" Leon asked, walking closer.

"Y-yes."

"What's the balance in the Kurilo account?"

"Four million Euros and sixty-nine cents."

"Right. I want you to transfer the four million to the International Fund for Orphans." He dredged the account details from memory and told Alexei. Over the years he'd coerced a number of the ungodly to contribute to this good cause.

"But—but—*all* of it?"

"Well, I'm leaving the account open."

"Sixty-nine cents!"

"Haven't you done it yet?"

Immediately, Alexei started keying in information.

"And before you close the laptop, show me the transaction."

Alexei sighed, pressed a final key, and then swiveled the machine on his knees to show Leon.

Transaction complete.

Carlota clutched Leon's arm and gave him a very broad smile.

"Very good," Leon told Alexei. "Now, come with us."

"Where are we going?"

"To the jetty. Bring the laptop as well."

It was a strange procession through the dining room, onto the patio, down the garden steps: Leon, Alexei, Carlota and two lost boys, eyes averted from the two dead security guards.

When they reached the jetty, Leon said, "Carlota, leave the boys here. Go below and free the others." He threw her the bunch of keys. "I reckon some of these might fit."

"OK." As Carlota boarded the yacht, Leon drew Alexei to one side. "Take the weight off your feet. Sit on that bollard." The two boys sat on two other bollards, far from Alexei.

Alexei shrugged and warily sat where directed, clutching the laptop to his chest.

Leon pulled out from the waterproof pouch the cell phone Mirko had supplied. He pressed the speed dial and Mirko answered immediately.

"That was prompt," Leon said. "Are you anxious to hear from me?"

"Well, how did it go?" Mirko asked breathlessly. "Did the equipment come up to scratch?"

"All worked perfectly. Now, there's a cleaner issue. I recall last time we had dealings you mentioned a specialist team who'd do the job, no questions asked."

"They're ex-Mafiya. And they are expensive."

"I have the funds, Mirko. Get them to bring a boat here. They need to make four corpses disappear—two in the villa and two on the jetty. And take off by boat Carlota and me plus fourteen children."

"Fourteen children? You have been busy—or did the lady help?"

"We don't divulge tactics, Mirko, you know that. Can you arrange this—and pronto?"

"Just hold a minute..." There was background noise, the clicking of keys being typed and murmuring, and then he was on the phone again. "They can be at the jetty and the front door in an hour."

"Well done." He closed the call.

Carlota was helping the children down the gangway. They all clustered round the two boys, gawking at both Leon and Carlota.

Leon returned the automatic to Carlota. "Watch our friend Alexei while I get our equipment."

"'Friend'...? Sure." She glared at Alexei and pointed the weapon threateningly. He looked away and sweat sprouted on his brow.

It took Leon a couple of trips to heave the air-tanks and other equipment onto the jetty. While doing that he contacted Mirko again to make further arrangements.

When he'd finished, he checked his watch.

They had about forty-five minutes before the cleaners arrived. "We're going to wait here for a while," he told everyone.

The children dozed, doubtless aided by the fresh air, a far cry from their recent confinement.

Finally, when fifty minutes elapsed, he spotted the bow wave of a large vessel cutting through the bay. It had to be them. Well done, Mirko.

Leon studied his watch. "The clean-up crew boat will be here in ten minutes. They'll take the children aboard." He went to the garden steps.

"What are you going to do?" Carlota asked.

"Welcome the removals men." He returned to the villa, passed through the rooms to the lobby. Beside the front door was a keypad, appropriately labeled. He pressed the button marked "gates" and opened the front door in time to see the gates opening automatically and a carpet-fitting van motor through and along the short drive.

It braked at the entrance and two burly broad-shouldered men jumped from the rear doors and carried a rolled carpet each. The driver stayed in the cab.

As they climbed the marble steps, one said, "Waste disposal. You're expecting us."

"So I am." Leon directed them to the bodies and the two men handled them with ease, rolling a body in each carpet and returning to the van; then they went to the jetty and boarded the yacht. Within minutes they appeared with two heavy carpets over their shoulders. The gangway bent slightly under their weight.

The talkative one said, "Is that it?"

"Yes, thanks. Mirko will settle with you."

"Right. We'll be off then."

Leon turned to Alexei and waved a hand at the yacht. "OK, you can go—sail off into the sunset."

Carlota gave him a dark look. "Seriously?"

"He's donated a lot of Kurilo's money to a good cause."

She said, "You know what you're doing, I guess."

With remarkable alacrity, Alexei jumped to his feet and hurried up the gangway.

"Can you sail the thing?" Leon asked.

"Sure. It's one of my many talents!" He unhitched the gangway and threw it sideways onto the jetty; it landed with a clatter. He reached the cockpit and turned a key, pressed a button and the engine started up, the props agitating the water.

Alexei called, "Will you cast off for me?"

"Sure." Leon strode to the forward bollard and tossed the looped rope over the bow, and then walked to the rear and did the same for the aft rope. As the craft edged away from the jetty, he shouted, "Bon voyage!" Then he pressed a button on his watch.

Carlota moved at his side, fingering her automatic. "Bon voyage? He was obviously complicit in all that Kurilo and his wife did."

Leon was non-committal.

The clean-up boat pulled alongside the jetty, gently buffeting the tire fenders; the crew didn't bother securing lines either fore or aft. They weren't sticking around. A gangway was lowered. Leon boarded first and climbed the companion ladder to the bridge wing of the wheel-house to meet the skipper. He slid the door open and stepped over the coaming. "Thanks for coming so promptly."

The skipper was bearded, weather-beaten and of a taci-turn nature. "Where do you want to take the kids?"

"When you clear the bay, head south and drop them off at St. Thomas's Bay."

"No problem."

Leon climbed down and joined Carlota and they both shepherded the children onto the craft's deck and helped them descend the stairs into a kind of state room. While they'd been doing that, crew members had obligingly put their diving equipment on the deck under the companion ladder.

Then Leon poked his head through the hatch and signed to the skipper in the wheel-house and the men pushed off from the jetty with billhooks. The boarding had taken barely two minutes. They motored into Marsaskala Bay, veering to the southern side.

Descending the stairs, Leon took out his cell phone and, taking care not to include Carlota, he photographed the children clustered near each other.

She came up to him.

"A souvenir snapshot?"

"No. I have an idea."

Without further explanation, he left her and went to the upper deck, and climbed to the wheel-house again.

The skipper nodded at him but said nothing.

Leon could see the red, green and white navigation lights of the yacht *Free* further ahead, moving north, to negotiate round the point of land called Il-Ponta Taz-Zonqor.

He looked at his watch.

Chapter 19

Rough Justice

Alexei grinned broadly at the steering wheel. He thought: *I really feared that guy was going to shoot me!*

What that guy didn't know was that there was another secret bank account, which was held in reserve.

He glanced behind him, at a bench where the laptop lay.

Money waiting to be accessed. And I've got the access codes!

The point of land on his left was lit up, as good a warning as a lighthouse.

Making a slight adjustment, he steered well clear of the coastline rocks. Surf shimmered phosphorescent in the moonlight as it hit the jagged rocks. He didn't want to founder now.

There was a lot of money for him to spend, spend, and spend.

And there was this yacht as well, to either use or sell...

His chest filled with pride.

I kept my cool. And it paid off!

That guy had done me a favor. It had been getting too intense with that couple. They'd become less obsessed about money and more obsessed with their dirty little games.

I'm well rid of them!

Briefly, he wondered what happened to the Kurilos in the basement.

He shrugged.

No longer my concern.

The vessel bounced on the waves as he started to round the point.

This is heaven!

———

LEON AND CARLOTA stood in the wheel-house behind the skipper. The stillness of the night was punctuated by the almost soporific regular beat from the boat's engines. They looked through the windshield.

Where the yacht *Free* sailed was a sudden bright flash and seconds later an explosion, loud, and yet muted by the distance.

Leon whispered, "Sabotaged the yacht. Activated it when I cast off. It blew more or less right on time."

"No prisoners," Carlota confirmed.

"Indeed. Alexei knew what was going on. Complicit," Leon agreed. "Now he's free...in Hell."

———

"MIRKO, ANY LUCK LOCATING BASIL DOUKAS?" Leon asked on his phone as he stood in the wheel-house.

"Yes, you're right, he's in Tangier. I've got the street and house address; I'm sending you a Google map and his phone number."

"Thanks."

"I've just had word that the coach is waiting for you."

Leon gazed out to the shore. Headlights flashed, once, twice. "I see it. Well done!" He closed the call.

The boat's engines stopped and an anchor was dropped.

Like finely honed sailors, the crew wordlessly lowered a large inflatable dinghy and then they helped the children down a dangling ladder into it. Leon and Carlota stood on the bridge wing and waved to them. They waved. Earlier, he'd explained to them what to expect.

The dinghy's outboard motor puttered and they headed for the shore.

A short while later Attard's plain-clothes men scuttled to the shoreline and helped the children into the surf. When they were all ashore, the dinghy turned and headed back for the boat.

Leon phoned Francis Attard. "They're safely delivered, thanks."

"And the Kurilos?"

"You'll find they must have had a serious domestic disagreement. Of the fatal kind."

"Oh?"

"Probably best if you don't go overboard with the scene-of-crime investigation. And prepare your people for plenty of unpleasant discoveries. Best if they don't have breakfast beforehand."

"That bad, is it?"

"Yes. For the media, you might want to put it down to black magic gone wrong."

Attard laughed. "What, on an island with a church for every day of the year? Very amusing. In case I need a statement from you, where can I find you?"

"Statement, Francis? I wasn't there, was I?"

"Silly me. And where will you be?"

"Tangier."

"And you can't fly since you have no passport at present, correct?"

"That's about the size of it. Regards to Monica. *Ciao!*"

―――――

THE SKIPPER HAD ALLOCATED a cabin with two bunks, one above the other. Earlier he had given them both a djellaba each, which smelled musty, and sandals. "You can't go wandering about in those wetsuits," he explained. "We have a stock of clothes for various eventualities. These should suit your purposes." Grateful, they bundled the North African clothing inside a polythene bag.

At first, Carlota, lying in the lower bunk, could not get to sleep. "I should be appalled by the way we have taken the law into our own hands..."

"It isn't the law we've taken into our own hands," he replied gently. "We've meted out rough justice—and saved tax payers oodles of money."

"Rough justice." She heaved a big sigh. "They died too quick, you know."

"I know. But torturing them, making them linger in agony, would only make us feel worse."

She sobbed briefly. "It really gets to me when I hear talk of those who preach abolishing the death penalty. They say: if banning the death penalty saves one innocent person from being executed, then it is worth it. Something like that. But they don't use the reverse argument, do they? What about the murderers who are let out and kill again? What about arguing: if locking up murderers for their entire life will save other innocent lives, then it is worth it. Eh, tell me that!"

"They make the rules, they don't suffer the consequences," he said. "If they did, I guess they'd alter their viewpoint."

"Yes, I think they might... Leon...?"

"Yes?"

"Thank you for bringing me along. We made a difference, didn't we?"

"We did. And we have more to do. Try to get some sleep."

She didn't answer. She had fallen asleep, finally succumbing to the influence of the oddly reassuring motion and sound of the vessel.

Leon closed his eyes and awoke as a crew member tentatively entered the cabin.

"Oh, you're awake," the man said.

"Yes. Everything alright?"

"Yes, sir. We've arrived. Skipper asks you to go up top."

It was dawn. A magical time floating off the coastline. Surf broke on the shore. The deep ultramarine sky was tinged with buttery light from the emerging sun. Rocks and cliffs loomed, dark, mysterious and potentially treacherous. Across the waves, in the distance sounded the muezzin, calling to the faithful for their *Fajr* prayer.

Standing on the bridge wing, Leon said, "I expected we'd be going against the tide of illegal immigrants crossing to Spain. Yet it's all clear."

The skipper grunted. "Those damned people smugglers pick their time and place, and today they're somewhere else along the coast, profiting on gullibility and misery!"

Before they left, the skipper had taken Leon to one side, clapped a hand on his back. "I know what you did."

Presumably the cleaners had nosed around, seen the bodies in the basement, and had let the skipper know.

"And," he went on, "I applaud you for it."

"I did it for the dead children..."

"I may be a crook, but for me anyone who can harm kids has crossed the line."

"I agree, Skipper. Will you be in the area for the next forty-eight hours?" Leon asked.

"I'll be berthing in Gib. Why?"

"Can I call on you if I need a way out?"

The skipper clapped his shoulder. "Just make sure your phone has plenty of juice."

The crew loaded the dinghy with their scuba gear and then Carlota and Leon climbed in awkwardly as the boat bobbed with waves caused by the tide.

The outboard motor spluttered to life and they were taken ashore. At last they stepped into the swirling surf. A crewman handed them their gear and they waved briefly and hefted it all to the concealment provided by several sand dunes.

Over on their left were a number of caves. Leon helped

Carlota over the rocks and they stashed the equipment there for the time being.

When they emerged from the cave, he saw the navigation lights of the skipper's craft moving away, probably heading for Gibraltar.

As daylight illuminated the area, they both stripped off their wetsuits and donned their djellabas and put on their sandals. The clothing was cumbersome as they clambered up through the rough ground from the rocky shore. Eventually they attained a rough road. They trudged for mile on mile along this and passed several dwellings and low-lying farmsteads. Finally they reached the main national road, the N16 and caught a coach that would take them into Tangier. Leon paid for the fare with Euros and spoke in Arabic.

The muezzin was calling faithful to noon prayer when the coach arrived in the city.

The shops were open for business and not surprisingly the shopkeeper was happy to accept payment by credit card.

He bought clothing and shoes suitable for a businessman and his assistant, and also a small leather briefcase. Carlota kept her automatic tucked in her waistband at the base of her spine.

At a general store he downloaded the photos of the children in the boat to a printer and made two copies of each. He also bought a street map.

They ate at a café and consulted the map. They soon located the house Mirko had identified.

Now refreshed, they set out to find the street.

Leon scanned the villa and surrounding buildings.

"Boldness be my friend," he said.

"What?" Carlota said.

"We'll walk in, I think. As planned. No need for scrambling over walls and breaking in."

"You're sure?"

"Sure." He produced his cell-phone and dialed the Doukas number. A woman answered.

Leon said, "I wish to speak to Mr. Basil Doukas. It is urgent."

"Mr. Doukas cannot be disturbed at present. What is it in connection with, sir?"

"It is a highly confidential matter. Señor Iglesias recommended me to Mr. Doukas."

"I'm sorry, Mr. Doukas has never had any dealings with anyone by that name."

"Ah, he may know him as Señor Fuentes..."

"Oh, I see... One moment, please." There was a lengthy pause and then she came on the line again. "He has a brief window. Who shall I say is calling?"

"Santos, Carlos Santos."

"Thank you, Señor Santos. I will put you through..."

"Hello, Señor Santos." A man's voice. "How is Tomás? I haven't heard from him since I shipped the last batch of merchandise. I trust he is satisfied with it?"

"He was very pleased. Unfortunately right now he has to keep a low profile. He's gone deep undercover." Unless the flood-water has receded and they have dug him out of the mud...

"What has happened?" Concern in his voice.

"Well, I don't know the full story. But I understand that one of his people was working for the authorities."

A pause. Then: "That is most unfortunate—for him, I mean."

"That is why I am approaching you, Mr. Doukas. As Tomás is not taking on merchandise at present, I hoped I could interest you in a boat-load. At reasonable prices. I want them off my hands, to be honest. Fourteen of them."

"Fourteen, you say? That is a good number." Another pause. "I would like to see them before making a decision, of course."

"I understand. However, bringing them to you is a big risk unless I have a contract to purchase."

"I cannot give you such a contract sight unseen. I need to

see if they will prove suitable for my clients, of which I have many."

Snagged on the line. "I agree. It is only fair." Leon could do a pause just as well. Then, he said, "I have a solution."

"Tell me your solution."

"At this early stage of bargaining, perhaps I can show you photographs to begin with. That would save us both time, no?"

"Yes, that would be acceptable. I will give you directions."

"No need. I know where you are. I am not far now, actually."

"You are clearly most keen. I will await your arrival. We can have a bite to eat and a drink."

"That would be most generous of you, Mr. Doukas."

"We Greeks are known for our hospitality."

"I will bring along my assistant, if that is alright?"

"Is he trustworthy?"

"I would be lost without her."

"Oh, a woman. Well, of course, you must both come."

"I look forward to it, Mr. Doukas."

———

THE VILLA WAS grand yet modern, three stories high, with its mainly glass façade including blocks of bronzed terracotta so that it changed color at different times and when viewed from different angles. People within doubtless could see out, but outsiders certainly could not see inside.

Carlota stood a pace behind Leon, holding the briefcase.

In answer to his pressing the bell button, a manservant appeared at the wired glass door. A speaker crackled then said, "State your business."

"Señor Santos and his assistant Señorita Friday to see Mr. Doukas."

The door buzzed and the lock was released. "Enter."

Leon pushed the door wide and stepped inside, followed by Carlota.

They were in a large modern atrium, with huge chandeliers suspended from a high ceiling. Gold-flecked marble tiles on the floor contrasted with the marble walls. A large mirror framed in gilt hung beneath the sweep of the central staircase. Copies of Greek statuary lined two sides of the atrium. A banana plant sprouted from a big pot at the foot of the stairs.

A burly man in a brown suit came forward. Leon noticed the bulge of a weapon under his left armpit. "Just a cursory search, if you don't mind, sir?"

"No, not at all. In this business you can't be too careful."

The man frisked him professionally. Then he turned to Carlota, raised an eyebrow.

She raised an eyebrow in response.

"There'll be no need to frisk the lady, I'm sure," the man said.

We were banking on that, Leon thought. If he'd found her gun, then the action would have started sooner than preferred.

Carlota had the grace to give the man the twitch of a smile. "How gallant."

"I will check the briefcase, though."

"Of course." She unclicked the fastening and passed it to him.

He stuck his big meaty hand inside and lifted out two A4 photographs. "Is this all?"

"Yes," Leon said. No secret compartments.

He put them back in the briefcase, handed it to Carlota. "This way, please." He led them to the right, into a high ceilinged room. Two walls were crammed with bookcases. On a glass and chrome table to the left were a number of plates filled with delicacies, both sweet and savory, bottles of champagne in ice buckets and slim-stemmed cut-glass flutes. Two sofas were placed in front of an old fireplace; between the sofas was a glass-topped coffee table with two drawers at each side.

Standing by a big window overlooking the port below was a short stocky man with coal black wavy hair graying over the ears. He wore taupe slacks and a mustard-yellow pullover. He turned to face them. Leon guessed he was in his forties. His complexion was light tan. Leon likened his eye-color to seaweed brown, and probably his nature was as slippery. He had a skewed nose and Leon wondered how that had been caused. There were also gray streaks at the temples. Mr. Doukas was clean-shaven which emphasized his jutting dimpled chin and hollow cheeks.

"Welcome, Señor Santos to my humble abode." He possessed a smooth soothing voice. Deceptive, no doubt, since here probably resided a ruthless mind.

"Thank you," Leon said. "This is Señorita Friday." Doukas ambled up to her and his thick fleshy lips smiled. He bowed slightly almost in Teutonic fashion; not very Latin, Leon thought. "Charmed, Miss...?"

"Just Friday," she responded with a delicate smile.

She reached for his extended hand and he quickly clasped hers, covering it with both of his. "Charmed." Then he let go abruptly and eyed Leon. "Shall we talk about business first?"

"I'd appreciate it, sir."

"Come, sit." He led them to the two sofas. He sat on one and Leon chose the other. Doukas patted the sofa by his side. "Please, Friday, join me here."

She sat next to him, the briefcase resting on her lap.

"Now, the photographs?" Doukas began, extending his hand to Leon.

Leon said, "Friday, if you will?"

She opened the briefcase and pulled out the two photographs. She passed them to Doukas.

His fleshy lips seemed suddenly more moist, as if he was drooling. He ran the back of his hand over his mouth, and then said, "They seem to be on a boat."

"That is correct," Leon said. "Waiting offshore—*if* you want them."

"Oh, I do, yes, I do."

"Do you have many already on the premises?"

Doukas shook his head. "No, I actually traded my last batch two days ago. Your call came at a propitious time."

"That's good, then, isn't it?" Leon coughed, and added, "Can we discuss a price?"

Studying the photographs, Doukas bit his lip. Then he said, "Twenty-eight thousand Euros."

Leon leaned forward. "Make it thirty thousand and we have a deal."

Doukas sighed. "Very well." He leaned across the coffee table and they shook hands. "When can I expect the shipment?"

"Tonight."

He let go of Leon's hand. "So soon?"

"As I said, I want to offload them... But I trust you will give me a deposit in advance. I am taking all the risk by landing them, after all."

"Name a figure."

"Ten percent?"

"Yes, I can agree to that. Wait while I call my accountant." He stood and pulled his cell-phone from his pants pocket, then dialed. "Ah, Tadeo, bring in the laptop. I have a transaction to make. Very good."

Less than a minute passed when a chubby short man entered the room carrying a gold-colored laptop. He wore large eye-glasses.

"Tadeo, my accountant," he introduced; "Señor Santos and Señorita Friday."

Tadeo nodded acknowledgement and then Doukas waved him to sit next to Leon.

"What do you want me to do, sir?" he asked Doukas.

"Open my account. I wish to make a payment to Señor Santos."

Key-taps later: "Done, sir." He turned to Leon. "Your bank details."

Leon gave him the account details of the International Fund for Orphans.

"How much?"

Doukas did a swift calculation. "Three thousand Euros."

As Tadeo was about to tap in the figure, Carlota withdrew her automatic from the small of her back and placed its snout against Doukas's cheek. "Make that three million, Tadeo," she instructed.

"You bitch! Jabez should have searched you!"

Tadeo blanched, hand hovering.

Leon leaned close to him, threatening. "Don't think about closing this transaction. Do as the lady says."

Tadeo removed his glasses and squinted at Doukas for guidance.

Doukas, his brow sprouting sweat, croaked, "Do what they say." The smooth timbre had vanished.

Leon watched Tadeo complete the transaction. Then he grabbed the laptop, shut it and stood up.

"Time to go," he said. Keeping her pistol leveled on Doukas, Carlota stood as well.

Doukas's complexion had transformed to a rust color. "You won't get away with this. I'll hunt you down, feed you to the fishes!"

Leon shook his head and sighed. "If you'd accepted this transaction with good grace, things could have turned out differently."

Doukas bent forward and pulled open a drawer in the coffee table, grabbed a revolver.

Carlota shot him before he could raise the weapon.

Doukas stared at her, his face twisted, as if she'd insulted him. He collapsed on top of the coffee table and the glass broke into a million tiny pieces. Tadeo gasped and whispered, "Oh, dear God!"

Carlota looked at Leon, a query in her eyes: *no prisoners?*

Leon grabbed the revolver from Doukas's limp hand as the door opened.

Jabez stood in the doorway, taking in the scene. He was already holding his pistol in readiness.

Moving sideways, Leon shot Jabez at the same time as the remiss frisker fired.

Leon's shot caught Jabez in the chest.

Tadeo screamed, "I'm shot!"

Always check the enemy's out of commission. Leon hurried over to Jabez and checked his pulse. No longer a threat. He was dead.

Then he returned to Tadeo who was slumped on the sofa, whimpering, "I've been shot..."

Leon checked the accountant's wound. "It's only your shoulder," he said. He examined the other side. The bullet had exited cleanly. "You'll live."

"Wh—what are you going to do?"

Leon eyed Carlota. "Enough..."

She gave him the ghost of a smile then asked Tadeo, "Where does Doukas keep his car and the keys?"

CHAPTER 20

CONSENTING ADULTS

LEON DROVE THE LEXUS LS500 TO THE VERY EDGE of the road, overlooking the sea. From here, they clambered to the shoreline and maneuvered over the rocks to the cave. They collected all their gear and placed it above the waterline. They changed into their wetsuits and put their business suits and shoes in the polythene bag. Then they climbed up to the road again and sat in the car's comfortable seats and waited.

It was night by the time they rendezvoused. The boat's skipper anchored off the same spot of coast.

Leon glimpsed his night lights and flashed the car's headlights. They had both been careful not to touch many surfaces in the vehicle on the journey. He'd made a point of wiping it clean with one of Doukas's towels which he'd brought for the purpose. He was reluctant to leave the luxury car, but they had no choice.

Now they climbed down to the shore for the last time, using their torches they'd left with the equipment.

The dinghy lingered a short distance off the rocks, the two crewmen waiting patiently.

Leon and Carlota carried their gear through the surf and dumped it in the dinghy and then, in ungainly fashion, clambered in.

"Welcome back!" said a crewman and started the outboard.

They soon steered alongside the boat and clambered up the rope ladder. The crewmen had said they'd bring the diving gear.

"Your cabin awaits," the skipper called from the bridge wing.

They dumped the polythene bag of clothes in the corner of the cabin. Then Carlota said, "We need to remove these wetsuits."

True enough. They were cold, shivering. And exhausted; both physically and mentally.

Unabashed, they had just finished peeling themselves out of their wetsuits when a sudden swell of the sea made the boat shudder and lurch, and the movement pushed them together. Naked, touching, flesh to flesh. They laughed and clung on to each other probably longer than the ship movement required. Both of them were clammy and in need of a shower, but that would have to wait.

It seemed the most natural thing in the world for them to lie down together on the bottom bunk. Share warmth. It was a tight fit to hold them both, so she half lay on the bunk and half on top of him.

"I'm your employer," he whispered. "This can't be right."

"I think it is very right," she replied.

The age difference didn't matter at all—for consenting adults.

In the early hours the boat docked at the port of Alicante and a man and a woman dressed in business clothes landed legally as they carried Spanish ID.

———

LEON DROVE WITH JEROEN. It was the aftermath of the flood. Nothing had returned to normal yet. A number of roads were unserviceable, having been washed away, and

Guardia vehicles were slewed across to deter further travel along them. Others were blocked with debris and mud that had been deposited by the fast-flowing water. On either side they passed what had once been dozens of fields; now, it was an enormous lake with the occasional tree or the upper story of a farmhouse poking out.

Matias Flores opened the door about a minute after Leon rang the buzzer. He looked worse than before, his eyes bloodshot. He hadn't shaved in a while; the stubble was ragged. He hung on the door as if he needed it for support.

"You," he said. "You're back."

"Yes. Very observant."

"What do you want now?"

"Don't you want to know if I found your daughter?"

"Oh, yes, of course I do. What a stupid question!"

"Can we come in?" Leon asked politely.

"We?" Clearly, he was more alert than he appeared.

Jeroen stepped into view from the side.

Leon said: "My associate and I—can we come in to talk?"

"I suppose." He waved them in and shut the door after them. "Go into the lounge. You know where it is."

It hadn't changed much. There were different clods of dried food on plates. Cigarette stubs overflowed the ashtray on the floor.

Matias gestured vaguely. "Find somewhere to sit if you like."

"We'll stand, we're not staying long."

"Whatever."

"It's about Nadia," Leon said.

"Any luck?" Matias didn't sound hopeful.

"Yes, actually, I found her," Leon said.

Matias moved back a pace and his mouth gaped open. "You did?" Abruptly, his eyes seemed furtive.

"I did. She told me everything."

"Everything?"

"Yes. Everything."

His eyes evaded Leon's penetrating gaze. "You can't believe an impressionable youngster."

Leon nodded at Jeroen.

Matias turned his head. "Hey, what are you doing?"

Jeroen swiftly pressed a hypodermic needle into Matias's neck and injected the contents of a vial before Matias could react.

He raised a hand to massage his neck. "What the fuck did he just give me?"

"A sedative," Leon explained.

"Is he a doctor?"

Leon didn't answer the question. "It's to ease your nerves."

"Yeah, my nerves have been shot to hell lately. More debts than I can handle..."

"Come with us. We can put things right."

"You can?" Trusting. An effect of the drug.

Jeroen held Matias's arm and gently walked him to the door. Leon followed.

————

Only wearing his boxer shorts, Matias lay on the couch in Jeroen's studio.

"Are you sure about this?" Jeroen asked.

"He pimped his own daughter. I'm sure."

"Very well. It won't take long."

When Matias woke from the drug he found himself in the back seat of the Yaris. Jeroen had driven them up into the hills, a good distance from the flood-plain of Vega Baja.

"What...?" Matias murmured. "My head, it aches." He blinked, finally saw Leon sitting in the front passenger seat. "I remember you... That drug... What the hell was it?"

"A sedative, like I said."

Matias glanced down, realizing he wore only shorts and not even his shoes. "Where are my clothes? What have you done?"

"So many questions!" Leon replied. "I've done only what I considered necessary. And I've donated all your clothes to people the flood has made homeless."

The movement of people caught Matias's eye. He looked through the side window.

The Yaris was parked at the high curbside in a typical Spanish hillside village at the top of a cobbled slope. Attractive whitewashed buildings lined the street on both sides, with high steps. High curbs and high steps were necessary when the rains came. Some doorways had strong metal brackets on each side, designed to retain a metal barrier to keep out the winter's snows. The sky was egg-shell blue, and totally clear of clouds. Washing hung from lines strung from balconies, flapping in the breeze that funneled down the hill.

People strolled, shopped, chatted, and milled around the small fountain in the center of the wide town's square. A couple of café-bars were open, the outside tables and chairs occupied. A couple of children jostled and fought over a hula-hoop while a bone-thin mongrel scampered out of their way.

Idyllic. Yet doubtless to Matias quite surreal.

Matias stared, his high forehead wrinkling in confusion.

Leon pointed through the windshield. "There's a police station at the bottom of the hill. On the left. I suggest you give yourself up to them."

"Eh," Matias said. "Why should I?"

"You sold your daughter to child abusers. That's reason enough, isn't it?"

"You don't know that for sure." Then his brow unwrinkled and it was as if a distant memory returned. "I remember now. You spoke to Nadia, didn't you?"

Without replying, Leon produced his Astra automatic with a silencer fitted.

"Jesus!"

"Shouldn't you get going?" Leon urged.

"Wh-what? Dressed like this?"

"Think yourself lucky we left your shorts on."

He cocked his head to one side. "Who is 'we'?"

Leon nodded at the driver with a ginger-haired ponytail. "The two of us."

"The doctor who drugged me?"

"Matias, I am getting impatient," Leon said. "Now, go, get out!"

"Can't you drive me to the police station?"

"No. Now, get out!"

Reluctantly, Matias opened the door and clambered out. He shut the door gently, as if not wanting to draw the attention of the people nearby. He stood hesitantly and shivered, wrapping his arms around his torso.

There was no real need to shiver, since it was a hot day. Just nerves.

He started to walk down the slope, wincing as his bare soles touched the hot cobbles.

Suddenly, a woman looked up from her shopping basket and stared at him in bewilderment. Then she pointed at him. Others noticed, too.

They shouted at him. Cursed him.

Matias glanced back at the car, puzzlement in his eyes, alarm in his pallid features.

It was quite plain to see why the women yelled. On Matias's forehead was a tattoo written in Spanish, '*Soy pedó-filo*'. I'm a pedophile.

He turned and hurried awkwardly toward the police station.

Women and some men hurled abuse and a few even started flinging stones at him.

He raised his hands to protect his face, and stumbled and cried out.

On his bare broad back was the tattoo: '*Abuso a niños.*'

A stone hit him in the temple and blood appeared on his shoulder.

He cried for them to stop, stop, *stop*!

A man stepped from a street café and lifted an aluminum tubular chair and hit him with it.

Matias fell to his knees and then he struggled to his feet and staggered away, further down the hill.

While stumbling forward, Matias peered over his shoulder, pleading in his eyes, blood dribbling from his nose.

He still had twenty or so yards to go to reach the police station.

"Will he make it, do you think?" Jeroen asked.

"He might," Leon replied. "But then again, is the police station open?"

"You did not check?"

"No. It's a sleepy village. Why stay open when you can enjoy a siesta?"

Jeroen shrugged and started the car. He reversed up the hill and drove into a side street that would lead out of the village.

———

As JEROEN DROVE, Leon fondly recalled Jacinta, his niece. When she was eight, he'd driven her and his sister Pilar to an Indian restaurant for a treat. As they approached a roundabout, Jacinta had leaned forward and gripped the back of his seat. "Uncle Leon, what is that lady doing sitting on the *glorieta*?" she'd asked.

Like most of the women who frequent the local roundabouts, this woman was attractive, highly tanned and toned, wearing a white tube to partially cover her prominent breasts but not her midriff and white boy's-style shorts. She had long black hair and read a magazine while sitting in a green plastic chair on the outside edge of the roundabout, long legs stretched out, the heels of her black boots resting on the metal crash barrier. Many of her sisters were Eastern European or South American and didn't read magazines or books but fingered their cell-phones instead.

He'd glanced sideways at Pilar, and she shook her head, clearly not wanting him to tell Jacinta the bald truth. He could live with that. In the wash of life, truth often comes out gray.

"Oh, that's Florence," he explained. "She's waiting for her boyfriend."

"*Sí, claro*," Jacinta said, satisfied and he grinned, not reacting to the poke in his ribs from Pilar.

Recently a wag, who had signed himself as Dougal, christened this woman and those like her with the name Florence. There was no sign of Zebedee or the magic roundabout. A dated joke for Brits. Then, the following week they negotiated that familiar roundabout again.

Jacinta exclaimed, "Uncle Leon, that lady's still waiting for her boyfriend! If I was her, I'd have dumped him by now!"

Only by superhuman effort did Pilar and Leon keep their faces straight. There was no answer to that.

The innocence of the young. May it always be preserved and cherished.

Afterword

An anonymous man was found at the bottom of a cliff beneath a small mountain village. His damaged features made identification virtually impossible. Unusually, he bore tattoos on his forehead and back, mostly incomprehensible writing since wild animals appeared to have mutilated the corpse. Nobody claimed Matias's body.

Seprona finally captured the lynx and her two cubs. They were tagged and released into the wild to join their brethren near Yecla in Murcia.

Inspector Teo Chávez arranged for two officers to call at a certain small villa. A man was accused of unlawfully imprisoning his daughter and duly arrested. Gaby and Tía Paloma were reunited. Subsequently, the ex-husband was jailed.

Following medical treatment at Torrevieja Hospital, Evan Tremayne returned to England where he underwent a course of therapy. At the conclusion of the course he resigned and changed his career path, opting for carpentry.

Police obtained hundreds of pedophile images from the Golf-Sur Golf Course; the majority were undamaged. Subsequent viewing revealed that no faces of the abusers were shown; but some tattoos were distinguishable. Jeroen and other tattooists were called in to identify the artwork and the artist where possible, and in a handful of cases the identification was positive and charges were issued.

The gota fria of 2019 was the most severe in decades. The rain began in earnest on September 11 and continued for four days and nights. In the twenty-four hours to September 12, 296.4 mm of rain fell, which equated to about half the yearly average. By September 12 several rivers had broken through their banks. Bodies were still being discovered on September 18. Roads and schools were closed along with Murcia and Almería and Alicante airports. Towns were left isolated for several days.

The financial cost of the flooding disaster which hit the Vega Baja and the south of Valencia province was estimated to be more than €1.5 billion; this would include property, vehicles and crops. Remarkably, the number of deaths, while tragic, was few. Thousands of people were evacuated; many as a precaution due to a controlled release from a local dam; several hundred were taken by boat or helicopter. Over 600 soldiers from the army's UME brigade and 1,000 Guardia Civil officers were drafted in. The police, fire service, the Civil Protection and Red Cross were also deployed. Tales of heroism abounded as members of the security forces and volunteers risked their lives to rescue residents and animals trapped by rising floodwater. Householders and farmers have made legal claims against the authorities for the catastrophic loss of crops blaming the controlled release. Compensation is still not settled in many cases.

GLOSSARY

Unless otherwise stated, the words listed are Spanish with English translation.

- Abogado—lawyer, solicitor
- ALPR—Automatic Licence Plate Recognition
- Amigo—friend
- Ayuntamiento—town hall
- Calle—street
- Claro—clear
- CV—Comunitat Valenciana
- Delfin—dolphin
- Denuncia—report to the police
- Finca—countryside house
- Glorieta—roundabout
- Golf: Birdie—one shot below par
- Golf: Cabbage patch—rough
- Golf: Eagle—score 3 on a hole
- Gota fria—literally "cold drop"
- Hola—hello
- La Primitiva—one of several lotteries
- Madre de Dios—Mother of God
- Madrileños—inhabitants of Madrid

- Menu del día—daily meal, designed for working man
- Mercadona—Spanish supermarket chain
- Niños— children
- Paseo—walk, stroll
- Reintegro—bonus win on lottery, usually 1 euro
- Seprona—Servicio de Protección de la Naturaleza (Guardia Civil)
- Tapas—assorted appetizers in restaurants and bars
- Tía—aunty
- Tío—uncle
- Triq—street (Maltese)

A Look at Book Three:
Organ Symphony

Organ harvesters are his prime target.

Leon Cazador is on FBI liaison duty in Charleston, South Carolina when a dead child is found with a kidney missing. Suspecting an old foe, he jumps into action when a convoy of trucks with kidnapped children hits a snag, and a boy escapes.

But what starts out as a simple cat and mouse chase turns into a convoluted web of deceit involving an underground organ transplant ring that surpasses Leon's wildest expectations—and abilities.

Years later—and carrying around the weight of unresolved burdens —Leon runs into suspicious activity in Córdoba, Spain that makes his heart stop cold. Organ traffickers are running rampant, and a three-man investigating team has gone missing.

Eager to put an end to this corrupt organization's misdeeds once and for all, Leon makes finding its leader his top priority. But will he have what it takes to bring an evil like no other to its knees?

AVAILABLE SEPTEMBER 2022

ABOUT THE AUTHOR

Nik Morton has sold over 100 short stories, edited periodicals and contributed to magazine articles, chaired writers' circles, run writing workshops, and judged competitions. He has edited many books and was sub-editor of the monthly magazine *Portsmouth Post* (2003-2007) and Editor in Chief of a U.S. Publisher (2011-2013). He has had 32 books published—including 3 books in the psychic spy *Tana Standish* series and 8 westerns—and co-written 4 books in the *Floreskand* fantasy series. His *Write a Western in 30 Days – with plenty of bullet points!* is a best-seller. With his wife Jennifer, Nik lived in Spain for several years (2003-2019). They have since returned to England, residing in Northumberland—near their daughter Hannah, son-in-law Harry and grandchildren Darius and Suri.